W9-BRP-712

Georgetown School
Indian Prairie School District
Aurora, Illinois

WEEDED

Genesis begins ......

Genesis Begins Again

Genesis Begins Again

Alicia D. Williams

A Caitlyn Dlouhy Book

THORNDIKE PRESS
A part of Gale, a Cengage Company

GALE
A Cengage Company

Copyright © 2019 by Alicia D. Williams.
Thorndike Press, a part of Gale, a Cengage Company.

ALL RIGHTS RESERVED
This book is a work of fiction. Any references to historical events, real people, or real places are used fictitiously. Other names, characters, places, and events are products of the author's imagination, and any resemblance to actual events or places or persons, living or dead, is entirely coincidental.

Thorndike Press® Large Print Striving Reader Collection.
The text of this Large Print edition is unabridged.
Other aspects of the book may vary from the original edition.
Set in 16 pt. Plantin.

LIBRARY OF CONGRESS CIP DATA ON FILE.
CATALOGUING IN PUBLICATION FOR THIS BOOK
IS AVAILABLE FROM THE LIBRARY OF CONGRESS.

ISBN-13: 978-1-4328-8220-4 (hardcover alk. paper)

Published in 2020 by arrangement with Atheneum Books for Young Readers, an imprint of Simon & Schuster Children's Publishing Division.

Printed in Mexico
Print Number: 01   Print Year: 2020

For every person who felt as if
they weren't good enough.
You were. And will always be.

ONE

Nobody could tell me that today wasn't gon' be my day. Even though I couldn't determine the correct term of equality in math, shanked the nearly airless volleyball in PE, and truly didn't care to discuss the effects of the Civil War in social studies, I was unshook, 'cause today my girls finally agreed to hang out with me — at my house!

And with Regina to my right cracking jokes, Fatima and Tasha and Angela to my left laughing insanely loud, shoot, every eye is on us. Boys jockin' us — well, actually jockin' *them.* Regardless, they're grinning like we're *all* a bag of M&M's. I'm so amped that I actually yell this to the guys. And don't you know — Regina uses *my* line as a jump off, cracking, "And y'all ain't 'bout to taste none of us either!" We all slap hands and keep it moving.

Regina's going on about her plans for us to watch music videos, 'cause Tasha's crushing on some new hot singer. And in my mind, we're all sitting on the couch debating which rapper is the finest. Then, we'll drink Sprite and eat the chips that Mama went out to buy especially for us.

But as soon as we round the corner of my block, my heart skips like a scratched CD. *Not again. Please, not again.* But yes, again. All our furniture sits in the front yard — but this time it's laid out exactly like it had been inside the house, as if the movers are playing a cruel joke. Our glass living room table sits in front of the couch with a cocktail table on each side. The kitchen chairs are properly placed with the dining table. Even our beds are still made with the blankets and pillows.

"This your house?" Regina says, flicking her long braids.

"Uh, no." *Dad.* Didn't he know today was epic for me? "I live over there," I say, pointing to a house where the metal bars on the security door swirl in an elegant design.

"She lying," Fatima butts in. "I saw her go in this one the other day." "This one" is a small brick house with peeling green trim, chipped up cement steps, and straight metal bars on the door and windows like a prison.

Now I understand what Grandma means when she says, "There's always one." Regina snorts, "Hey, y'all, Genesis gotta pee outside!" Then she throws back her head and bursts out laughing. The other three start laughing too. A bunch of copycats.

I open my mouth, but nothing comes out. They're whispering and pointing, and my family's STUFF IS SITTING IN THE YARD! "You know what?" I finally come up with. "I forgot, my mama said we were getting new furniture."

Angela raises an eyebrow. High. "Not with that big ol' metal thing covering the doorknob, you ain't."

They all swivel their heads at the same time and mutter, *"Danggggg."*

"Nobody's getting through that door besides the landlord," Angela jabs.

Regina turns to me, smirking. "Just

9

admit your folks are bums."

I search their faces, hoping at least one of them will stick up for me. But no one, not even Tasha — whose mama's car was repossessed in the middle of the night just the other week! — says a peep. Yes, I know a repossessed car ain't as serious as finding your stuff spread out in the yard for everybody to see, but still. "No, uhm . . ." I'm out of lies. *Dad. Dad. Dad.* "It's just that —"

"It's just that it is what it *is,* ain't that right, y'all?" They all "yep" as Regina now roams around the couch and tables, stalking. "Furniture so busted even the Goodwill don't want it."

The copycats "hee-hee-hee" again. This time I force myself to laugh right along with them. "I know, right!" I agree, trailing her.

"I knew you were poor, but dang . . ." Regina struts past our kitchen set, pokes at a wobbly chair. "This is pitiful, Char."

I try hard to not visibly wince. Char. Short for Charcoal. Since I started at this school, I've laughed at their jokes and sucked it all up to make friends. And I'd made progress; just this last week they stopped calling me Eggplant. And then they'd agreed to come over. . . .

Regina beelines toward a cluster of furniture that had clearly been in my bedroom. "Y'all wanna see some of Char's hand-me-downs?"

"Don't!" I slip in front of my dresser, stretching my arms across it protectively.

Regina shoves at me, but I'm not budging. "Move it, CharCOAL!"

And now I'm mad. And when I get mad, my mouth shoots off before it can connect to my brain. And now my mouth's dishing out a response faster than I can stop it, because how could she? How dare she?!

"You know what?" I shoot back. "Forget you! You're not all that with yo' ratchet Black Barbie wannabe self."

Silence.

Dead silence.

Now I've done it. Good-bye, Regina. Good-bye, Tasha, Fatima, and Angela. Good-bye, any chance at — *stop it!* I tell myself. Maybe she won't take too much offense to my clap-back.

No chance. Regina stands rigid, her

hands ball into fists. Her posse rallies closer. "What did you say?" she says, her voice low, dangerous. All four of them edge toward me. Slow. Steady. "Say it again."

No way am I saying it again.

Regina narrows her eyes. One fist starts coming up. And then, oh merciful Lord, a screen door slams. My neighbor. My neighbor who's never said two words to me since we moved in now stands, wide-legged, on her porch. She sizes up the furniture, me, Regina, and the girls. Regina glowers back, maybe waiting for her to leave so they can pummel the living daylights out of me. My neighbor doesn't leave. She stares us down.

Finally, Regina raises her chin. "Don't let me catch you around, Eggplant. Come on, y'all," and in unison the other three turn and march out of my yard. Down the sidewalk.

Bang! The screen door closes as my neighbor goes back into her house.

And now I'm left with, well, with this! I fall on my bed — which is OUTSIDE — and pray I don't ever have to see Regina and 'em again. Then I curse Dad for not paying the rent. Again. I curse him for making me wait out here while passing spectators stare stupidly, like maybe I don't realize furniture is supposed to be inside a house.

Then I curse myself. For believing someone like Regina would even be friends with *me*.

But I'm not gon' cry. I'm not. Especially 'cause even though our neighbor might be back inside, she's watching from her window. It's getting chilly now, so I reach over and dig in my drawer for a sweatshirt. But my hand first finds a sheet of paper — The List. I pull it out.

The List. Even though the paper's wrinkled and worn, I review and add to it all the time. Back in fifth grade, Chyna and Porsche slid a note onto my desk. Gullible me thought it was an invitation. And then I read the title: 100 REASONS WHY WE HATE GENESIS.

Stupid girls. Couldn't even count. They only listed sixty reasons; and they were stretching it, too, because some were really dumb, like #1: She smiles too much, or #39: She thinks she got pretty writing, and even #46: She bumped into me and acted like she didn't know it.

Shoot, they should've just asked me for the rest. Because I've already added twenty-four others, like #73: Because she's always getting put out of her house. Or, what I'll add now, #85: Because her friends dump her when they see her stuff on the curb like a Salvation Army pickup.

After reading over the entire list, my fingers refuse to fold the paper back up. Thoughts of how badly I wanted to strut down the halls with Regina and her girls keep needling me. Of course I'd never actually be one of them, but just being with them was good enough, you know? When I'm with them, someone else is on the sidelines admiring me, no clue I'm fronting like my life's *all that.* But now I picture Regina's face from fifteen minutes ago and how I laughed at myself to prove I could take a joke, because yes, I really could. Except none of that was a joke. So, I guess I proved I'm great at frontin'. Now, my fingers tremble as I add #86:

Because she let them call her Charcoal, Eggplant, and Blackie.

I bury the note back in my dresser and pull out that sweatshirt. Then I patrol around the yard like a security guard. On my third round, a cab pulls up. Mama jumps out wearing pink scrubs, and the cab speeds off. "You all right?" she calls, immediately wading through the "rooms," inspecting each item.

"I'm cold, and I gotta go," I say, nodding at that big device covering the doorknob.

"Anybody bother our stuff?" Mama rummages through her dresser drawer.

"Not since I've been here. Why we get put out again?"

"Not now, Genesis." Mama removes some papers from the drawer and shoves them into her purse, picks up her jewelry box and tucks it under her arm. "Well, this is a first." Mama's surveying the yard, turning in a complete circle. "I don't think we've ever been put out so neatly before."

After what seems like forever, but actually is only five minutes later, a silver Cadillac parks in front of the house. Mama checks her watch and says, "Right on time, thank God."

An old man climbs out. "Mrs. Anderson . . ."

"Mr. Myers, thank you so much for meeting me." Mama blinks her big brown eyes.

"Ordinarily, I wouldn't because it's your husband's name that's on the lease, and —" His eyes meet Mama's and just like that, his clenched jaw softens. "I hate to do this, Mrs. Anderson, I really do, but you all haven't paid in months."

"I know, cutbacks at the plant. My husband lost half his hours, half his paycheck." Mama gives that same reason every time, but never confesses where the other half of Dad's paycheck goes. "We're awfully sorry."

We follow him to the porch and up the cracked steps. Mr. Myers gives Mama a gentle smile as he unbolts the metal lockout device. "I'll do this favor . . . only for you."

"I'm truly grateful," says Mama, stepping inside. "I really am."

I race to the bathroom and my bladder's grateful that the movers left behind the tissue. When I come out, Mama's searching the kitchen cabinets. She turns to me, instructing, "Genesis, do a final sweep of your room, just to make sure the movers got everything. Okay?"

In my room, a mirror hangs on the other side of the closet door. No matter how many times I shut it, that door cracks back open. Now, as I check inside to make sure nothing's been left behind, the mirror faces me. It hates me too.

We stand in a stare-off like Celie did in *The Color Purple,* this old movie that Mama watches every dang time it comes on TV. In the movie, gorgeous Shug Avery makes Celie face herself in the mirror to convince her she's beautiful, even though Shug called Celie ugly in the first place. "You *sho'* is *ugly.*" That's exactly how Shug said it too. And here I am, facing myself like Celie. "Well?" I say. "Get on with it."

Look at you, with that wide nose, my reflection says.

I pinch my nostrils down.

And those big lips.

I smash my lips tight.

And that nappy head.

I finger the tangles loose.

Don't get me started on how black you are.

I want to say something, but what? That I think I'm cute? 'Cause I'm not. That I have good hair? 'Cause I don't. That I'm not dark? 'Cause I am.

Who you think's gonna love you with the way you look? Cackling echoes through the mirror so loud it could shatter.

"I can't stand you," I say to my reflection.

I slam the door, trapping the voices inside.

When we're done, Mr. Myers ushers us back outside, then covers the door handle with the lockout device. Mama holds a box full of spices and canned foods that she found in the kitchen. My search came up empty. She apologizes again for the inconvenience, and for not paying the rent. Mr. Myers kindly shakes his head. He feels bad for us, I can tell. He doesn't have steely eyes like the last three landlords. They looked at us like we were dirt, even though they're probably only mad about being cheated out of their money.

18

Which is fair, I guess. But Mr. Myers's eyes are sad, even as he drives away from the curb. I wave good-bye, but he doesn't see it.

Mama finds the trash bags and hands me one. "Get your clothes out of the drawers and put 'em in these." She does the same. When we're done, we both sink onto the couch and wait for Dad. I shiver and Mama takes the couch's throw blanket and wraps it around my shoulders. She checks her watch again.

"What time is it?" I ask.

"Almost five." Mama rubs the chill from her legs. Her scrubs are no match for the cold. I take the throw from my shoulders and cover us both. She digs her cell phone from her purse and checks it. More cars drive past, folks looking at us like we're crazy.

"Mama . . . ," I say hesitantly. She looks at me, confused, so I add, "Did you forget? Today my friends were coming over."

Mama slaps her forehead. "Oh, Genesis, I'm so sorry. I'm so sorry." She asks what happened, and I tell her everything besides the confrontation part. She apologizes again and promises to make it up to me when things get back to normal. Things are never "normal," but I make a mental note to remind her, if they ever are.

For another half hour we sit on the couch, cuddled up. Mama calls Dad twice, and each time he says he's on his way. She's about to hit his number for a third time when he drives up, followed by a U-Haul truck.

Before Dad can step a foot on the curb, Mama's already up, fussing. "What took you so long? You know how cold it is? Guess you want us to catch the death of pneumonia, huh?"

"Calm down! I told you I had to pick up Dwight and Mike." Dwight and Mike stand next to the U-Haul and nod when Dad says their names. "Then we had to go back 'cross town to get the truck."

"From the looks of your red eyes, you been doing more than that," Mama says, all sly. Then she points a finger at him saying, "You told me the rent was taken care of, then you have me leave my job to cover your mess — YOURS."

Dad opens and closes his mouth. I wait

a few seconds for his reaction, and when he doesn't go off, then I get up too.

"Hey, you did say this wasn't gon' happen again," I echo, wrapping the throw around me, and standing next to Mama. Just to think, Dad was off somewhere drinking while Regina and her crew were tryna' drag me. So I add, "And we were called bums, and I almost got into a fight."

Mama turns to me. "A fight?"

"Almost," I cover. Now I'm mad all over again. "How would you like to be called a bum?"

For a second time, Dad seems at a loss for words. But he recovers and finally says, "But you okay, right?"

I nod, but Mama . . . if her eyes were lasers, she'd surely roast Dad with the look she's giving him.

"What?" he says, acting clueless. "She said she was okay."

"Your child is out here about to fight over this mess? Is this what you want for Genesis?"

"I hope not," I mumble under my breath.

"Come on, Gen. Let's get you warm." Mama holds out a hand. "Give me the keys, so I can start the car."

"So, you mad? You lookin' at me like this is all my fault!" Dad's left eye squints, like a tick. *Here it comes.* This is when the alcohol usually starts talking. Mama doesn't respond, and I take two steps back. But Dad, he just reaches into his pocket, pulls out the keychain, and drops it into Mama's hand. Then he jogs over to Dwight and Mike, gestures to the yard, and they get to work loading the truck.

Whaaa? Whew, Dad's response was . . . chill. Then I think, *Dang, the night ain't over.*

We say good-bye to Euclid Avenue, and hello to — where are we going now? I buckle my seat belt, my hands a little shaky. Here's the thing. The first time we got put out we stayed at a motel, and all night long we heard arguing, cussing, and police sirens. No biggie. The second time, well, we went to Grandma's, but Mama said she never ever wants to do that again. And the third time we got evicted — five months ago — we stayed in Dad's friend's basement. That's when Dad . . . drunk Dad . . . went off on me. I mean like, really, *really* went off. His words still ring in my head.

You were supposed to come out lookin' like her . . . look at you with yo' black —

I plug my fingertips into my ears to block out his voice. But his slurry words are still there. At first I was more scared than hurt. Like, you know how you can't see dust drifting in the air, but you see the filthiness after it's settled? That's something like how Dad's words were for me. And you know what? I started studying myself in the mirror and, yeah, he's right.

The radio is on, and it's now safe to remove my fingers. My coal-black fingers. I remembered overhearing Mama once telling her friend that milk baths were good for the skin, and she'd shown off her arms proudly. *That's why Mama's skin is so light,* I'd thought. I know, I know, of course that's not why. But it didn't stop me from sneaking a gallon of milk from the fridge and pouring it in the tub. I rolled back and forth, trying to get that little bit of milk all over my body. But after the second time, Mama griped: "Who's drinking up all the milk? Ain't nobody that thirsty!" That ended that — and I was no closer to looking like Mama.

Part of me believes that Dad might not have said those things if it wasn't for us being stuck staying in a basement. So I know I'm being selfish, but I'd be happier if we stayed at Grandma's — even if her snaps are sharper than an alligator's.

"Ma?" I hesitate. "Uhm . . . where we staying?" I grip the seat cushion, bracing for an answer. *Please not in that basement. Please not in that basement.*

Dad glances at me through the rearview mirror. "Your grandmother's."

"Really?" I breathe out, "Yesssss."

"Shouldn't we talk about this first?" says Mama, the hard look back on her face. "You know how I feel about going there —"

"I know," Dad interrupts, "but —"

"And where exactly will *you* be?" Mama interrupts back.

"At Dwight's. Somebody has to keep an eye on our stuff." Dad anxiously drums his thumbs on the steering wheel as he explains that our furniture will stay in the U-Haul until he finds us a new place.

Why would he want to stay with Dwight? Besides the fact that Grandma has made it clear that a man who can't provide a roof for her daughter can't sleep under hers. But still, Dwight only keeps mayonnaise and ketchup in his refrigerator and has three German shepherds that bark all night long. Dad would be better off at a motel.

After a few seconds, he mutters, "And I'm gon' need to borrow some money, too."

"Really, Emory?" Mama shifts away from him, glaring out the window.

Yep, that's why he's staying with those three barking dogs.

TWO

Mama and I wait forever for Grandma to answer the door. The porch light beams down on us as if announcing to the entire block that *The lost ones are now found, praise the Lord.*

"Who is it?" comes her voice at last.

"It's me," says Mama.

Two locks click, and the door cracks open. Grandma peeps from behind it. She has big eyes like Mama's, but hers are even prettier. They're gray. "Have mercy, Sharon. You have that child out here at this hour?" Mama waves Dad off; he toots the horn and drives away. "Where's Emory going?" Grandma asks, sharp.

Mama stammers, "He's . . . he's —"

"Honestly, I don't care to hear it." Grandma motions us in, and we wrestle the trash bags past her. "Seems to me you should be tired of this foolishness by now."

"It's just for the night, Mama."

"Hmph, and you're fine with that?" Grandma gives me a side-hug. "Genesis, go on up to bed. Say your prayers first . . . on your knees, none of that praying in bed stuff, you hear? And, pull your shoulders up, stop slouching."

I climb the stairs, already praying for God to bless Mama for having us stop at the drive-thru. Shoot, after the day we've had, being sent to bed without a meal would've been, like, torture.

Grandma has four bedrooms, but I always sleep in the same one. Mama's. Her room still has the dated flower wallpaper and pink canopy bed from when she was a kid, as if it's waiting for her to come back home. As I dig through one of the bags of clothes for something to sleep in, Grandma's and Mama's voices get louder and louder. I'm not one to eavesdrop, but technically I'm not eavesdropping when they're talking loud enough to wake a bear knocked out by a tranquilizer.

"Sharon, please, don't compare that man to your father." Grandma is always getting on Ma about Dad, and sometimes she throws Grandpa in for extra guilt. *Your father would die of another stroke if he knew. . . .*

The teakettle whistles and a chair scrapes the floor. I move to the top of the steps.

Mama doesn't reply.

"And, you wouldn't *be* in this situation if you'd gone back to school, gotten a degree. But here you are wiping up after folks at that nursing home. For *minimum* wage. Nobody can live decently off that, and we both know that you simply cannot rely on that husband of yours." Grandma's voice now breaks exactly where it always does, then she adds like she always does, "I know I sound like a broken record. But nothing ever changes with that *man!*"

"And how am I supposed to do any of those things *now*? I have Genesis to consider," Mama shoots back.

"Well," Grandma says, softer, "you could come back and live here, for starters."

Uh-uh. UH-UH! I can't imagine living with Grandma every single day. Mama says Grandma can nitpick the wool off a lamb. I can't even use the toothpaste without her instructing me how to properly squeeze the tube.

I don't hear Mama's response, so I scooch down a few steps.

Grandma has cleared her throat and is charging on. "And, I warned you that he wasn't the type of man for you to marry, didn't I?"

"*Mama,* please." A teacup chinks against its saucer a little too hard. "Genesis is right upstairs," Mama says, low.

I back up the steps in case Mama decides to check on me. Actually, I should be putting on my T-shirt, folding up my clothes, and getting into bed. But there's a traffic jam of questions inside my head. Like really, what kind of man *should* Mama have married, and why isn't Dad it? Is it his drinking? Or that his hours'd been cut and he's been hitting the casinos? But, he wasn't doing those things when they met, this I know. I quickly change and sneak back to the door.

"Sometimes I think you only married him to spite me —"

"I can't do this right now." A chair scrapes back.

"Go on, run away. You refuse to see the truth," Grandma says. "Lord, my child is blind in one eye and can't see out the other."

Mama climbs the stairs fast. I leap into bed. The door opens. "Genesis?" I fake sleep. After a few minutes, Mama cuts off the light, climbs into bed, and cuddles real close. "I sure hope your Dad'll come for us tomorrow," she whispers.

Dad will come. He always does — not always the very next day, but who knows? Maybe he'll not only come, but also run up Grandma's walkway, pull me in his arms, and tell me he misses me. Maybe Grandma'll talk nicely, no preaching. Maybe, just maybe.

But I doubt it.

When Grandma calls me to breakfast, I ask where's Mama.

"Oh, she left for work about seven or so," says Grandma. "Must've been tired, too, because she woke up late. Had to borrow my car to make it on time."

Then it comes to me that I've got to face Regina and the girls at school today! "How am I getting to school?" I ask, but what I really want to know is, *Do I have to go to school?*

Grandma slides a bowl of oatmeal in front of me and spoons a little bit of brown sugar over the top. "Your mother said she couldn't wait to drive you across town — she had to be in early today, because she left early yesterday — and by the time you catch a bus and transfer, you'll have missed half the morning."

What's weird is that yesterday, for one moment, I was fly — yes, I know it wasn't real — but still, my swag was smooth, my laugh was chill, and my snaps — my snaps had everybody rollin'. Then I think of our face-to-face standoff. *Don't let me catch you around, Eggplant.* No Regina drama for me today; I ain't mad about that.

I reach for the spoon and Grandma snaps, "Don't pick up that spoon till you thanked the Lord."

I put the spoon back down and clasp

my hands together. "God is great, God is good, let us thank him for our food. Amen."

"That's it? Hasn't Grandma taught you how to give a respectable grace?"

Only one hundred times. Even though I'm sure God won't mind if I say a simple prayer every now and then, I clasp my hands together and say another grace for Grandma's sake. "Dear Father God, thank you for this breakfast of fine oats and the water to boil them. Thank you for the sugar to sweeten them, the cows that made the milk, and the farmer that churns the milk to make the butter. And finally, bless Grandma for preparing it. Amen."

She studies me, as if determining whether I was being disrespectful or not. Finally she says, "That'll do," and takes her seat across from me.

With Grandma eyeing me, I remember her and Mama's conversation last night, but I'm afraid if I ask her about it, she'll start lecturing me, too.

I take my bowl to the sink, and a big bag of lemons on the counter catches my eye. There must be twenty in there! "Why you have all those lemons?" I ask.

"A sweet girl from church dropped off a whole bag. Fresh lemon juice, nothing better! I'll use some for lemonade . . . some for tea . . . my dark spots . . ." Grandma runs her fingers over her hands, hands pale like Mama's. "And, my cough tonic. It helps with my bronchitis. You know, lemons are God's healing food."

"Dark spots?" Lemons help with dark spots? Immediately, my mind starts buzzing.

"For these marks. See here?" Grandma points to small light brown dots sprinkled across her hands, like freckles. "That doctor on the TV, now, what's his name?" Grandma thinks for a second and then says, "Never mind. But he said that juice from lemons makes them fade."

"It works?"

"Would I waste my time if it didn't?" Grandma says, gathering up her dishes. "Now, go get yourself dressed, it's already after nine," she says, as if I actually have some place to be.

Back in my room, I get to thinking about lemons fading Grandma's spots. I have a glimmer of an idea, and it's making me feel happy. Then, while searching through the trash bag for some clothes, Regina's stupid cracks pop in my ear. *Y'all wanna see some of Char's hand-me-downs?* Charcoal. And right then, my little idea turns into a need-to-do.

I take two towels out of the linen closet and two lemons — *that should be enough* — from the kitchen. I almost forget the knife, and turn back for it before locking myself in the bathroom.

So that rolling around in milk thing was stupid. So was the baking soda experiment. And I'm embarrassed to confess that for three months straight, I'd sit with yogurt on my face for fifteen minutes every night — yogurt 'cause I read something about the acid being good for lightening skin — but nothing happened. Now, even though this lemon thing sounds a lot like the milk thing, Grandma trusts it, so maybe?

Once I'm out of the shower, I slice a lemon in half and smear it over my face, ears, neck, and shoulders. Little bits of pulp settle on my cheeks like acne. I take another half and rub it down my arms, elbows, and hands. I don't stop rubbing till lemon juice is on every area of my body. I stick a rind over my gums, for good measure. I'm not even going to *talk* about the color of my gums! Then, I sit on the edge of the toilet and wait, hardly daring to feel hopeful, but yeah, in truth, I am. "Please, Lord, let this work," I repeat over and over, like a chant, till Grandma tells me I've been in here long enough. The lemon dries, and at least it's not sticky. So I get dressed, without washing it off. The used peels I wrap in tissue and bury at the bottom of the wastebasket; the rest I tuck in a washcloth for later.

Grandma sniffs at me when I enter the den. "You've been in my lotions?"

"No." I sniff myself. Man, Grandma has the nose of a bloodhound.

"Hmph, you smell nice anyway." She flicks her finger toward the preacher on TV and says, "Lord ah mercy, this man can hardly move due to his gout."

Whaaa? But I know not to ask.

We watch *Dr. Oz* next, and I suspect he's the guy who recommended the lemon idea. I sure would like to ask him when to expect a change, 'cause my arms are just as dark as they were an hour ago. This leads me to ask, "Grandma, how're your hands doing?"

"Oh, this arthritis is something else." Grandma rubs her knuckles as if they've been aching all day.

"What about the spots?"

"Spots?" Grandma inspects her hands. "Getting lighter, I suppose."

"How long it takes?"

"How long does what take?"

"The lemons."

"Not long, I expect."

"You rub it on and that's it?"

"What time is it?" She picks up the remote. "You're going to make me miss my program."

If there is one show Grandma absolutely cannot miss, it's *In the Heat of the Night*. Why she loves this show, I have no idea. It's so old all the action looks fake. Still, I check the clock in the kitchen. "Little after twelve thirty," I say, then press on: "So, what else you do?"

"Nothing else." Grandma's changing

the channel. "Except a little exfoliation." She finds her show and rests the remote in her lap.

"Exfoliate?" We've seen this episode at least one hundred times already. Ugh. "Grandma, exfoliate?"

"Genesis, I can't talk and watch this, too. You're being worrisome, you know that? Why don't you go vacuum or something, make yourself useful?"

That settles it. I take my worrisome self and make myself useful, all the while figuring out this exfoliating business.

When Mama comes home from work, she tells us that Dad's "working on a surprise," and we'll find it out tomorrow. Of course, Grandma snorts, "A surprise? Hmph, we shall see." Mama doesn't defend Dad, and it was his fault we were called "bums," so I won't either. Like Grandma, I snort, "Yep, we'll see." A surprise, after all, ain't always *good*.

But then I do get a good surprise! In one of Grandma's bathroom cabinets, I find this stuff called apricot scrub, and on the tube is the word "exfoliate." Score! So, right before bed I rub the scrub on my skin — which feels like tiny, ground-up walnut shells — and rinse it off, then I spread the lemon on again. Finally, I get back to bed feeling hopeful.

THREE

First thing I do this morning is check my hands, and guess what? No difference, unless you count that I'm ashier. Okay, my knuckles and elbows might be tough, but the smoother parts like my face and neck? *Come on.* My glimmer of hope is starting to fade, when I hear Mama on the phone.

"Yeah, we'll be ready in an hour," she says, which hints that she's talking to Dad. But I'm not gon' believe he's coming till he's here. Mama isn't either, judging by her dry tone.

But an hour later, sure enough, the horn honks. I hurry to the front picture window to see for myself that it's indeed Dad. And yep, it's him. Mama scrambles to the bedroom and stuffs bags like the house is on fire. I pack, too, but slower, letting him wait like I had to outside on the couch Thursday. Grandma hovers by Mama like a mosquito, buzzing about Dad not having the decency to knock on the door like a proper gentleman.

"Will you listen to him," she harps. "Out there waking the neighborhood with his horn."

Mama hurries to the bathroom and washes her face.

Grandma's right behind her. "Where to now?"

"Well, he says he's got us a nice, big house with a big backyard. And a fireplace."

"He tell you that on the phone?" I ask, surprised. She didn't tell *me*.

"Yes, Genesis," Mama says, short. When Mama answers me like that, it means don't ask no more about it.

"Where is this nice, big house, anyway?" Grandma huffs.

"Farmington Hills." Mama squeezes a glob of toothpaste onto her brush.

Grandma says, "Farmington Hills? How did he manage a place out there?"

"Emory says a coworker owns it. We're renting from him."

"You plan on riding the bus back and forth to work from way out there?"

Mama stalls for a second. "Suppose we'll have to work that out."

I shove my head between the door and Grandma's body. "What about school? I ain't so sure about going —"

"How many times I tell you not to say 'ain't'?" Grandma says, harsh. Then, "Lord, I hope he doesn't get y'all evicted in front of all those white Farmington Hills folks."

White Farmington Hills folks?

Mama brushes quick then spits into the sink. "Because getting put out in front of *Black* Detroit folks is better? Real nice, Ma." She moves past Grandma, grabs my bag, thrusts it into my arms, and snatches up her own.

"You know I don't mean no harm." Grandma trails after us to the door. When she sees my dad now standing on the sidewalk, she adjusts her shawl like a superhero cape, like she's going to fly over and beat him with her Bible till he

41

falls to his knees and repents. "After all these years, I see you still haven't learned the proper way to pick up my daughter," she spouts instead.

Dad stands tall, straight. His dark skin shines, like he rubbed on a little too much Vaseline. His full lips, wide nose, and thick eyebrows make him look strong. Handsome. A cigarette hangs loosely at the corner of his mouth, threatening to fall any second. Mama's already at the car when he reaches for her bag, opens the door, and helps her inside. "I didn't want to disturb you this early, Mrs. Foster," he says once Mama's door is closed.

"I see." Grandma steps out to the porch railing. "You'd rather disturb my neighbors?"

Dad takes a quick puff from his cigarette, drops it to the ground, and stubs it out. Then he finally reaches for my bag. "Hey, Gen-Gen."

"Hey," I say, handing it to him. I'm wishing the lemons suddenly did their magic and Dad'll rave about how pretty I've gotten since Thursday.

Grandma calls out, "I hear you're moving to Farmington Hills."

"You heard correct." Dad smiles, showing dark gums. I inherited his gums. I used to rinse my mouth with hydrogen peroxide to try to turn them pink like Mama's. They're still dark as plums. "You should see it. Plenty of space, huge backyard, clean neighborhood with lots of working folks."

"Hope you manage to hold on to this one, for a change," Grandma snarks.

Dad's eyes narrow. "Genesis, get in the car."

But before I can take two steps, Grandma calls out again. "Genesis, aren't you going to give Grandma a good-bye hug?"

I glance at Dad. I glance at Grandma. Tension creeps in like a shadow. Finally, I drag myself back up the sidewalk, up the stairs, and give Grandma a quick squeeze. Then I drag myself all the way to the car and climb in. I scrunch down in the backseat, done with being the rope in a tug-o'-war game.

"Surprise or no surprise, I can't take much more of this," is what Mama says once we're all in the car. She flicks at his arm, and Dad catches her hand and kisses it.

"This is the last time. I promise." He kisses her hand again.

The last time was supposed to be the last time. He promised.

Now Dad grins back at me.

I sit up and start to return his smile. Then I quickly sink back down.

"Why you so quiet, Gen-Gen?"

See, Dad has a way of making you forget that you're mad at him and what you're mad about in the first place. But today I want him to notice that even though I'm glad to see him, I'm still salty. So I turn to the window and simply say, " 'Cause."

" 'Cause?" Dad waits for me to elaborate, but I don't. "Oh, okay, it's like that? The silent treatment?" Dad fumbles around the console, when he should be keeping both hands on the wheel, and puts a CD in the player. At the first snare of the drum, my ears tune in. All on their own, my lips curl up, but I tighten them back down into a grimace.

*Listen, baby . . . ain't no mountain high,
ain't no valley low . . .*

Dad curls his fingers in Mama's hair
and croons the guy part of the song. His
voice is deep and mellow. When the
female part comes on, Dad balls one fist
into a pretend microphone and holds it
to Mama's mouth. She smacks his hand
away.

"You're not gonna sing? Forget it.
Come on, baby girl, let's show your
mama how it's done." Dad starts the
song all over again.

When I was little, Dad used to sing me
old Motown songs to stop my crying.
Only Motown. "The old songs have lyrics worth singing," he'd say. Singing
together used to be our thing; but he
hasn't asked me to sing in forever. So
now, half of me wants to stay mad. The
other . . . loves to sing. And even though
I'm salty, it ain't enough to stop me from
singing loud, so Dad can hear how much
I miss those times.

"Ain't no river wide enough, baby. . . ."

Soon, our voices drown out the CD.
Before I know it, I'm no longer in an
Impala with a dented bumper, but on-

stage in a short sequined gold dress and spiky heels, a giant fan blowing out my long blond weave like a horizontal halo, just like Beyoncé's. The crowd shouts, "Genesis, we love you!"

"Damn it!" Dad suddenly swerves around a pothole, but hits another one instead. "Gon' knock my wheels outta alignment again!"

The roads are so full of holes that it makes me bounce all over the place even with the seat belt on. Every year the mayor promises to clean up Detroit, but the potholes keep getting deeper no matter how much black gunk they fill them up with.

Forty-five minutes later, dead brown grass, overgrown foliage, and litter-lined streets are replaced by perfectly manicured lawns, sun-sheltering trees, and green recycle bins. We're apparently in Farmington Hills. "And here we are!" Dad says excitedly as we enter a development sectioned off with tall trees that stand like a row of police, guarding the place. A huge white wood sign with carved blue letters reads, WELCOME TO FARMINGTON ACRES.

"Dwight, Mike, and Chico helped me move everything early this morning. We even got the beds set up." Dad drives slowly down the street. "Nice, ain't it?"

Mama gasps. "Sure is." It's true. There's not a single boarded-up building, vacant lot, or ditched car in sight.

"And this here" — Dad parks in the driveway of a white brick house — "is ours, what you call a ranch-style house."

"*White* bricks?" I say, gunning to get a close-up.

"It's called 'white washed.' Like it?"

Now, I'm not gon' lie, I'm pretty psyched. . . . You know how you're watching a TV show and they flash to the outside of the character's rich-looking house? This house could be one of those flashes, for real.

"Look at that grass!" Mama exclaims, scrambling out of her seat belt. Dad's out of the car faster than Mama, and I'm not too far behind. "It's so thick and pretty."

This is true too. Not a single bald patch to be found.

"And these houses, they're beautiful,"

Mama goes on, noting niceties up and down the road. Shiny cars are parked in driveways, cute mailboxes posted at the curbs, and small lawn flags wave in the wind. It's fancier than Grandma's Sherwood Forest neighborhood.

Dad grabs Mama's hand and pulls her up the front steps. "Wait till you see the inside." He unlocks the door, swings it open and sings, "Ta-da!"

Mama's the first in, leading us into the living room. "Wow, it's a lot of space, Emory," she says giddily. The floors are hardwood. I can slide on them if I want to, but I'm way too old for that, so I probably won't. The room is long and wide, with a fireplace, not one of those fake ones that's bricked over, but a real Ho-Ho-Ho-Here-Comes-Santa kind. The dining room has a high ceiling with a chandelier hanging in the center. *A chandelier!* A million diamonds dangle from it; I'm not bragging, but if we had company, we could sit under it drinking swanky tea, holding our pinkies in the air.

"Yeah, it is a lot," I calmly chime in, but inside I'm screaming, *Oh my gosh,*

"That's not all." Dad beckons us to the kitchen. It's big too, with white cabinets and silver knobs, a cabinet that you give a swirl to open — which Dad calls a lazy Susan — both above and below the countertop, and a double sink with a spray faucet.

"Whoa, this is a big closet," I say, opening two doors.

"That's a pantry," Dad corrects. "Nice, huh?"

"All for food?" I step into it. "We can only put high-quality stuff in here like Grey Poupon and Evian water," I joke.

Dad raises his chin high. "Oh, yes, ma'am, we must stock Grey Poupon," he says snootily. We both laugh, taking turns mimicking his bougie interpretation, until Mama calls us silly.

"Stainless steel," she says, checking out the refrigerator. We've never had a silver refrigerator before. And definitely not one with a water and ice maker right on the door!

"Sharon" — Dad is beaming big time — "remember how we used to dream about having a house like this?" Mama remembers, because her eyes get glassy. "This is real marble, feel!" Dad knocks on the counters to prove how hard they are.

"It's like — from a magazine," I admit.

"Gen-Gen, you ain't seen nothin' yet." Dad opens the backdoor and steps out onto the deck. "There's so much we can do with a yard this size. We can finally have a barbecue with all our friends. Whaddaya think about that?"

At the mention of friends, my mind flashes back to Thursday's beef with Regina and the girls. I'm about to remind Dad that I don't *have* any friends, thanks to him, but I decide not to ruin this moment because for one — *this house!*

"I don't know," Mama says. "Let's just take one step at a time."

"I'll be right back." Dad disappears into the house humming "Ain't No Mountain High Enough," leaving Mama and me outside, letting this all settle in. Could this place really be ours? After a few minutes, Dad comes back saying, "Okay, y'all ready to see the rest yet?" Then he shows us the laundry room with a washer and dryer already in it — which Mama goes gaga about — then he takes us to a different door and opens it.

"This is our room, Sharon. The master bedroom. We even have our own bathroom. Check it out."

"Wow," I can't help but say. "It's . . . it's as big as our old living room."

"And see here," Dad says, going over to the window. "You can even sit on this little ledge, drink coffee, and read the paper. We can throw some cushions on there and make it real nice. What do you say?"

"It *is* . . . comfy," says Mama, trying out the ledge, her voice sounding uncertain. "But . . . can we afford this place? Your cut hours and my thirty-two don't add up."

Dad hesitates just a beat and then says, "I got it all under control."

"A place this size . . ." Mom glances around. "The cost of heat alone will eat up my paycheck, and then you add on electricity, water, cable, and groceries. . . ."

"Sharon . . ."

"You forget about the car note and insurance? Then there're the other expenses —"

"Sharon?"

"I don't know. . . ." She pauses, then adds carefully, "Plus, the weekly bus fare for catching the bus from out here —"

"Sharon?" Dad places a hand gently on her shoulder. "I've got one more surprise. . . . There's a high position opening up, with more money —" Mama's face stays worried, but Dad keeps talking. "I've got the years and experience; I'm a shoo-in for it."

Dad's never discussed a promotion before. A promotion — hey — maybe things could go back to the way they used to be, before the budgeting and the "we've got to make do."

"Dad, you're getting a new job? Like a real new job?"

"Yep, Gen-Gen." He laughs. "A real one." Then Dad lifts Mama's chin and peers into her eyes. "So stop worrying. Just have my back, like you used to, okay?"

"Yeah, of course." But not three seconds after Dad plants a sweet kiss on Mama's cheek, she asks, "But are you sure? Because, it never fails, every month there's some unforeseen bill — a tire's blown out, car tax due, insurance deductible for —"

"I said 'I got it,' didn't I?" But Dad rubs his forehead like he does when he's getting stressed.

I remind Mama that Dad's a shoo-in. "He'll be collecting those baller paychecks, right, Dad?"

"Yeah, Gen-Gen! See, that's what I'm talking about. I got it." Dad drapes his arm across my shoulders, saying, "Come on, let me show you your room." That's when he tells me the best part of this place is that the school's in walking distance. *New school?* I gotta be the new kid *again*? An attitude instantly creeps up my spine. But just as quick, my 'tude vanishes when we get to my room. So big! Huge! My bed, dresser, and bookcase fit with plenty of room to spare. I could turn up my music and give a whole concert, pretend to have a band plus backup dancers, and still have tons of space.

"It's dope, right? Didn't I tell you?" Dad hugs Mama. "Get settled. I've gotta make a run."

"Wait, you're leaving?" All the excitement drains out of me. "We just got here."

"Where're you going already?" Mama's tone gets real serious, real fast.

Dad scratches his head, stalling for an answer. One comes because he says, "Well, this house can't pay for itself," and then laughs as if it's funny.

I don't laugh. Neither does Mama. She repeats, "Where are you going, Emory?" But before she can launch into a rant, Dad flashes a dazzling smile. "I'll be back soon, trust me."

FOUR

With Dad gone, Mom and I mill around the house as if we're at a fancy department store, afraid to get attached to the big bedrooms, schmancy chandelier, and washer and dryer. We resist putting sheets on the beds, towels in the bathroom, or dishes in the cabinets. We take turns shaking our heads in disbelief 'cause *we* know what we're both thinking — we're sure we've made a mistake giving Dad another chance but maybe we could — for once, if only for a little while — chuck our worries and enjoy this unbelievable house.

"Should we wait till he comes back . . . ," I suggest, "to unpack?"

Mama runs her hand along the marble countertop and looks dreamy. "No, let's do it," she says, suddenly going to a box and ripping off the tape.

The boxes and bags are all unmarked, so we attack at random. Mama finds our cleaning supplies and unloads them. And then she starts unpacking so fast it's as if she's afraid Dad'll race back and say, "Sorry, babe, but we've gotta load it all back up," before she even gets everything *out* of the boxes. I'm just as fast 'cause in barely an hour I'm done cleaning and unpacking my room and the bathroom. Four hours later, it looks like we've lived here for months.

The house is stuffy like it's been shut up for a while, so Mama's opening all the windows. She tells me to get the broom to sweep the living room. When I get back, she's standing by a window, letting the wind catch her hair.

"I like the yard next door. Their flowers are pretty," she says. "I'd love to plant some, or hey, maybe we could start a garden with vegetables and stuff. I've always wanted to do something like that."

Mama looks real happy in her dream home. I mean, who wouldn't want to not have to haul their dirty clothes to the Laundromat or live with bars on the front door? As if living next to an abandoned building or lot is something we *want* to do. So yeah, it's not only Mama's dream to have a house like this, either. And now, here we are. So I answer, "Yeah, flowers would be cool."

What's not so cool is that Dad's still not back. And now I'm hungry, but I keep on pushing the broom around getting hungrier and madder about having been evicted, and scared of it happening again, and I finally burst out with, "It's not fair how we got to up and move."

"Why don't you take a break and go find some kids to hang out with?"

I won't tell Mama that there's no way I'm going to bother looking for new friends. Instead, I empty the dustpan and then find some saltines that made it here from our old place. I grab a packet of crackers, then flop on the sofa and stare at the fabric, remembering how Regina trash-talked it. It *is* sorta worn. "We need new furniture. This stuff doesn't fit with this house," I inform Mama.

"This *is* a beautiful place," Mama says. "Clean neighborhood, too."

"Yep and yep," I agree. "Mama?" I

hesitate 'cause one issue is still bugging me. "You think we'll have to move again?"

Mama takes a good look at me, as if deciding whether to answer or not. Then she says, "I don't know, Genesis," in her no-more-questions voice.

But just when I think she's done, Mama continues, "Monday I'll have to get a copy of your latest school transcript and request a transfer." Mama rummages through a box and pulls out a big brown envelope and some other papers. She's learned to keep her own files on me, including my birth certificate, previous transcripts, and immunization records. "I'll take this to the new school while your paperwork is being processed." Again. "Walking distance to the school is a plus. So, no more public bus passes or transfers." Is this supposed to make me want to go to school more? Mama adds, "Think of it as a new beginning. An adventure."

An adventure? Was she kidding? First of all, there's nothing remotely fun about standing in front of a room full of students staring me down like I stole something. And second of all, the teacher always makes me announce my name to a bunch of stank-faced kids. I might as well put a bull's-eye on my forehead. And third, the teacher almost always sits me in one of two places: the very front of the class or the very back. If I'm in front, I'm doomed because my head is target practice for every kid behind me. If I'm in back, I'm doubly doomed because then I have to walk the walk of nervousness, praying that some clown doesn't try to trip me on the way to my seat.

Yeah, great adventure.

Mama doesn't seem to notice my lack of response. She just looks around, pleased, until it hits her that Dad's not back. For another hour, we do a bit more cleaning, distracting ourselves from speculating where he might be. Mama dials him, but he doesn't pick up. My stomach growls, the crackers digested an hour ago. "Maybe we should order a pizza," she says, searching for restaurants in her phone. "Gosh, I don't even know this zip code."

Once she locates a pizza place and calls, Mama repeats the topping choices to me.

My mouth is already watering in anticipation. "Yes, let's go with breadsticks, too," she says into the phone. "Let me make sure I have enough, hold one second." Mama grabs her purse and takes out her wallet. "How much is the total again? Wait a minute . . ." Her fingers go frantic, going through each small section, and then repeating it all over again. "I'll have to call you back."

"What's the matter?" I ask.

"I could've sworn I had some money . . . no, I'm almost positive I had thirty-something dollars in here," she says, now searching her purse.

"Could you have spent it and forgot?" I ask, checking her wallet.

"I know a lot has been going on, but I ain't losing my mind, I don't think."

Then, as if on cue, we hear the familiar hum of Dad's car. "Dad's back?" I say, shocked. We both dash to the window, and we're even more shocked: He's filling his arms full of bags. I run to the door and open it.

"Why're you staring at me like you've seen a ghost?" Dad says, coming up the sidewalk, grinning like a maniac. "I told you that things would be different, didn't I? Now, come help put this stuff away."

"Okay, but Mama . . . hey, what's that smell?" I start poking into the bags as he steps around me. "Chinese food?"

Mama lags behind, closely observing him shelve the groceries. She's wearing a serious frown, but when Dad blows her a kiss, she relaxes a bit. "Emory, did you —"

"See," Dad says, cutting her off. He's stocking the pantry with cereal, pancake mix, rice, crackers, and canned vegetables. "We're going to fill this thing up, plus the cabinets, too," he says, a little too happily.

I put the milk and pop in the fridge, a little miffed that Dad didn't inform us he was going grocery shopping. I would've asked for lemons, if I'd known.

"Hmph." Mama raises an eyebrow. "Chinese food? You bought it because you know I'm nicer with a full stomach."

"I bought *all* this food 'cause I know y'all hungry," he says, wiping sweat from his brow.

"He's right about that," I say, moving past my irritation and forgetting about Mama's wallet. The table is loaded with all our favorites. Chicken and broccoli for Mama, sweet-and-sour chicken for me, General Tso's chicken for him, and shrimp fried rice for all of us. And orange Faygo, too. He brought the good stuff, as if he just won the lottery.

"You know, Gen, we might not've had Chinese food if it wasn't for the Gold Rush."

"The Gold Rush?" I ready myself for one of Dad's mini history lessons. I set the table, listening as he explains how rumors of gold nuggets drove folks to California, some coming from as far as China. I'm thankful for those rumors 'cause now I can chow down on this good meal.

Dad goes to the kitchen sink and washes his hands. "Yep, the miners loved it," he says, grabbing a paper towel. "Good food and cheap prices." Before he sits down, Dad takes off his jacket and swings it onto the back of his chair. And four flat circles fall out of his pocket and clink to the floor.

"Chips? Poker chips?" One split second passes before Mama flies off the handle. "Is this how you paid for all this food?"

Dad's forehead goes sweatier, and it's not from putting away groceries.

"You rather I have you starve?" Dad says, defensively snatching up the chips and stuffing them back into his jacket pocket.

"Have us starve?" Mama echoes. "Emory, please. What you did ain't about starving."

It sure isn't because Dad could've been like, "Babe, I've gotta do something that'll piss you off. . . ." But naw, he waltzes in like a champ with dinner — and now — busted.

"Listen, I have to make sacrifices —"

"Playing Blackjack or Craps or whatever the heck you've been playing is hardly a sacrifice," Mama says, real serious. "I'm gon' ask you one time, did you take money from my wallet?"

"Why you even trippin'? I won, didn't I?" Mean Dad scratches at the surface. I can see him in the reddening of Dad's eyes.

"I don't give a da—" Mama stops, editing herself.

Mama almost cursed. The thing is, Mama doesn't curse — at all. She could've cursed when we got put out in the snow, or the time some crackheads stole our flat-screen. She really should've cursed when we had to stay in Dad's friend's dusty basement, plus him going off on me — boy was she mad then, but she didn't curse.

"You thieving money from me now?" Mama gets up from the table.

"Would you just hear me out?" Dad pleads.

"Eat your dinner, Emory. Don't want your 'sacrifice' getting cold." With that, Mama stalks out of the kitchen.

Dad and I sit at the table. Close-mouthed. Finally, Dad grabs his jacket, pulls out a bottle, and drinks straight from it. I gape at him.

He wipes sweat from his brow again and says, "What? You got something you wanna say too?"

Yeah. You ain't ever gon' learn, are you? is what my mouth wants to shoot out, but instead I quietly say, "Naw, I'm good," shovel in four forkfuls of chicken, and then escape from the table before Dad's liquor takes effect.

It's a good thing I left. Because a half hour later he's drunk — mean drunk — and the shouting has started.

I try to block it out, but Mama's voice reaches clear to my room. "I've tried to help you. For the last five years! I thought if I could just love you enough, then you could kick it. But you need help, help I can't give you." Mama now sounds real stern. "Emory, there's only one thing that I can think of . . . Alcoholics Anonymous. You've got to go, Em. Otherwise . . ."

Mama lets her last word hang in the air. *Otherwise.* Even though she doesn't say it, we all know what "otherwise" means. And you know what else? We all know that she means it, for real.

FIVE

In the new school's main office, my right foot will not stop tapping. My stomach is cramping up too because of this thing I do: I hold my stomach in without even realizing it. And when I do realize it, I take deep breaths to relax. But all on its own my stomach goes right back, squeezing tight again. *Stop it, stomach!* I focus on a poster of an eagle soaring over the mountains that reads YOUR ATTITUDE DETERMINES YOUR ALTITUDE. A cross-eyed bulldog, the school's mascot, is painted on the wall beside it. Even though it's only a painting, I don't like the way his left eye stares at me.

"So, you're requesting transcripts, correct? And even brought a file of your own," says the lady behind the counter — Ms. Bramble, her nametag says. "Very

66

sufficient, indeed. Let me just finish putting you into the system." After a little while, she hands Mama back the big manila envelope.

"Now, Genesis," Ms. Bramble addresses me, "you'll take this schedule to your first class. You have Ms. Luctenburg for language arts. She's in A-8. She's also your homeroom teacher."

Mama scans the paper and nods her approval. "I would come along, but I'm running late for work. 'Sides, you're probably too old for that, right?" She looks around warily. She, too, notices the newness, the foreignness of this place. So far we haven't spotted a broken window or even a single ceiling tile caving in. Shoot, a school like this probably will never have lead in their water fountains. Mama smooths down my eyebrows. "You need a little lotion on your face" — she starts digging into her purse — "and your lips are chapped."

"Stop, you're making me nervous," I say, backing away.

"Sorry," she says, now fingering the unruly edges around my forehead before giving me a tight hug. "You'll be fine."

She thanks Ms. Bramble and leaves me standing there.

Mama's right. I'm old enough to go alone and ordinarily I wouldn't care, but today I wouldn't mind having her by my side at this fancy school. "Which way?" I ask the lady.

"Out the door, to the left, and down the hall, sweetie." Her voice is gentle — makes my stomach relax. "And welcome to Farmington Oaks Middle, have a good first day. First days can be scary."

If she only knew about my last three first days, this swanky school should be a cakewalk. These kids probably cried if their pencils didn't have erasers or if their markers ran dry. Shoot, I've been to schools where there are no markers. Like I said, cakewalk.

The hall's crazy with kids. I've never seen so many white faces all in one place in my entire life. I search the crowd. It seems like forty kids shuffle pass before I finally find some kids who look like me. I smile. They look at me weird.

So much for solidarity.

I force myself into the current. Under a

TOGETHER WE STOMP OUT BULLYING sign, an old man stands waving, warning us to stop running, slow down, and have a good day. No one pays him any attention. Two guys cruise in front of me with pants sagging. Pfft. Like seriously, nobody's that hard out here in Farmington Hills. A tall, white lady stands by a classroom door eyeing everyone passing by.

"Boys!" She's calling out to the pants-at-knees guys. They just about skid to a stop. "If you dress like you're less than nothing, then you will be treated like you're less than nothing. Sadly, this is not an option for you to choose. You will have some decency about you and pull up your pants."

Guess what? They do it! And guess what else? She's standing in front of classroom A-8. I flatten back my hair, step up to her, and hold out my schedule.

She peers over her silver frames. "Good morning, may I help you?"

You know those old movies where the wind's kicking up dust and big tumbleweeds roll across the TV screen? That's how dry my throat feels. "I'm new."

69

"Speak up, please. You will have to learn to use your voice, young lady."

"I'm new," I say again, louder, showing her my paper.

"Genesis Anderson," she says, reading over the sheet. "I am Ms. Luctenburg." She hands my schedule back, directing, "Go on in and wait by my desk, please. I'll be there shortly."

Wait by her desk? Really? Everyone in the entire class will inspect me like I'm a freak show. And of course, that's exactly what they do, too, as I stare at the back wall, cheeks burning.

"Cute outfit," one girl says. I can't be sure who, but I glance over in time to see the smug look on the face of a red-haired girl. She's leaning on her desk, as if challenging me to say something. Before I dare part my lips to respond, she adds, "Where'd you get it? Goodwill?"

And everyone laughs. Instantly, I regret not wearing my blousy printed shirt — the only one that Regina has ever complimented me on — but dang, I thought this pink camo T-shirt was decent. Now I'm faced with a new-kid dilemma — should I clap-back? Red-haired girl is leaning, anticipating. No, it's better to keep my mouth shut until I can figure out how to deal with these suburban kids.

As I wait by the stupid desk pretending not to hear a thing, more kids drift in — mostly white kids. One white girl with glasses brushes by fast. She takes a seat by the wall, moves her desk a little to the left and then a little to the right, and back and forth like two more times before sitting down. As I watch her, a girl with light brown skin breezes past smelling like Grandma's Avon creams. Jasmine, maybe? And this girl has dreadlocks. The locs aren't even all the same size, some fat and some thin. Trust me, ain't no boys checkin' for her with that never-seen-a-comb hair, 'cause where I'm from, if your hair's not straight, bobbed, pixied, or even braided, then you can forget it. It's a waste to be a Lite-Brite with a nappy hairstyle like dreadlocks.

The classroom is just about full when a boy — dark as me, *thank you!* — passes by with a low: "Excuse me." He must be into sports because his arm muscles nearly burst through his sweater. And two more brown-faced boys stroll in, a real dark boy, but without the muscles — two in one class, *double thank you!* — and the other, he looks mixed.

Just then, Ms. Luctenburg steps inside the room and everyone simmers down. She stands beside me and says, "As you have noticed, we have with us a new student. Her name is Genesis Anderson." She waits as if expecting applause. "Would you like to share anything, Miss Anderson?"

I shake my head.

"In this class, we use our words to communicate." A few kids snicker. "Who would like detention with me?" she adds, glaring out at the snickerers. Immediate silence. She turns back to me. "What school are you joining us from?"

Right then, my mind draws a blank on the last school's name and before I know it I blurt, "Detroit."

Over-the-top laughter.

Ms. Luctenburg's lip curls as if she smells old pinto beans, and everyone again hushes. She explains to me that the class is currently finishing book reports, then releases me with, "You may take the desk in row two, seat three."

Great, near the front.

"Dang, she's burnt," the no-muscled boy says under his breath, and I quickly roll my eyes at him. Mixed-boy laughs, and I turn to glare at him, and meet his hazel eyes. He has good hair, soft and wavy. He opens his mouth and —

"Mr. Jason Smithy," Ms. Luctenburg calls out. "Do you have a joke you would like to share with the class?"

"No."

"Perhaps you would like to be the first person to volunteer to read your book report?"

He hisses and then shuffles to the front of the class. "Mr. Smithy" covers his face with his paper and reads really fast.

"Paper down in front of you. Slow down and start again, please."

He clears his throat. His hands shake. "My paper is on *No More Dead Dogs* by Gordon Korman. The main charac-ter, Wallace Wallace, is assigned to write a book review, which happens to be on his teacher's favorite book from when she was a kid." He glances at Ms.

Luctenburg, then clears his throat. "But he hates the story because it is extremely boring."

Ms. Luctenburg makes him stop and start about five more times, urging him to speak up and articulate for the sake of public speaking. By the time Jason is done, his cheeks are red and shiny. I feel sorry for him because it's a pretty good report. Three more kids present after him, but I wouldn't be able to name the titles of their books if you asked. What I can tell you is that Ms. Luctenburg seems to be one of those teachers who was born without a single funny bone in her body.

When class is dismissed, Jason is in front of me as we file out. He doesn't even glance my way, and he doesn't say anything smart, either. And well . . . let's just say that I'm all the more determined to get more lemons.

My math teacher, Mr. Benjamin, reminds me of Albert Einstein, like, a Hollywood character of a math teacher. He hands me an assessment and rattles something about it being standard. "First, answer the questions that you know, and then go back and answer the rest as best you can.

The grade won't count against you."

An assessment on the very first day? He can't be serious. I mean, I've taken assessments before, but never on the first day. What kind of teacher puts a new student through a traumatic experience like this? Mr. Benjamin, that's who. It must be a mistake. Any teacher with hair as wild as his has to be kind of screwy. "Mr. Benjamin? Am I supposed to be taking this *now*?"

"Yes, of course." He gestures to the class. "Take any available seat you'd like."

I choose a desk toward the rear of the first row. Then, I flip open the cover sheet. Multiple choice. Amen. Multiplication — I got that. Why was I even buggin'? Division — easy breezy, except the double digits slow me down. Multiply fractions — skip. Decimals — just count the decimal places, right? Percents — how many pages is this thing? Word problems — screech to a halt. I have a stare down with the first question:

Michael bought 8 ball caps for 8 friends at $8.95 each. The sales clerk charged him an additional $12.07 in sales tax. He left the store with only $6.28. How much money *did Michael start with?*

Michael bought eight ball caps. Got it. For eight friends. He has eight friends? I bet they're not best friends. That's unrealistic. Eight caps, $8.95 each, plus $12.07 in tax. $12.07 for tax? What a rip-off. He probably won't even have enough money left to buy his own self a cap. Michael is a darn fool for spending all that money on people he thinks will be his friends. How much money did Michael start with? A lot. Must be rich. Rich and stupid. Evidently, Michael doesn't have a grandma to tell him that "money buys everything but good sense."

All around me kids pack and leave the classroom. The dark-skin muscle guy is in this class, too, and he stops to talk to the teacher. I quickly go back through the test. I skipped half the questions! There's no way I'm turning this in and having Mr. Benjamin thinking I'm dumb, so, real fast, I randomly circle answers.

Mr. Benjamin comes over. "Aren't you dedicated! I like that. However, I'm afraid you'll be late to your next class."

I hand him the paper, front side down, and tell him that I didn't have enough time to finish.

"Would you like to complete it tomorrow?"

"No, I made educated guesses."

"I see." He turns the paper over, scanning it. "I'm sure you did fine."

Hmph. Mr. Benjamin doesn't have a clue.

On my way to finding the gym, I can hardly move without bumping someone. My schedule's damp with hand sweat, and the room number is now smeared and hard to read. Then I catch a whiff of rubber and B.O. — phew — the gym! I join the pack of kids surging in. The padded walls make the gym look like a room for crazy people. And I must be one because I wanna bash my body against them until my nervousness goes away; in PE there are always some kids waiting to size up us newbies.

Girls and boys split away to opposite sides of the gym and disappear through doors that have the words LOCKER ROOM above them. There's no way I'm going in there — especially without clothes to change into. Can you say creepy? An office is in the back corner, and that's the direction my feet go. A woman spots me through the window and gets up. "Well, here's a new face," she says, closing the door behind her. "Do you have your schedule?"

I hand her the soggy paper.

She checks her clipboard and makes a mark. "Welcome to PE, Anderson. I'm Coach Singletary. And over there with the boys is Coach Baynor. Play any sports?"

"A little bit . . . double Dutch." Technically, double Dutch is an official sport, and I turned the ropes two and a half times in sixth grade.

She gives me a once-over and chuckles. *Chuckles.* "Did you order a PE uniform?"

"I don't think so."

"We'll have it ready for next time. I suppose you didn't bring any gym clothes?"

I tell her I didn't, tugging at my jeans that suddenly feel too snug to be trying to show off my non-game.

Coach Singletary instructs me to take a

seat against the wall. She strides over to the half-court line and blows her whistle as the last few girls straggle out from the locker room. "Listen up. We're shooting hoops again today. Get back into your assigned groups and get started." Girls randomly run over to a rack of balls. Coach tells me that my street clothes shouldn't get in the way of my having fun, so go ahead, join a group or grab a ball.

Basketball is not my sport of choice. Still, I grab a ball and go to a less occupied net at the far end of the court, hoping not to be checked out as I check out everybody else. The girl with glasses from Ms. Luctenburg's class dribbles deliberately. I watch her for a few minutes, noticing how she inspects the ball closely before each shot like she's examining it for germs or something. Her team shouts for her to shoot already, but she takes her sweet time. That's when she sees me staring, and I immediately throw my ball, which clearly doesn't fly anywhere near the net. I chase after it, ignoring the chuckles that are surely happening.

Someone calls out "Yvette," and a dark girl with bangs swivels around. She's what Grandma would call "plump" — not fat, just a little pudgy — or what guys call "thick." And her hair is long and bone straight. The girl passing her the ball has good hair like Mama's, except hers is sandy brown. They dribble and shoot as if a bunch of boys are watching — hard enough to appear to be playing, but hardly enough to work up a sweat.

And wanna know something? None of these girls seem to be paying me any mind, which means that once I figure out the group that, you know, I wanna hang with, then I probably won't have to jump through any hoops — not like at my last school. *Jump through hoops* — now, that's funny. I bounce the ball more relaxed now. You know why? 'Cause my day just got better.

Or so I thought. Getting to the next class is a disaster. Why? First, I get so twisted around trying to find Wing C that I have to go to the office. Ms. Bramble high-lights a map, but once I leave, all I see is a maze of boxes and lines. Just as tears of frustration start to prick my eyes, a voice says, "You need help with that?" It's the sweater-wearing dude from my first class. "You're new, right?"

I nod.

"You're in my English and math classes. I'm Troy."

Just then, another Black dude runs up and punches Troy in the arm. "Yo! What's up with those science notes, Bill Nye."

"I asked you to not call me that," Troy tells him.

"Stop acting so sensitive," the boy teases, rubbing Troy's head.

He pushes the boy's hand away. "I'm not."

"Man, I'm only playing. But seriously, I need those notes," the boy says, before running off.

I almost don't want to put Troy on the spot, but I can't help myself. "Why he call you Bill?"

"Inside joke," Troy says dismissively. "Anyway, what's your next class?"

I hand him my schedule, dropping the issue.

"Chorus. Oh, Mrs. Hill. Go down this hall. . . ." As he gives me directions, I try to focus real hard on his words, but I can't stop geeking inside that he stopped to help me. After getting me on track, Troy dashes off as quickly as he'd shown up.

When I find C-4, it's as if I've landed in a Bruno Mars rehearsal. Music's blaring, and xylophones, drums, maracas, and practically any instrument you can imagine are scattered all over the room. Black-and-white photographs of musicians and singers hang on the walls. Students are taking seats situated in a half circle. The smart-mouthed kid from English strolls in; he better not crack on me, if he knows what's good for him. He doesn't, thank goodness. Jason's in this class too. He approaches that Yvette girl from gym with a bounce harder than any dude in Detroit, and they start snickering.

I venture a little farther into the room. A closet door is open, and a rump sticks out. Then a Black lady straightens up and closes the door. I haven't seen any other Black adults here. Well, not in any of *my* classes, and I pray right then that she's the teacher. When the lady notices me, she immediately comes over. "Well, hello. I'm Mrs. Hill."

"You are?" I manage to say, handing her my schedule while doing a happy dance inside.

"Why yes. Were you expecting someone else?" Mrs. Hill says, checking over my course list. I can't stop staring. Her cheeks are big and round with deep dimples. Her face is caramel brown, and her hair's cut into a short, curly Afro, which is okay for her because she's old. And this lady teaches my chorus class.

I exhale and three butterflies fly out.

"Please excuse me for a moment," she says. She turns off the music and proceeds to the center of the room. "Class." She waits for their attention. Here it comes. I concentrate on a photograph of a lady singing into a microphone.

"Take a few minutes to warm up your voices, and then sing 'The Drinking Gourd' three times in its entirety. Let's go, sopranos, altos, tenors. . . ." Chairs scrape against the floor as kids turn their seats toward each other.

A blond girl raises her hand. "Mrs. Hill, which exercises do you want us to do?"

"Sing the alphabet using the five-note scale up and down, twice. And then start on the song, got it?"

"Can I lead us?" Yvette says.

"We don't need a leader," says Smart-Mouthed Kid. He gets a few laughs.

Yvette throws up one hand, saying, "Whatev." Her friend with the sandy-brown hair, who she had called Belinda, whispers something and they giggle.

"Thank you, Yvette, for volunteering." Then Mrs. Hill says to the boy, "Terrance, I expect you to follow Yvette's lead, understand?" He nods, frowning.

Mrs. Hill then comes back to me. She hands me my schedule and says, "Now, Miss Genesis." She says my name like a pretty song, then assesses me as if I'm a piece of sheet music. "Let me guess. You're like slow jazz from Miles Davis. Observant, endearing, yet complex." She points to a poster of a man blowing real hard on a horn. "Have you heard of him?"

Should I take this as a compliment or

insult because this man is midnight black. Bottom of your shoe black. Burnt rubber on Grand River Boulevard black. He's so black that he makes *me* look light. If I have heard of him, I'd never admit it. "No."

"I'll have to play him for you one day. His music is truly remarkable." Then she nods toward the other students. "Listen to that." The voices harmonize, echoing through the room, and I have to admit, they sound good singing something as simple as the alphabet.

I steal a chance to scope out the class. The flowery-smelling girl from language arts, Nia Kincaid, sits with the sopranos sharing a music sheet with two white girls. Yvette sings above everyone as she's up front, directing. Jason sits back in his chair, hardly moving his lips like he's too cool. His boy Terrance mean-mugs me, so I frown back.

Mrs. Hill leaves me again and goes to the piano. All I can think is: *Lady, would you please let me go sit down?*

But then she's back, handing me a sheet of paper. "This is the song we're working on, 'Follow the Drinking Gourd.'

Here's some background: The drinking gourd represents the Big Dipper in the night sky. As I've already shared with the class, folklorists explain that the song tells the tale of Peg Leg Joe, who would wait on the banks of the Ohio River to sail runaways across to the other side. But in actuality, it was a roadmap for slaves to follow to freedom." She then tells me about the Underground Railroad and how it's said that trees were secretly marked with charcoal or mud with the symbol of a left foot and peg foot. "The whole song's a secret message."

The class is on their second round of the song, and Mrs. Hill still doesn't have me sit down.

"Beautiful, isn't it?" I don't answer because I don't want her thinking I like standing here listening to her speech. She continues anyway. "Not just the singing, but the words, too."

"When the sun comes back and the first
    quail calls,
Follow the Drinking Gourd,
For the old man is a-waiting for to carry

86

you to freedom,
If you follow the Drinking Gourd."

"Jason, I need you to enunciate, please," she suddenly calls out. "You too, Terrance. Remember to breathe, Susan." Mrs. Hill then confesses, "There's something about spirituals that gets to me. This song in particular is special to my family. When I was a little girl, my grandpa would sit me on his knee and sing it to me, tell me the story of his daddy's great-grandpa who was a slave in Kentucky and how he escaped to Philadelphia. Can you imagine singing a song that your great-great-great grandpa sang to cling to the hope of freedom?"

No, I can't. Mama rarely shares stories about the old, old days. Dad tells me tales, but never about family. Grandma recites the same old stuff, but it doesn't go back that far. And apparently no one told Mrs. Hill that we don't talk about slavery anymore, because she goes on like she's proud to know her ancestors were picking cotton.

The song ends. Yvette's riding boots clack on the floor all the way back to her seat. Now all eyes are on Mrs. Hill and me. Here goes, Mrs. Hill will finally make me introduce myself. But shockingly, she doesn't. She whispers for me to take the open seat in the soprano section, immediately makes everyone stand, and leads us through the song herself.

I hold the music sheet out in front of me. Even though it seems like I'm singing, my mind is on Mrs. Hill's story. Her grandpa's great-great grandpa must've made it to freedom; otherwise she wouldn't be broadcasting that information. Her family probably sits around the table every Thanksgiving recounting that same tale. Shoot, if my great-great-great-great grandpa made it all the way to freedom, and had survived all the terrible stuff slaves had to endure, guess I'd blab the story too. Makes me wish Mama or Dad would tell me our family history, no matter how bad it might be.

When class is over, Mrs. Hill stops me. "Now, I know it's your first day. And you may be a bit nervous, but I'd like to find your key. Do you sing much?"

"A little . . . in my room." For some reason, I share this secret with her.

"That's the best place, isn't it? Come over here, this'll only take a few minutes." Mrs. Hill goes to the piano and sits. "Stand right there, perfect." She presses one key at a time and hums. Then she has me repeat after her. Every time I do, she says, "That's good, real good." About ten keys later she closes the piano and declares, "You're an alto. I want you to learn the words, sing what you remember, but don't worry about the musical notes unless you read music."

"Yes, ma'am." Then I add, "I can't read music."

"That's fine." Mrs. Hill escorts me to the door. "And, Genesis," she says, taking my hand, "when you practice, I don't want you to just sing it. I want you to embrace it."

"Yes, ma'am." I feel a smile creeping on my face, the first one all day.

Mrs. Hill wants me to sing. I'm down for that, just as long as she doesn't ever have me sing by myself. Having people gawk and talk about me every time I start a new school is bad enough, but singing in front of everybody? Alone? I can see myself now, adding to my list. # *What-*

ever: Because she acted like she was Beyoncé and they laughed her right out of Farmington Hills. No, thank you.

SIX

Day one of school — conquered. Even with the red-haired girl dissin' my clothes and Terrance giving me dirty looks, it still was nothing compared with my other first days. Trust me, I've been mean-mugged by the scariest, shoved by the toughest, picked on, made friends, then dumped by the best of 'em. Never mind that two girls hated me so much — *for no reason at all!* — they made a list full of stupid stuff just to inform me that they hated me.

Once inside my house and in my new room, I turn on my old trusty CD player's radio — one of the things I've managed to keep during our moves — and immediately start digging in my junk box in the closet. I push past a bag of nail polish, my Rihanna CDs, and an iPod that's missing its charger, till it's in my hands: my black button-down shirt, had it since I was seven. For the first time all day I let myself really relax. I drape the shirt over my head, pull it back into a ponytail, and tie it with a ribbon. It sways to the right and left, cascading down my back just like Rihanna's. It feels kinda silly — I'm not seven anymore — but I don't care. It lets me pretend to have good hair. It makes me beautiful. Even my skin looks lighter against the dark fabric.

Next, I sneak into Mama's bathroom, steal her makeup bag, and slide out her foundation. The cream glides over my skin like icing. Now I'm light-skinned. I turn up the volume on my CD player. And I can't stop myself: I start singing along, letting my voice — the voice that won't ever come out if anyone's listening — loose. Everyone in the audience begins to wave their arms and dance in the aisles. Then from behind the curtain comes a rare and special appearance — Dad. He grins at me — *for* me — and joins me onstage, a microphone in his hand, and the drums thump and the horns blare.

The song ends. A commercial comes on, and just like that — my fantasy's over for now. I pull the shirt off my head, wash my face, and do my social studies homework. When I'm done, I turn off my music and go sit in the picture window — I can't believe we have a picture window! — and watch the street. Then I get to thinking that, yeah, we should have flowers in our yard. After a while, all on its own, my body starts to rock side to side and before I know it, I'm humming. Humming Mrs. Hill's song. Then singing.

"When the sun comes back and the first
    quail calls,
Follow the Drinking Gourd,
For the old man is a-waiting for to carry
    you to freedom,
If you follow the Drinking Gourd."

This reminds me of when, oh, about two schools ago, I read a book about a family of slaves who tried to escape over the Cincinnati River in the winter. They didn't even have coats or boots. Nothing except the clothes on their backs. It had to be really unbearable to drop everything and run off like that. I can't help but wonder how it feels to be so bound up that you can't be or do what you want. Bound so tight that you'd take a huge risk like that, crossing a river in the snow.

One day. That's all it takes for Mr. Benjamin to discover that I know nearly nothing about math. He discreetly lays the assessment facedown on my desk. I flip over a corner. Forty-nine percent. *Great.* I stuff the stupid test in my backpack, knowing what's to come. At the end of class, Mr. Benjamin's sure to tell me that he's moving me to the low math class. Not zoning out is hard 'cause my mind keeps asking, *What's the point?* And I keep answering, *I know. I'll never get math.*

But then Mr. Benjamin excitedly posts himself in front of the class and scribbles marks on the smart screen that look like hieroglyphics. "My friends, today we'll be starting a new unit." He extends his arm and announces, "The slope and *y* intercept."

Mute. We all stare.

"The sooner you all embrace math, the less painful it will be. I promise."

We all grunt. Loud.

"Before you start groaning and moaning, my friends, let me explain. Math is like a chess game, or . . . or a puzzle. Even the Rubik's Cube can be solved by using algorithms."

"That's why I never got that cube," says a boy with a surfer haircut.

Hilarious. We all laugh.

"Allow me to show you." Mr. Benjamin draws formulas, connects lines, waves his hands and joggles his eyebrows. Everyone in class copies examples, asks questions, solves equations, and gets excited. Even me.

When class is over, Mr. Benjamin calls me to his desk. *I knew it!* "I believe I've worked out a solution that'll help you catch up."

"A . . . solution?"

"Yes, I have a wonderful student who'll tutor you."

Okay, this is something new. But hold up — the last thing I need is some nerdy white kid trying to make me out to be a dumb Detroit girl. "What do you mean?" I ask cautiously.

"Here, meet Troy Benson. Troy?"

Troy, the one who helped me in the hallway and is in my language arts class, too. Here's the thing — all of a sudden I'm a tiny bit nervous, I mean, because he is a boy. I mean, I knew he was a boy. Obviously . . . but this is me, Genesis, working one-on-one with a boy.

Troy strides over, grinning. His teeth are crazy white. *He'd be half cute if he weren't so dark,* is what Grandma would say. Me? He's definitely half cute.

"My classroom is open for use during lunch or after school, if you like," says Mr. Benjamin. "Well, I must leave you two to figure out timing — I have to prepare for my next class."

"I can take it from here, Mr. B." Troy turns to me and says, "Hello, again."

"Hey," I say, ignoring the fact that my hands have gone clammy.

"Genesis, right?"

My cheeks get hot. *Chill, girl.* "Yeah."

"So, we can meet either during lunch

or after school, it doesn't matter," Troy tells me. "We can start out with three days a week, see how you do."

"How 'bout lunch?" I say.

"Great, let's start tomorrow," Troy says, going back to his desk and packing up his things.

I feel silly just standing there watching, so I ask, "Do you tutor a lot?"

He slings the bag's strap over his shoulder and hurries back. "Sometimes, for extra credit." He stops, pulls out a comic book, and tucks it under his arm.

"We were doing something else at my other school. And I just made some dumb mistakes on that assessment, that's all," I say, covering; I don't want him to think I'm some moron. All these different lessons from the different schools are jumbled in my head, and I can't sort them out.

"Don't worry, we'll straighten you out; a lot of people get tripped up on math."

Troy and I are walking down the hall — talking. I can feel a stupid grin on my face, and I can't stop it, can't even say something cool like, *Hey, thanks for look-*

ing out yesterday, when I was turned around. Well, that's not exactly cool, but still, I can't say it because my lips are frozen. And the grin's still there even after Troy leaves for class.

I'm totally killin' it on day two. Not.

I hate these shorts.

The PE uniforms must be made weird because no matter how much I shimmy the shorts down my thighs, they still creep up when I sit, totally failing to protect my butt from the cold, hard gym floor.

Coach Singletary is pacing back and forth in front of us, blabbing about some physical fitness test that'll count as 75 percent of our grade. "You'll be expected to run a full mile. Timed." A mile? I ain't never run that much unless I was being chased. Then she goes on about curl-ups, push-ups, and flexibility tests. "Any questions?"

Someone raises a hand. "Does the test start today?"

"No, but pre-testing does. The boys will start with curl-ups and push-ups with

Coach Baynor. And the girls will have the pleasure of running outside in my company."

"But that's not fair," another girl protests. "It's freezing out there!"

"Life's not fair," answers Coach. "And yes, it's a little brisk. Just remember to pace yourselves. Don't want you on the sidelines upchucking." A few kids laugh. "Move. Once you get your blood flowing, you'll warm up."

While the boys grab mats, we girls grudgingly follow Coach Singletary. The gym doors burst open, and a blast of chill air sends goose bumps racing up my arms. When we get to the track, I stand to the side and pretend to tie my shoes as clusters of girls jog off. Yvette and Belinda sprint away, with a few girls encircling them. Once they're all ahead of me, I start. It takes forever to complete one puny, little lap. No, it's not puny. It's enormous. It's so big that Usain Bolt himself would stop and say, "Now wait a minute."

By the second lap, I'm gasping for air. My arms pump harder, my entire body aches, and only the momentum carries me forward. Sweat rolls down my back. I wipe my forehead.

My forehead.

My hair.

Sweat is like kryptonite to pressed hair, kinks it right up.

"What's the problem, Anderson?"

"Cramp," I lie.

"Walk it out."

Coach doesn't need to tell me twice. I mosey along, fanning my face and praying silently that my hair doesn't get any worse than it is already. Not too far ahead, the basketball-inspecting girl with glasses from yesterday runs alone. Every so often she stops and ties her shoes, but I keep my distance. She's not weird looking from what I can tell. She must have crooked teeth or a wandering eye or something strange about her. Why else would she be by herself? Before I know it, I find myself jogging a few feet behind her. I hang back — she's even slower than I am — and soon my pace falls in sync with hers.

Suddenly, as if she has eyes in the back of her head, she spins around. "There are other lanes; can't you find one to run in instead of following me?"

I freeze. But no way am I gonna act afraid of a white suburban girl. "For your info," I say, "I wasn't following you. There're a million girls on this track — someone's bound to be behind you."

"And you just happen to be the lucky one." She talks with a sharp twang. "Don't think I haven't noticed you watching me."

I put my hand on my hip and say, "Girl, I ain't been paying you no attention." But I do check her out quickly — she doesn't have a wandering eye or crooked teeth. She's actually kinda pretty.

The girl keeps at it. "What about on your first day, huh?"

"I don't know. I might've glanced your way."

"Might've? Really?" She raises one eyebrow.

And I raise one too.

We stand facing each other, ignoring the whistles and screams of Coach warning us to get back to running. Ignoring the other girls on the track who're slowing down to examine the scene, ready to shout, *Fight, fight.*

Then the girl does something unpredictable.

She yells at the gawkers, "What're you looking at? Haven't you seen two people talking before? Geez!"

Then she says, "I hate this track."

And I say, "We didn't have to do this at my old school."

"You didn't? You're lucky." White girl with glasses unties and reties her shoes, and then we walk-jog again.

"What's up with them making us run in the cold?" I say. "We could get the flu."

"Or walking pneumonia," she adds, "and die."

"Well, that's a little extreme," I say. "But I feel you."

"Get outta the way!" a girl says from behind. Waves of blond and brown tresses bounce past us. "Move it, freak!" They all giggle that mean-girl giggle. I'm not sure which one of us — me, or what *is* her name? — they're talking to, because we both go silent.

Coach whistles for us to pick up the pace. We don't. Instead, the glasses girl fools around with her shoestrings again, and I fuss with my hair. Coach is yelling and her face is getting redder and redder, and this girl is tying and retying each shoe. Just as Coach is about to have a conniption, she stands up and says, "You know what's the worst?" She jerks her head toward the girls in front of us. "Them."

"No doubt," I agree. We watch them run to the same beat like a pack of clones. Then I glance at Coach, who is now yelling at a different set of girls.

The girl adds, "They think they're all that, like they're better than you or something."

"Me?" I ask, suddenly panicking — how did I already become their target.

"No, other girls, in general," she explains.

We start back jogging. And it's now clear to me that the girls were dissing *her.*

Glasses girl is thin but not skinny. Her nose is regular, her mouth's regular, and she has nice brown eyes. I don't get it.

Why are they slamming her? So I ask, "Why you think they be trippin' like that?"

She jogs a few more steps before answering. "Jealous maybe?" She adds, "Who knows?"

Now I jog without answering because I sure as heck don't know.

Coach's "Move It!" yells get louder as we round the track. "Anderson and Papageorgiou, move those legs!"

We step it up before Coach can run behind us blowing her whistle.

"What she call you?"

"My name. Papageorgiou, and I don't wanna hear a joke about it."

Now I know I like her. She's tired of jokes too.

"Just wanna know what to call you, that's all."

"Sophia. Sophia Papa-gee-or-gee-oh." She watches me.

I don't crack a smile or anything. "Genesis . . . Genesis Anderson. And I don't want to hear a joke about it either."

And we run. My lungs feel like they're

exploding, sending sparks all through my body. But I don't slow down. We run together. Me and Sophia.

"See you found a friend, Papa John's pizza," says the red-haired girl from Ms. Luctenburg's class.

"I see you're still a skinny puke face!" Sophia shouts back.

Skinny puke face? Sophia's comebacks are worse than mine. Regina and the girls would've laughed me off the block with a corny crack like that.

"What's the matter, Detroit?" says red's sidekick. "Girls don't run where you come from?"

"Ignore them," Sophia tells me.

But I don't. Might was well rep my city with a smooth-as-ice dis. Here're a few tips learned over the last several years that I'm sure will fly out here in the 'burbs.

Throw them off with a question while laughing like you're wildin' out.

"Oh snap, did she just try to clown me?" I say to Sophia, who obviously doesn't know the rules.

Make strong eye contact and don't be the

first to break it.

My eyes lock in with the red-hair girl, and she's good. So good that I'm reminded of the stare down with Regina. But she ain't Regina, and we're not on a block in Detroit. Red-hair girl looks away.

Say something bad to make them back off.

"Keep talking. I can show you how we run in my neighborhood." *I can show you? Might as well add a "please" and "thank-you." Ugh.*

The girls laugh, mimicking us, and trot off. I peek again at Sophia and try to figure out why she's getting hated on. And I have no clue. Maybe I should've stayed alone. Alone and invisible.

SEVEN

When I get home from school on Friday, Dad's car is in the driveway. He's been home every day this week, but never this early. I pause on the porch, thinking how Sophia's cool to talk to and how Troy's tutoring is actually helping. Too bad this fancy house was only temporary. But dang, I hoped it'd be more than one-week temporary! I unlock the door and go in. Huh. The furniture seems to be all in place. No boxes stacked in the middle of the room either. "Ma?"

But still, Dad took Mama's money, and even though she's been chill so far, things could've just now hit the roof. I call out again. "Ma?"

Mama comes out from her bedroom. "Hey, babe." Her long ponytail swishes. "Didn't hear you come in."

"Why's Dad home so early?" Here it comes, the bad news.

"They switched his hours on him." Mama leans against the wall, folding her arms. "So, how was your day?"

"Fine." *That's it? No "we gotta move"?* "I'll be right back," I say and bolt to my room and make sure my hair's not a mess, my skin's not ashy, and my lips aren't cracked. I smooth and brush every part of me into place and scramble back into the living room, 'cause even though Dad hasn't drunk heavily all week, I ain't taking any chances. But when I finish, he's not around, so I take a seat at the base of the couch and pull out my homework. Alcoholics Anonymous pamphlets are spread out on the table. Just as I'm about to reach for one, Mama's at my side.

"What were you doing?" Mama asks.

"Nothing, just had to go to the bathroom."

She looks at me sideways but doesn't ask anything else. Before I get a chance to tell her about Sophia, Dad enters the room. I sit up straight and smile.

"Chubby Cheeks" is what he greets me with.

Hate that nickname.

"What? You ain't happy to see me?" he says, setting a glass on the table. The liquid is light brown, and it's not pop.

"Yeah." I scoot back, gauging his mood.

"What's your homework?" Dad takes a seat a few feet from me.

"Math, language arts, and stuff."

"History?"

"Nope."

"Sharon, the girl's got no history."

"Okay, Emory." Mama goes to the kitchen.

"It's called social studies," I correct him, relaxing a notch.

"History's important, remember that. Nobody taught me anything . . . no history or nothing. I had to learn it on my own. That's why I teach you what I know." Dad nods hard, as if agreeing with himself, then says, "In your history class, you should protest, start a demonstration or something."

Mama sneaks up behind Dad and tags

him on the arm with a dish towel. "Emory, why you putting that foolishness in her head? A demonstration, really? You're so full of it." Then she heads back to the kitchen.

"I'm just teasing the girl." Teasing is what I don't want. I smooth my hair down again, even though right now he's cool. "Your mama can hear trees fall in the forest." He leans over to me and says, "You don't have to start a big protest, just a small peaceful one."

"I can still hear you," Mama calls out.

"All right, all right, I'm done messing." Dad leans back and closes his eyes, or "checks the inside of his eyelids" as he calls it.

"Hey, Dad, what's up with that new job?"

"I'm working on it," he says, opening his eyes.

"She doesn't understand what 'working on it' means," Mama says loudly.

"These things take time," he hollers back, then presses his lips together. I've got those same lips. They're dark. Real dark. As soon as I'm old enough, I'm gon' keep them covered with pink or maybe purple lip gloss.

Dad starts nodding again, then raises his head. "Gen-Gen, did I ever tell you —"

"Wait," I interrupt him. "I got one. Have you ever heard of Peg Leg Joe?"

He pulls on his mustache, mulling it over. "Naw, can't say I have."

"What about the drinking gourd?"

"The drinking gourd?"

I grin because I can't believe I'm stumping Dad. "Time's up! The drinking gourd is the code name for the Big Dipper that the slaves used to escape."

"Yeah, I heard of the Big Dipper, but you threw me off with the Peg Leg part." Dad adds, "That ain't something that was taught when I was in school, you know? 'Sides, don't nobody wanna be reminded we were slaves. You feel me? I don't even watch movies with 'em in it . . . makes me mad."

"But this is a good story." I then repeat all of what Mrs. Hill told me.

"Yeah, that's a good one, Gen-Gen,"

Dad agrees when I'm done. "Now, have I ever told you about someone who fasted for twenty-one days?" He gives me a smile just like he gives Mama. "Come here . . ."

I slide closer and sit at his feet. "Twenty-one days is like forever. I bet you it wasn't a kid," I guess.

"You're right. It was this dude named Gandhi, and he fasted as a means of protest."

"No kid in their right mind would commit to starving just to make a point. Heck, my protest wouldn't last five minutes." And Dad *laughs*. He does. He laughs!

My dad's a talking, walking Wikipedia. When he's in a good mood he teaches me all types of stuff. He told me why a marching band parades down the streets in New Orleans during a funeral. How a girl named Anne Frank hid in an attic with her family because she was Jewish. And that Christopher Columbus didn't really discover America, since Native Americans were already living here.

"But you see," Wikipedia Dad goes on, "Gandhi had a vision of peace . . . way across the ocean in India, with all the hustle and bustle of cars driving through crowded streets and cows crossing right in the middle of roads, there was this little man . . ."

Closing my eyes, I imagine what this Gandhi guy looks like. My father's deep voice carries me across the wide waters. And I soar across India, catch a delicious whiff of chicken from a vendor, watch men driving motorbikes through crammed roads, and hear hypnotic music from stringed instruments. I land beside Gandhi, sitting cross-legged on a rug. He's a small, brown, bald man.

"Emory, you talk like you were Gandhi's right-hand man or something." Mama's interruption lands me back into our living room. I was so into the story that I didn't even hear her creeping up on us.

"How you know I wasn't?" He turns back to me. "Ay, Gen, I was like, 'Yo, Gandhi, if you wanna gain worldwide attention, don't eat the food. People'll get suspicious thinking the government planted something in it, and they'll fast with you.' See, that's what they don't tell you in those history books."

"Emory, stop talking crazy. I don't want Genesis repeating that nonsense at school."

"It's better than what they're teaching her." Dad squeezes my elbow, asking, "They ever teach you about Gandhi?"

"No."

"See what I mean, Sharon? She can learn more from me than them." Dad winks at me.

"Not with you sprinkling in only half the truth. I don't want my baby going around talking outta the side of her neck." Mama smiles though, and I know she's just giving him the business.

"Yeah, I hear you." Dad reaches for his glass, but then he pauses. For a few seconds it's as if he's hypnotized, then he shakes his head, breaking free. Dad doesn't take a drink, surprisingly, but instead pulls out a pack of cigarettes from his shirt pocket and slides one out.

I'm stumped, wondering what that was all about. Does he feel bad for stealing from Mama, and trying to really slow his drinking roll? Or, have the lemons worked, and I'm too blind to notice? *Yeah, I wish.*

"Emory," Mama says, her voice going high. "You agreed not to smoke in this house . . . it's too nice to be smelling up."

"Yep, that's what I promised." Dad stands, thrusting out his arms, stretching. "I'll smoke in the backyard."

Mama shut down our precious moment, but before he leaves I try to grab it back. "Wait, Dad, what happened to him? That Gandhi guy?"

"Not much, I told you the important parts for now, anyway."

"Got another story?"

"Naw, baby girl. I've got nothing else. 'Sides, I don't want your mama mad at me. You see the way she beat me with that dish towel?" He rubs his tagged arm and starts humming a tune unfamiliar to me.

"Dad, did you know someone fasted even longer than Gandhi?"

"Who?"

"Jesus. For forty days and forty nights. That's what the Bible says, anyway."

He winks at me. Again. To be real with you, one of Dad's winks is worth putting up with him calling me Chubby Cheeks.

It's late at night, maybe already early morning, when I smell it. The aroma travels down the hall, slips under my bedroom door, and circles my nose. Toward the kitchen I creep, taking extra care not to creak the floorboards. Dad stands barefoot with flour powdering his fingers, singing. I want to sing right along like that Black girl did in the movie *Annie.* A couple of years ago, Mama rented the DVD. Anyway, in my imagination, I'd be Annie and Dad'll play the man part, and we'd hold hands and tap-dance all over these wooden floors.

Even though I can't tap-dance, I join in singing, quiet at first, *"I've got so much honey, the bees envy me."* Dad cocks his head and listens. Then a little louder, *"Oh, ooh . . ."*

"I've got a sweeter song," Dad sings.

"Than the birds in the trees." I make sure my hair scarf is tight and in place on my head, and then step into the kitchen.

Dad laughs and says, "Baby girl, what

you doing up?"

"About to eat some shrimp."

"You love some food, just like your daddy." Dad picks up a raw plump piece and hands it to me. "The trick to getting the shrimp just right is all in the batter. You've got to add just the right amount of seasoning" — he holds open a brown paper bag and I dump the shrimp in, a small cloud of flour puffs out — "and the right amount of shaking." He shakes the bag four times. He pulls out the flour-coated shrimp and drops it in the hot grease. "Then, the right amount of cooking. Shrimp cooks up fast. Two minutes tops."

I get the plates and hot sauce and set them on the table. "Dad, it's like you don't listen to the radio at all. You do know there're some modern songs out, right?"

"Gen, how I look like trying to sing Trey Songz without a six-pack?" Dad says, patting his stomach.

"You got a point," I joke.

Dad spoons out the shrimp and lays them on a pan lined with paper towels to catch the grease. "Back when I was a knuckle-headed teenager, I used to hang out at this auto repair garage owned by this old man named Luther. Anyway, Ol' Luther tried to teach me about cars and stuff, keep me out of trouble. He played Motown all the time . . . couldn't stand it at first." I nodded, but I had no clue where Dad was going with the story. He continues, "Now it makes me remember those times, those good times, see?"

"I guess," I say, yawning. "Hey, what's that song, the other song, you always humming to yourself?"

Dad gazes up at the ceiling, like he's trying to remember which one. "Oh, that's an old blues song. Used to be my mama's favorite." Before I can ask him the name, he tells me to take my seat at the kitchen table, and then he sets six big shrimp on my plate.

"Blow 'em, they're hot," he warns.

I bite into one. The outside's crispy and spicy, and the inside's soft and juicy. The shrimp's so good that I wiggle my toes. He laughs and takes a bite of his; crumbs hang from the tip of his mustache and jiggle as he chews.

Dad's a better cook than Mama. He tells me he learned as a little boy growing up down south, in Arkansas. It's true because a long time ago he showed me an old, beat-up photo of him, his brother, and his mom at the stove cooking. Even though I never met them, their faces are etched in my mind.

This, for whatever reason, makes me think of Mrs. Hill sitting on her grandpa's lap. I'm not about to sit on Dad's legs, but it seems like a good time for some family history. Dad won't ever talk about his mother, but he could at least tell me about his brother.

"Dad?"

He raises his head, licking hot sauce from his fingertips.

"How come you never talk about your brother? Mama told me he died from rabies, is that why?"

I don't know if it's because the shrimp's so good or because it's just us two, but Dad actually lets loose. "No, it's because . . ." Dad pauses, as if his words are stuck. "Charlie was my best friend."

In my mind, I see Charlie. He was

119

taller, thinner, and much, much lighter than Dad.

Dad spends a long time sucking the little bitty meat out of a shrimp tail, probably picturing his brother too, and now the story's most likely going to end. Then Dad stuns me by adding, "He was 'bout eleven. I was eight. We used to play in this old abandoned house, a lot of kids played there. But this day, we climbed into the attic . . . and we got to throwing rocks and pieces of wood, busting out the last of the windows. Just messing around, you know. Then . . ." Dad rubs his head like the next thought hurt it. "All of a sudden, there was fluttering all around; we thought it was just birds. Until Charlie screamed. He was screaming, 'Get 'em away! Get 'em away!' They were bats." Dad waves his hand, fighting imaginary bats. "So many of 'em . . . flying around his head, and I was trying to get them away . . . get him away."

"Dang," I say, visualizing the whole scene. "I thought he got rabies from a dog. He got it from bats?"

Dad nods.

"Well, how come y'all just didn't take

him to a doctor?"

"He was so busy jumping that he didn't even *know* he actually got bit." Dad's voice chokes up for real now. "Not till it was too late."

Rabies from a bat? No wonder Dad doesn't talk about it; he's still fighting bats.

Dad clears his throat and goes on. "Charlie was fine, at first. Then he started complaining about his brain, said it wasn't thinking right. My mama gave him aspirin. This happened more times, but we couldn't make heads or tails of it, you know. Then a few weeks later he got real sick. It was too late by then."

"Too late for what?"

"To help him." Dad's face goes tight. "That's what the doctor said. . . ."

Hold up, I got more questions — how long after until Charlie died, what did his mama do, and what else happened after Charlie's mind wasn't thinking? But it doesn't look like Dad can handle any more, because he takes out his cigarettes, lights one, and takes a long drag. An end of conversation drag. And I'm not about to remind him that he's not supposed to be smoking inside. He probably needs it right about now.

When Dad stubs out the cigarette, I try to make him feel better, complimenting, "Your shrimp's the best." Then smile big.

He stares at me.

"What?" I ask, bracing myself.

"You've got your mama's smile. Never really noticed before."

I got Mama's smile? My heart's knocking in my chest. *I got Mama's smile?* Right then, I'm aching to tell Dad about Troy and my tutoring, about Jason and his stupid sidekick. I want him to know how Mrs. Hill had the nerve to compare me to Miles Davis.

"Your mama got a smile that'll make a man spend all his money." He eases back in the chair and his big, round belly rises and falls with each breath. His sad eyes get brighter as he goes on. "I couldn't take my eyes off her . . . simply divine."

Even though my hair scarf is tied on my head like an old maid's and the lemons hadn't changed me in the least, I dare ask, "Am I simply divine? Like

Mama?"

Dad reaches over and covers my hand with his. But he doesn't answer my question. Just as I'm about to cop an attitude and be like, "Forget it," I hear his brother Charlie's screams, *Get 'em away!* Now, how can I get mad when Dad's got all that inside him? So I settle with at least knowing I got Mama's smile.

EIGHT

Another week flies by without any arguing. It's as if Mama's forgotten about Dad thieving, 'cause all she does is rave about the washer and dryer. "Thank God I don't have to haul these clothes to the Laundromat and spend the whole day fighting for a machine!" Me? Well, I'm finding my rhythm at school, and have yet to be called Blackie or Ratchet. Plus, Sophia and I are getting along pretty well. But I'm still struggling with math. Troy's been patient with me; I'll give him that.

"So, what's the first thing you'll do to solve for x?"

Troy's waiting for an answer, and I remind myself to focus. "Add five?"

"I told you! You know this!" he says happily.

"How'd you get so good at this stuff?" I ask, hardly believing I can answer a math question like this after just a week of tutoring. Troy's good.

"I didn't have much choice. My parents are kind of strict."

I'm about to say that he doesn't look like the type who'd have strict parents, but then realize I don't know what that type actually looks like. I say, "Really?"

"Yeah, it's just me and my sister, Drew. We both have to have straight As or else."

"Or else what?" I ask, my mind's buzzing with consequences: no video games, no TV, no hanging out, no cell phone, no what?

"I don't know. We never chance it." Troy laughs. "I remember when I was in fourth grade and Drew was in sixth, my mom made us read two books."

"What do you mean 'she made you'?"

"I mean, she didn't let us choose our own. We had to read *The Souls of Black Folk* by W. E. B. Du Bois."

"No offense, but that sounds kinda boring," I say, wondering why the heck his mother would make him read something like that.

Troy laughs again.

"For real. I don't even know who he is," I add.

He shakes his head like he doesn't believe me.

"Don't look at me like that! All they ever teach during Black History Month is Martin Luther King, Rosa Parks, and Harriet Tubman. Anybody else, then you're on your own."

"You're right," Troy agrees. "Just so you'll know, W. E. B. Du Bois was one of the founders of the NAACP. And it really wasn't all that boring, but my mom wasn't making us read it for entertainment. Her thing was, she wanted us to know that no matter where we came from, we can still be great, you know?"

I wonder if Dad ever heard of this W. E. B. Du Bois. "But in fourth grade?" I ask. "She couldn't wait till you were in high school? Dang."

"You don't know my mom."

"Okay, what was the other book?"

"The other one was *The Autobiography*

of Malcolm X."

"Malcolm X? Okay, I heard of him. There're always 'Brothers of the Nation' at a corner selling bean pies or their *Final Call* newspapers." Troy eyes me funny, so I add, "Well, not out here in *Farmington Hills,* they don't. But in Detroit — whatever, never mind. So, why'd you have to read that one?"

"Well, my dad wanted me to 'cause he says the book changed his life. And my mom went along with it because she wants me to know what it feels like to question things and think for myself."

"That's wild." For some reason, maybe 'cause Troy's so smart, I assumed they'd be sitting around the house reading stuff like Shakespeare.

"Yep, kind of wild. My mom is no joke. My dad is hard-core, too." Troy refocuses on my homework, pointing to the next problem, but I keep talking.

"What do they do?"

"My mom, she's a chemical engineer, and my dad's a graphic designer." Suddenly I'm hoping like mad that he doesn't ask me the same question. I don't want to answer with my dad's a plant worker and my mom cleans up old people.

"So." Troy taps the paper again. "What will it be?"

"I'll add five to both sides." I scribble $+5$ on each side of $3x - 5 = 13$.

"Then?"

I picture the numbers in my head and struggle not to use my fingers. "Then I'll divide by three?" Troy raises an eyebrow. "I'll then divide by three," I say more confidently.

Troy nudges me with his elbow. "See, you've got this!" I hold in a grin that's threatening to pop open. "You should be proud," he goes on. "You're catching on quick."

"I guess I am," I say, flashing him my best "Mama" smile. "I never could understand this stuff before, but you explain it way better than any teacher."

And I can't quit cheesing because I'm feeling pretty stoked for understanding this stuff — finally.

■ ■ ■ ■

There are two more things that are different about Farmington Oaks Middle. One, at my old schools, you only ate in the cafeteria. Period. Here, we can leave the lunchroom after we've finished eating or even take food to go (some kids eat outside!). And two: the library. When Sophia first asked me to meet her here, I had no idea what to expect. This place is gigantic! Like a real public library, with computers and wall-to-wall books, and hardly any empty spaces on the shelves! I find myself still getting lost in the titles. *Breadcrumbs. York. Out of My Mind.* And, they even have a lot with Black people on the covers. *Bud, Not Buddy. As Brave As You. Brown Girl Dreaming. The Jumbies. Gone Crazy in Alabama.* Farmington Oaks has all the Harry Potters, too! Every one of them! So many books to choose that I snatch several from the shelves and stack them in my arms.

"You're checking out all those books?" Sophia takes the top one, examining its cover.

"Yep."

"How're you going to read 'em all before they're due?" Sophia puts the book back. "You only need one."

She's right. I only need one, so I check out *Brown Girl Dreaming* because . . . well, the title. I'll have to read twice as fast to get through all these before we have to move again. We find two beanbags in an isolated corner. Sophia arranges and rearranges her seat about ten times before she actually sits. I try to read, but what the heck is she doing? When she finally starts reading, Sophia turns a page, then she almost immediately flips back as if she has to read the last passage again because it's that good.

"Why're you watching me?" Sophia says, without looking up from her book.

"I'm not watching you . . . I was . . . thinking," I cover.

"Fine then, about what?"

I pause.

Sophia says, "See, you weren't thinking, you were watching me."

"I was too thinking. It's just . . . corny, that's all."

"All right, let's hear it." She sits up on

one elbow.

"Well," I say, quickly making up my response, "I was thinking that it's awesome here, you know . . . with the beanbags . . . and computers . . . and the colors." Sophia waits for me, that one eyebrow cocked, and I decide to be real. "Okay, so what's up with you not hanging out with any of the other girls?"

"Whatever!" She catches herself and lowers her voice. "These girls are so fake. They'll smile in your face and stab you in the back with a butcher's knife."

"Tell me about it," I say, remembering how Regina went right back to calling me Char when she saw our furniture on the curb. Still, I can't help picturing girl cliques strutting down the halls together, and how I'm usually the one standing on the sidelines, watching instead of being watched. And I *had* that with Regina and them, even if it was just for a hot minute. And it felt great. So I say, "But wouldn't it be kinda cool to have a crew?"

"You're kidding me, right?" She takes off her glasses and rubs the lenses vigorously with a small cloth. "I don't need a bunch of fake friends. I only need one.

One real friend." She holds her glasses to the light and rubs the lenses again. "Really, it's like, one minute you're 'BFFs' and then the next . . ." Sophia shakes her head.

"That's the story of my life," I agree.

"Besides, I've got five brothers, my grandma, my ma, my dad, and my aunts, uncles, and their kids at our house almost all the time." Sophia wriggles around, adjusting herself until she's just right and says, "This place is a good place to just . . . chill."

"Hold on, five brothers?" If I had five brothers, man, I'd rule Detroit. "That's what's up."

"Not always," Sophia says. "It gets pretty loud."

It's sort of the opposite at my house. Sometimes it's too quiet with just me, Mama, and Dad. Well, unless he's drunk or something. Otherwise — quiet-ville. Which makes me curious — if Sophia comes here for quiet, then won't all our yakking disturb it? "If you want chill, then why'd you invite me here?"

"Maybe because . . . you're new?"

Sophia fusses with her glasses again, even though they appear to be spotless. "I don't know. Maybe because you don't know me, and I don't know you."

My mind flashes back to how she ran alone on the track that first day, now I feel guilty for having thought she was weird in some way. And I get it: Sophia likes that we're on an even playing field. No outsiders. No third party. Just us.

NINE

Mrs. Hill is not in the classroom when I enter.

"Here she comes," says Smart-Mouth Terrance, who happens to be brown as mud. I glance behind me, but Mrs. Hill isn't there. "Our first international student!"

He sweeps his hand in my direction. "All the way from Africa!" He's so wack that he doesn't even know that African jokes are played out. He's still probably calling kids African booty-scratcher, and I haven't heard that since second grade. I could crack about how dark he is, but my grandma taught me not to be talking ignorant like that in front of white folks. Anyway, I've heard all these lame jokes a million times already. There're plenty to throw back at him. *You so black that you leave fingerprints on charcoal. . . . When you go swimming, it looks like an oil spill. . . . When you showed up at night school, the teacher marked you absent.*

"Shut up, Terrance. You're such a jerk." Yvette flips her hand at him as if he's a pesky gnat. "Ignore him," she says to me. "He's a jerk to everyone."

I offer a small smile as thanks, and she gives me a "No problem, I've got your back" nod. Then she turns to her friend as I hurry to my seat.

Even though Terrance tried to play me, I'm feeling pretty good because:

#1. A dark girl stood up for me. Solidarity!
#2. That's never ever happened before.
#3. The jerk actually shuts up.
#4. No one's paying me any attention.
#5. No one's paying him any attention.
#6. Yvette gets me.

Mrs. Hill finally arrives, chatting with Nia like they're good friends. I've never peeped Nia talking to any of the other students. What's up with that? In sixth grade, this girl named Shatasha said that light-skin girls think they're better than everybody else. She wasn't the only one who said it, either. That's probably Nia's deal.

Mrs. Hill settles the class, and we get started. "I'll hear if you all practiced," she says with a smile, standing behind her music stand. After she leads us through vocal warm-ups, she holds up her hands like an orchestra leader and says, "Let's begin." Everyone starts singing "The Drinking Gourd." I sing, but not loud, because even though Mrs. Hill says to leave all worries outside the door, it's kind of hard to do now that the song reminds me of Uncle Charlie's story. Heck, it was because of Mrs. Hill talking about family history that I even pried in the first place.

"Stop, stop, stop. Something's not quite right." Mrs. Hill presses her fingertips together under her chin like she's praying. "Jeremy, let me hear you sing it."

"By myself?"

"Yes, of course." She does this with several more students. "Eloise, breathe deep into your diaphragm like I showed you . . . that's better. Belinda, let's hear you . . . good pitch. All together now . . . stop, stop, stop."

Yvette raises her hand. "Mrs. Hill, I think we sound good. At least, I do anyways." She shakes her bangs out of her face.

"You all sound good, I agree, but it's more than just sounding good. When it comes to a song like this, it's about reaching deep into your personal experiences and using your emotions to sing. Try recalling a moment in your life that has made an impact, whether it be hurtful, shameful, or even joyous. . . . Can you see how there's a passion and desperation in it?" Mrs. Hill pauses and gives us time to meditate on that.

"What if you can't think of anything?" asks Eloise.

"I have an idea. I have a little imagery exercise that might help you connect with a strong emotion." Mrs. Hill picks up a drum from the corner of the room. "Okay, so, everyone, close your eyes." She waits a moment, probably until every eye is shut, and then she begins tapping the drum. *Bum-badum-bum-bum-badum-bum* . . .

"Imagine if you can, that you're running for your life. You're hungry and exhausted and your feet are blistered and bloodied. If you're caught that means death to you, your mother, father . . . and your little sister or brother will receive the worst lashing of their lives."

Mrs. Hill leads us to visualize ourselves running through woods and bushes. At first, there're a few giggles and yawns. She thumps the drum harder, and soon my heart is pounding along with the beat. Then Mrs. Hill begins to hum. I try to dig deep and picture myself running through trees, but I only see me on the stupid track at gym with my hair kinking up. I open my eyes. One of the guys is staring off into space.

"Keep your eyes closed," Mrs. Hill says. "Now, see yourself hiding in the swamp. Hear the hooves of horses and barking of dogs. They're getting closer and closer. You're stuck with no way out. Are you well hidden?"

I've been in two other chorus classes and none of the teachers ever did anything like this.

Fine. I close my eyes again.

Bum-badum-bum-bum-badum-bum . . .

There's Regina and her silly squad parading through my house laughing and pointing. I want to run and shut my bedroom door. Except, there aren't doors on lawns.

I squeeze my eyes tight. And now I see bats . . . bats swarming around little Charlie's head. And Dad's small arms waving frantically. I hear Charlie screaming, *Get 'em away! Get 'em away!* Quick, I open my eyes.

Bum-badum-bum-bum-badum-bum . . .

"Your heart beats hard and fast. You're so close to freedom. . . ."

The *boom, boom, tap* of the drum sounds like menacing footsteps.

Again, I close my eyes.

Bum-badum-bum-bum-badum-bum . . .

This time I'm running from a place. A basement. My daddy's friend's basement. We'd come here last October, after being evicted. A washing machine sat in the corner hidden by piles of stinky clothes. A hot-water tank was perched like a monster under the stairs creak, creak, creaking all night long. No windows. No fresh air. Flat mattresses thrown on a cold cement floor were our beds. Our clean clothes stashed in black garbage bags.

Dad's hand gripped dice and crumbled dollars. Three friends surrounded him like he was the Pied Piper, listening to his stories and laughing at his jokes. Mama kept her focus on him. I sat, invisible. A wrinkled brown bag was being passed. Hand to mouth. Hand to mouth. All around the circle.

"Now, start singing quietly," Mrs. Hill says. The buzz of voices pulses through the floor and up the walls.

"When the sun comes back and the first quail calls, Follow the drinking gourd."

"Good, now as you sing, tap into that moment. . . ."

I was thirsty. Hungry. Tired, too. And I just had to get up from that mattress and ask for something to drink. I just had to interrupt Dad's best story ever . . . just had to disrupt the flow of the brown bag and rolling dice.

"What do you want? Can't you see

grown folks talking?" he thundered.

"Emory!" Mama said in a hushed voice, then turned to me. "What is it, honey?"

The words fought with my mouth to get out. "Can I have something to drink?"

"Let me get you some juice and chips. I'll be right back." Mama hurried up the stairs, careful not to disturb this house that didn't belong to us.

"Emory, man, she looks just like you," said a man with shiny, pointy shoes, nodding toward me. "Can't deny her even if you wanted to."

Dad glared in my direction, his eyes blood red. "Naw, she ain't nothin' like me." The word *nothing* lingered in the air like their musty cigarette smoke.

The bag stopped. Fingers itched. Hands fretfully rubbed foreheads. Then Dad. Dad laughed. His dark lips broke into laughter. Nervous chuckles joined in. Dice rolled and the bag started its travels again. It reached Dad. He took it, saying, "Man, here I go marrying a fine thing like Sharon." He tilted back his head and took a long swig. "And she ain't give me no pretty baby. She gives me . . .

nothin' but Chubby Cheeks." He motioned my way, almost falling out of his chair. They caught him and sat him back up.

"Emory Anderson, that's your child," said a short, round woman. "So if she's ugly, then you're a hot mess."

The tables turned.

"Emory, yo' hair's so nappy, I can shoot the bucks off yo' head with a BB gun."

"Come on, man, don't get mad. . . . It's already dark in here. Smile so we can see you."

"Somebody rub Emory's belly for good luck."

As they ragged on him, they couldn't see it. But I could. The vibration started deep in his gut. It worked its way up his chest. It crawled down his arm and spread through each one of his fingers like a virus. Finally, they recognized it. Too late. Just as Mama came back down the stairs with a cup in one hand, and a bowl in the other, Dad hurled the bottle against the wall.

Everyone froze.

Dad stood up, and came at me. "You!"

His breath rancid.

"What I do?" I stammered, scrambling backward like a crab.

Mama dropped the dishes and they clattered to the floor, juice and chips spilled everywhere.

"You were supposed to come out looking like her!" Dad pointed angrily behind him. "Look at you with your black —"

Mama ran over. "Stop it! You're drunk!" She pushed him away and pulled me behind her. "You will NOT talk to my child this way!" She grabbed my hand and practically dragged me up the stairs, away from my dad.

In the kitchen, Mama held me tight. "He didn't mean it, Gen. His drinking . . . it's a sickness, understand?"

No, I didn't. I don't.

"For the old man is a-waiting for to carry you to freedom, If you follow the drinking gourd."

Too late, too late, too late. His words have already shackled me.

I force back the rumble in my throat while the class sings.

"I thought I heard the angels say
Follow the drinking gourd.
The stars in the heavens gonna show
      you the way
Follow the drinking gourd."

I can no longer hold back, my mouth
opens and I sing. I sing. And sing.

After a while, I don't hear the drumbeat
or the other voices. I don't hear the
hooves or the crunching of leaves. I open
my eyes. Mrs. Hill stands directly in front
of me. Everybody's staring.

What? No one else was singing? They'd
all *stopped*? My face burns. "Can I go to
the restroom, please?" I barely get the
words out.

"Yes," Mrs. Hill says with a nod. As I
pass her, she grabs hold of my shoulder
and squeezes.

I make it out the door, down the hall,
and around the corner to the girls' room.
Unbelievably, it's empty. I duck into the
stall farthest from the door and fall back
against the wall. No matter how many
times I've come home and our furniture
was on the lawn, I didn't cry. With all the

144

teasing and name calling from other kids, none of them have seen me cry. Every time the voices in the mirror scream to me what I'm not, I have not cried. But right now, I'm going to cry. I'm going to cry for the time Dad told me I was ugly. I'm going to cry because I keep having to start all over again. I'm going to cry because everyone in chorus left me singing — alone.

Girls come in and out of the bathroom, and each time I strangle back my sobs. The whole class is probably laughing at the girl singing with her eyes closed. I don't even understand how I sang like that. I've never even sung like that in my room, by myself — ever! I force myself to get a grip.

And when the halls are absolutely still, then and only then do I come out of the restroom. But I have to go back to chorus; I left my stuff. When I get there, Mrs. Hill is straightening the chairs.

"I hoped you wouldn't leave without your things. Let me get them for you." Mrs. Hill brings me my binder.

"Thanks." Without making eye contact — especially with my crybaby red eyes

— I quickly turn to escape.

"You know, I was totally wrong." Mrs. Hill's voice is so gentle that I have to stop to listen. "Turns out you're not a Miles Davis. Could be a Billie Holiday? Have you heard of her?"

It's kind of hard to follow what she means, but at least I'm together enough to respond.

"Yeah. I mean, yes. She's that lady up on the wall, right?" I point to a picture of a light-brown lady with her lipsticked mouth open, singing.

Mrs. Hill smiles up at the photo. "That's her, the lady herself," she says, going to her closet.

"My father, he told me a little bit about her," I add, remembering Wikipedia Dad's story about why she always sported a gardenia in her hair. "I'm not sure if I've heard her songs, though."

After a few seconds of rummaging around, Mrs. Hill hands me an old worn album. "This is one of hers." On the cover is the singing lady with, of course, a big white flower on the side of her head. She seems to be pondering something deep, like man's existence.

"I didn't know people still owned these," I say, flipping the cover to read the song list.

"Indeed! The sound is superbly authentic. I wish I still had my old record player."

"You had a *record* player?" I keep my puffy, red eyes on the album.

"Yes," Mrs. Hill says with a laugh. "And don't say it like it was centuries ago; you're making me feel old." She opens the top of what looks like a box. "I picked this one up at a bookstore. Apparently, record players are making a comeback. A retro thing." She takes the record out of its sleeve, puts it on the turntable, and gently places the needle on the vinyl. "This one is called 'God Bless the Child.' It's kind of scratchy, but not too bad." Mrs. Hill hands me a set of headphones that totally cover my ears, just like deejays wear.

As soon as I slip them on, the muted horns draw me into their melody, and I'm instantly swaying. Then Billie Holiday's voice slips in and I'm immediately transported to an old-time jazz club, the kind they have in the movies. Cigarette fog drapes the room. Billie Holiday stands under a dull light nodding to the piano's tunes. She tilts her head back and gritty raw sugar spills out. Now I understand what Mrs. Hill was saying about "putting yourself in the music."

As the record plays, the music tells stories of the child who's got her own; the one haunted in solitude; the one who's heartache hangs around every day. When she sings, she doesn't explain the meaning of her lyrics, but you get it. *How does she do that?* Maybe memories are trapped in *her* voice? I press the headphones closer. I can't put my finger on it, but something's there, for sure.

A tap on my shoulder makes me jump.

"Didn't mean to scare you. But your parents are going to wonder where you are. It's just about four o'clock."

What? How do almost forty-five minutes go by without me noticing?

"Yeah, probably," I mutter. I'd rather stay here, hidden in Billie Holiday. "Guess I ought to be going," I say out loud, reluctantly. "She's good," I add. "Billie. She's real good."

"Here, take this with you." Mrs. Hill hands me a CD. "Thought you might want to listen to her at home."

"Really?" I finally look up.

"Sure, take it."

"Mrs. Hill?"

Mrs. Hill regards me so attentively that I want to tell her secrets that I can't tell anybody. Like how I was brave enough to stand up to Regina and the girls, but terrified inside. Or that Dad finally told me some family history, even though it was sad. I wish I could tell her I'm grateful to be a light-skin Billie Holiday–type rather than a Miles Davis. If I could, I'd admit that I appreciate her acting like she hasn't noticed my eyes. Mostly, I want to explain what happened earlier — my singing — so we can bury it forever. But the only word I can manage is: "Thanks." How come the right stuff *never* comes out?

"I'm just glad you like Lady Day. Keep it as long as you need." Mrs. Hill smiles with her eyes. I leave the classroom wondering if she somehow knows — knows that I've never sung like *that* before, too scared to sing like that again, in front of everybody, and not sure if I could if I actually wanted to — yeah, I wonder if she knows, even though I couldn't tell her.

TEN

In the solitude of our backyard, I sit on the deck's steps, thinking. I think of how the jerk Terrance clowned me today. And how in the world I got caught slipping, singing in front of everybody. I'm feeling all down till I think about how, for the first time, I have a real friend — Sophia. And —

"Girl, what're you doing out here?" Mama says, almost making me jump out of my skin. "Scared me half to death finding this back door cracked open."

"Shoot, you scared *me*," I say, easing back down in my spot. "I was about to make a run for it."

She steps out onto the deck. "You wouldn't've gotten far, not with this fence." Mama rests her elbows on the railing and takes in the fresh air. She still wears her scrubs, but with house slippers. "Lord, I hope your dad gets that new job soon. Patio furniture would be amazing come summer. I could sit out here and just relax."

"Me too," I agree.

"Looks like I won't be the only one soaking up all this calmness." Mama lightly kicks Dad's can of cigarette butts that's sitting on the first step of the deck. At least he's keeping his promise. Well, except for that night when he lit up in the kitchen. Dang, now I'm thinking about Charlie all over again.

Mama takes a seat next to me, and the moment feels right to share about me and Dad's late-night shrimp dinner. Maybe she can help me understand the deal with Dad's family. "Ma? How come you never told me the whole story about Dad's brother?"

Mama whistles softly. "That's a hard one, Gen. It's just that . . . your father never got over it. So it's something we never talk about, I guess."

The not-talking-about-it part doesn't make sense. But Mama doesn't offer more, so I let it go for now and listen to the birds and watch the squirrels. I never knew how birds could fill the air with so much sound. Where were these singing birds during chorus?

Then Mama, surprisingly, tugs my hair. "Come on, it's too breezy out here. Besides, it's time to tackle this stuff." She wants to do my hair!

I jump up, forgetting all about my solo in Mrs. Hill's class. "About time!"

"My fault, Gen. . . . I know a woman's hair is her crowning glory," Mama says, going inside, sweeping into the bathroom, and scavenging through the closet.

" 'Crowning glory'? Where'd you hear that one?" I ask.

"Oh, it's something your grandma used to say." She hands me shampoo, conditioner, and a towel. She takes the pressing comb and some elastic bands out of a drawer, then is off to the kitchen.

Grandma knows that my hair's never brought me any glory and maybe that's why she doesn't say it to me, and huh, come to think of it, maybe that's why Mama works so hard to change it. Shoot, before things got bad, we'd be in the beauty salon every two weeks without fail. But now, 'cause of Dad, we're on a budget, and Mama has to do it — and our two-week schedule is more like three and a half, and ain't no glory in that.

Still, when Mama washes my hair, I know for sure she loves me, because she does it even though she reminds me over and over how much she hates doing it. Yet, even though we both know I'm old enough to wash my own hair, she claims I don't get all the soap out, and insists on doing it herself. Her fingers are strong and firm as she scrubs my scalp. Warm water runs through my hair and down my face as I bend over the kitchen sink. The smell of sweet peaches fills the room.

Mama's love stops at blow-drying, though. My hair's a mess of tangles and knots. I jerk and pull. Jerk and pull. Jerk and pull the dryer comb through my wooly head. This she makes me do myself; we've had too many "emotional outbursts" with her yanking and me crying. Now I yank my own head, mad at no one but the Lord for giving me hair like this.

After an hour of agony, I find Mama in

the kitchen flipping through circulars. She takes one look at me and her eyes go wide.

"What?"

"Sweetheart, I've told you time and again, you're supposed to dry your hair down, not up like a rooster." She reaches for the comb in my hand. "That's some demented 'fro you got going on." Now she laughs, touching it.

"What am I supposed to do? It's too hard to dry any other way. And quit laughing!"

"I know, I'm sorry," says Mama. "It's just that — with that big, wild hair you look like you're in the Jackson 5."

"Seriously, Mama? A bunch of guys? Not to mention they're, like, ancient."

"Let me think." Mama tries again. "How 'bout Angela Davis?"

"Who?"

"Your father never told you about Angela Davis? Oh, Angela was this activist associated with the Black Panthers." Mama tells me how Angela fought for civil rights, but she doesn't tell stories like Dad, so I make a mental note to ask him about her later. Mama fluffs my hair, laughing again. "I can't help it, honey. The Jackson 5 is what comes to mind. Sorry."

"Fine, I'll give you all five of the Jacksons!" In a high-pitched Michael voice, I break into an old Motown song and all of a sudden, I'm playing guitar like Tito, spinning like Jackie, doing a two-step like Jermaine, a side rock like Marlon, and a moonwalk like Michael. Ol' school!

"Stop, Genesis. . . . You are hilarious," Mama says, laughing so hard she's fanning herself. "Girl, you are funny like your father."

Dad *can* be funny. Sometimes.

"That man used to always crack me up." Now Mama drags a chair to the stove. That means it's time for straightening. " 'Course that's one of the things that attracted me to him."

When Mama does my hair, she spills all the tea. One time she told me she wanted to go to college, dreamed of being a newscaster. "Then I met your daddy," she'd said. "He was determined, charismatic, plus that man could dance!" Another time she said Grandma *didn't like that* trifling man *sniffing around her.* Mama had gotten real reflective that time, but then she added in a rush, "But I don't regret anything. If we wouldn't have married, I wouldn't have had you, now, would I?"

The way Mama had said those words made me wonder if she truly meant them. In moments like right now, my heart believes she wouldn't trade me for anything in the world, especially since she's told me that plenty of times. But every now and again, my brain still questions if it's completely true, that she doesn't regret anything — not going to college, marrying dad, and having me.

Mama now combs through my hair, as if I hadn't just spent a half hour doing the same thing, and starts parting it into four sections.

"Yep, your dad won me over with his sense of humor," she says, gathering a section in the front of my hair and twisting a band around it.

"Dad was really funny?" I question. "Like, *how* funny?"

Her hands move fast, putting bands around two more sections of my hair, leaving the one in the back. Now I have three big Afro puffs, two in the front, one in the back.

She turns on the stove and puts the pressing comb on the burner. "He may not tell many jokes now, but he used to. . . . Like when he first told me that Gandhi story, he said he was the one who shaved Gandhi's head!" she says, laughing.

I don't laugh.

"Well, it was the *way* he said it."

Listening to Mama distracts me from the fact that a zillion degree hot comb will be millimeters away from my brain for the next forty minutes. She gently pushes down my head, and starts with the back-right side. The pressing comb is hot as heck; the heat attacks my neck. Slowly Mama slides the hot comb through the roots of my hair and pulls it to the ends, turning it from kinky to straight. Then she repeats the same movement, but this time she nicks me.

"Ow, Mama!"

"Stop moving. You wanna go to school all marked up?"

"No," I say, gingerly touching the burnt spot.

"Then be still." Mama places the comb back on the burner and puts a little grease on my hair for sheen.

"Why can't we get a flat iron?" I say, trying not to squirm, braced for another potential nick. "This is abuse."

Mama ignores me, as usual. The comb's now hot again. She takes it and pulls it through my hair. The grease melts, runs to my scalp and singes me, and I jump clear out the seat. The kitchen reeks with the smell of burnt hair.

"Genesis, you should be used to this by now!"

"No one should ever get used to this, Mama," I tell her, rubbing the new burnt spot.

"Sit back down here; we don't have all night." Mama brushes my hand away and parts another small section of hair. "Gosh, your hair's so thick."

"That's why you should let me have a relaxer."

"We've been through this before."

"Seriously, Mama, I'm the only girl in

America who doesn't have one. How many thirteen-year-olds you know still have to have their mama press their hair? No one owns a hot comb anymore! Or even knows what it is! And you've seen the kids at this new school! Everybody's hair is straight." I hope Mama won't see Nia; she wouldn't help my case at all.

"Hold your ear." Mama cocks my head to the side. As her fingers grasp the tiny hairs behind my ear, I feel my neck and shoulders and thigh and butt muscles all tensing up. *Don't burn me, don't burn me,* I chant in my head. "Be *still,*" Mama chides. She blows on the comb as she gets the iron insanely close to my scalp.

When she places the comb back down, I relax and start my argument again. "Everybody and their mama have weaves or relaxers or braids, or *something.* I'm too old for a stupid blowout and press."

"How many times do I have to tell you, Genesis?"

Mama only *has* to tell me once, but it'll never matter. I'll always ask, and she'll always answer with "You wanna get a relaxer and lose your hair again?"

I'll say "no" because I never told Mama

that the bald spots were actually because I used Nair hair-removing cream to take out the unrelaxed nappy hair once the new-growth started growing in. I'll say "no" because I'm still ashamed that I wanted the coily part gone so badly that I didn't even stop to consider what that stupid cream would do. I'll say "no" because I remember when my hair fell out in patches and Mama drove herself nuts questioning why, and the beautician insisted that it was the relaxer and cut my hair almost to my ears, and I cried and cried and cried. Now I wonder if I should tell her and maybe she'd let me try a relaxer again.

Mama doesn't need a relaxer. Her hair's naturally straight and long, and sometimes she curls it in big, round ringlets. It's so pretty that total strangers comment on it. This one time, we were at the Laundromat and someone asked if she was Alicia Keys. What a stupid question. Why in the world would Alicia Keys be washing her clothes in a public laundry — in Detroit?

Mama pushes my head back down. "Gotta get the kitchen."

The *kitchen* is at the nape of the neck. Why grown folks call it that I have no idea. Maybe because it's messy, like a kitchen can get? Plus, it's the worst part to straighten and the first part to kink back up.

I silently pray for Mama not to burn me. "Owww!" God doesn't listen.

"Sorry," says Mama. "Well, if having two little burns is the worst that happens today, it's not such a bad day."

If only she knew.

ELEVEN

When people say stuff like: "What else can go wrong?" well, that usually translates to: "Waaaiit for it. . . ." It only takes about five minutes before my burns seem like a treat, 'cause that's when Dad gets home.

Please, God, let me have enough shine on my hair.

"What up, doe?" Split shift, my big toe. Dad's been hanging out with his crew, still stuck in Detroit mode, using the official greeting. He positions himself at the kitchen entrance and watches us. A sweat towel hangs from his shoulder.

He comes over and tries to kiss Mama on the cheek. She turns her face away, waves the hot comb in the air. "Been drinking, haven't you? Sweating like you've been working harder than a fire-

163

man on Devil's Night."

Devil's Night? Whoa. Mama's throwin' some serious shade. The night before Halloween, prankster kids and arsonists light fires all over the city. It's gotten so bad that the firemen get so hot and exhausted that sometimes they just let the old abandoned houses burn. Hmph, he might be sweating like it, but Daddy ain't been working that hard.

Mama's snap bounces right off him, though, because he stands by the stove, grinning away. She sets the comb back on the burner, and I can tell pressure is building by the way she rubs her forehead. And Dad cheeses even harder. "Wanna know why?" he says, a little slurry.

Mama folds her arms tight, furious.

"I'm celebrating," he tells her, thrusting his hands up like he's shooting a basket. "And I went out with Chico and 'em . . . to celebrate my *new job.*"

"You got the job?" I turn to Mama repeating, "He got the job!"

Dad nods. Mama takes up the hot comb and presses it against the towel. It sizzles. And I swear Dad shifts around, as if he's the one getting his hair straightened.

"Dad, you *really* got the promotion? For real, for real?" I ask, only because he doesn't look as happy as I'd be looking if it happened to me. Shoot, I'd be dancing all over the place.

"Ain't that what I said?" Dad says, now sounding edgy. "Ain't you happy, Sharon?"

Mama takes her time rearranging the hot comb, grease, and towel on the stove before answering. "Seems to me that celebrating with family would've been your priority."

"Priority? That all you got to say?" Dad says, drying his face with his sweat towel.

Is that all she's got to say? Boy, is he begging for an argument or what?

"Congratulations," Mama finally says, but it comes out sounding more like *Con. Grad. You. Lay. Shuns.* Then she wipes her hands roughly on the towel.

"Thanks, but you don't sound too thrilled," he says, stepping away from the stove.

I pipe in with a cheerier-sounding con-grats, and add a: "You did it, Dad!"

"Thanks, Gen," he says, going back to grin-mode. "See, at least my baby girl is happy —"

"So." Mama cuts my props off. Dad was giving *me* props. "You got the same hours? How much more money is it? And what happened to AA? Those meetings approve of your drinking?" Mama rattles off questions without taking a breath.

"Whoa, whoa, why you third-degreeing me?" Dad now turns his attention to me, not answering any of Mama's questions. "Chubby Cheeks, you think I'm wrong for going out too?"

Now I'm the one folding my arms, 'cause my chorus bad mood was turned good, and now it's quickly swinging back to bad.

Mama pushes my head down, undoes another poof, and gets back to pulling the hot comb through my hair. I can feel the tension in her arms, and I'm back to chanting, *Don't burn me.* Dad stares, weaving, near unnoticeably, but weaving. And nobody mentions the fact that he still hasn't answered Mama's questions.

"Ain't you glad you never have to press your hair, Sharon?" he asks, wiping at his forehead again.

Here we go.

"Emory." Mama points the comb right at him. "We happy for you and all, but nobody's in the mood for your drunk foolishness tonight."

And I now understand Sophia's need for the library — I wish I could escape there this instant. Except Sophia doesn't seek peace because of a drunken dad.

"I'm just sayin'. . . ." Dad goes to the refrigerator. "Anyone ever say you look like your mama, Gen-Gen? I can't remember."

No one *ever* says I look like Mama, and he knows it. But I do think of something. "I got her smile," I say, reminding him of his own words from a week ago. He acts like he doesn't hear me as he closes the fridge door without getting anything out and leans against it, not saying a word.

"You just don't know when to quit, do you?" Mama's voice rises from level one to level two — the tread lightly voice. Truth is, I kinda hope she lays into him, makes him regret drinking. She pulls the comb through the final poof, then draws my hair back into a ponytail and tells me to get ready for bed.

"Baby girl, look at you," Dad says, "hair as straight as an Indian's." Indian. I sigh. Every Black girl I know, at one point or another, stands with friends on the playground and claims to have Cherokee in her family. Somebody's always trying to prove they're connected to beauty. When Dad comes over and stretches his hand out toward my head, I know that he knows I'm no different.

I pop up and duck past him. "They're called Native Americans, not Indians," I say, avoiding his eyes. Same eyes as mine. People who see us together say, "Emory, it looks like you spit that child out."

"Emory — enough! You're not about to stir up this" — Mama swishes her hand in the air — "mess. You promised me 'Things'll be different' and 'I'll stop drinking.' " She's dipping into level three, her voice isn't raised, but she's starting to blow up.

"Sharon, relax. Ain't we been *waiting* for this — our big break? That's got to be worth one celebration drink."

Mama's screwing the cap on the grease, tight, like she means to strangle it.

"I know what one drink looks like," Mama argues. "One drink doesn't make you mean. And right now, you're mean, and you're not about to be mean to Genesis!"

This is my cue to slink down the hall to my room and close the door. I bet Sophia doesn't have to go through stuff like this.

"Genesis?" Dad calls out. "You know I'm just playing with you, right?"

Even though I pull my pillow over my head, I still hear him. He always has to say something. Always. And he *isn't* just playing. I also bet Sophia's Dad doesn't *play* like this.

When Mama's fussing quiets, I climb out of bed and put my ear to the door. Nothing. I stuff my blanket around the bottom real good to make sure light doesn't escape. Then I turn the light on and stand in front of the dresser with my eyes closed. When I open them, Dad's face appears with a twisted smile. *Look at you, hair as straight as an Indian's.*

I pull out my brush. Years of hair, lint, grease, and fantasies are stuck deep down in the bristles. Childish dreams of looking like Cinderella, Belle, and Pocahontas are trapped in there. I undo my stubby ponytail, and brush my hair one hundred times like Rapunzel. Except I don't want hair long enough to trip over. I want hair like Mama's. So I pray over and over, "Lord, turn it good. . . . Lord, please turn it good. . . ." After a gazillion strokes, my hair hangs stiff and straight, and it still looks nothing like Mama's. So I slick my edges down and tie my scarf on real tight.

I take out the list from my sock drawer and put a star by #64: Because her dad's right, no one says she looks like her mama.

If people did, then Mama wouldn't have to torture me. Dad would lay eyes on me and smile like he does at Mama. Then he would croon to both of us as we ride in his car with the windows down and our hair — soft, soft hair — blowing in the wind.

TWELVE

"Genesis, didn't I say cut that TV off?"

"No, you asked if I was done with my homework." I press the power button on the remote and the TV goes black.

"Don't get smart; it's the same thing." Mama's already freshly showered from a day's work. "As a matter of fact, bring your homework to the kitchen table and work on it in here."

"Why?"

"Because I said so."

"Said so" is technically not an answer, but still I gather my books and drop them on the table. Even though Dad got the promotion, Mama's still annoyed that he came home drunk last night. And, I'm still annoyed about his teasing. And because he's not here, we only have each other to let out puffs of madness to.

Mama darts about the kitchen, whipping up dinner. When she's done, she fixes our plates. I slide my books to the floor, get the silverware, and Mama finally sits down. She takes a breath before asking, "How was school?" as if nothing's bothering her at all.

"Fine," I say, as if nothing's bothering me, either. "I've made a few friends, Sophia and Troy, he's my math tutor —"

Mom suddenly looks alarmed. "You have a math tutor? Why didn't you tell me?"

"Because it's not a big deal, they're on a different math level at this school is all."

"So, a boy, huh?" Mama smiles. Big. And *this* is the reason why I don't talk about school much.

"A tutor, who happens to be a boy." I make swirls in my mashed potatoes. "That's all."

"Okay, okay." She holds both hands up, surrendering.

"Dad still at work?" I mutter.

Mama glances at her watch. "I think so. He says he's in training, so his hours are longer. He's supposed to go to the

AA meeting tonight, I believe."

I notice with sudden dread a few folded-up moving boxes stuffed between the refrigerator and wall. She's not saving those boxes for us to move again, is she? But no, Dad's new job will make everything all work out. Right? I pinch off a piece of my chicken, but can't eat it. I hate those ever-ready moving boxes. I wonder if we'll ever not have to have them ready.

Then out of the blue Mama says, "Genesis, we need to talk."

Whoa, did she just read my mind about the boxes? I'm not sure I even want to hear what's coming: "We need to talk" is *never* good.

"I've been thinking . . . things may not change with your daddy." There's worry in her eyes as she studies me, and then she totally throws a curveball. "What's clear to me is that my mother's right . . . about me getting my degree, and I need a better paying job to take care of you — us. So — I've started applying to different companies." Then, even though it's just us two, she lowers her voice and says, "And I've been saving money, for school.

I'm praying not to have to use it for anything else."

Mama's never mentioned going back to school, and she's never ever admitted that Grandma's right. And I hope Mama's only meaning is that Grandma's right about her education and a better job. 'Cause it sounds awfully like Mama's planning to leave Dad, but that can't be the case, could it?

She's staring at me. Oh. She wants me to respond.

"Genesis, I have to do this. . . . I need to do this," she presses.

"That's cool, you should totally go for it," I assure her. "I could help out around here, do more chores and stuff. Hey, we can even do homework together, right here at the table."

"Thank you, honey," Mama says, her face lighting up. "And, Genesis, let's just . . . let's just keep this between us, okay?"

I nod. We all have secrets, but Mama's aren't like Dad's — secretly smoking in the house or sneaking off to the casinos. Or mine, singing in the mirror. All of a sudden I wonder if Billie Holiday ever sang in front of the mirror.

"Mama?" I say. "You heard of Billie Holiday, right?"

"Lady Day, of course! Why?"

"My teacher let me borrow her CD."

"Yeah? I didn't grow up on her music, but I like it. There's an old movie about her life, *Lady Sings the Blues.*" Mama goes on describing the movie. She tells me that Billie Holiday was addicted to drugs and her husband kept trying to help her beat it. Then Mama describes how the doctors strapped her in a straitjacket. Yikes! And *that's* who Mrs. Hill pegs me like?

"We should rent it," Mama says, getting up to fill her water glass. "I swear I drink more simply because it comes straight from the refrigerator's door." She takes a sip before continuing. "That Billie, she had a hard life, a real hard life."

Sure sounds like it! Then it hits me. Billie Holiday's husband must be to Billie Holiday what Mama and I are to Dad. Did Billie's husband ever get tired of helping her? Mama always accepts Dad's promises and stays, but now that she's planning to go back to school, does it mean his apologies are wearing thin? So I ask point-blank if she'd ever leave him.

My question catches her off guard because she quickly says, "Huh?" When I used to say "huh," she'd say, *If you can "huh," you can hear.* But I ask her again, anyway.

Then she starts with a dragged out, "Welllllll, Gen . . . it is a possibility . . . if things don't change."

Mama must've been doing some heavy-duty thinking. And Dad's stupid antics haven't helped his cause. But we can't move yet. We just can't. Yeah, chorus sucked, but . . . I *like* it here.

My conversation with Mama was deep, so you already know that when it's time for me to sleep, my brain won't shut off. I get out of bed, turn on my CD player and slide Billie Holiday's silver disk inside. And I really listen. Her voice . . . her voice is incredible. It swings up to the high note so smoothly — how does she *do* that? And then it hovers over the piano chords gently, gently. She sounds sad. But something else, too. Hopeful. I want to belt out Billie's lyrics. But Billie doesn't belt. She lets her pain ooze out slow. I wonder what caused *her* "sickness." I pick up the CD cover, and Billie's eyes are lonely, as if she wants someone to notice.

I notice, Billie.

The next day at school, Billie's songs keep humming in my brain. It's like I have my own soundtrack; in language arts I wanted solitude and by the time I got to PE, heartache was waiting on the track. So, when my last class is done, I stop at the library to find a book to match my miserable mood. As if it's my destiny, I spy a hardcover biography about . . . Lady Day! Sitting right there on the shelf. This is way too cool of a coincidence to keep to myself. Who else to tell other than Sophia?

But she isn't at her locker. I backtrack to the library; she's not there, either. Not in Ms. Luctenburg's class, the locker room, the office — where the heck is she? Just as I've convinced myself that she left without me, I decide to check the one place I didn't. The bathrooms. Each one

— by our locker and homeroom — is empty. Sophia's gone. It's probably my fault for taking so long in the first place.

I stuff Billie Holiday's biography in my backpack and fling it over my shoulder, already itching to read it, and on my way to the front doors — there's one more bathroom. If she's not in here, I'm gonna feel real stupid for wasting all this time searching for her. Still, I push the door open, calling out, "Sophia, are you in —"

Sophia's standing at the sink. Just standing there, with her face bright red. And I'm no expert, but it looks like she's been crying. And instantly I get a flash-back of me crying in the bathroom just two days ago.

"What's the matter? What happened?"

"There're no more paper towels," she says, washing her hands.

"What? Paper towels?" I check, and okay, there aren't. "So, just wipe your hands on your pants and come on."

She doesn't move. These suburb kids need what Dad calls street smarts. You'll never find a Detroit kid wiggin' out about the lack of paper towels. Shoot, we'd be

178

lucky if there was toilet tissue. Sophia still doesn't move. I start to worry that there's something seriously wrong. There's only one real reason that someone would be hiding out in the restroom with a flushed face. And it's called "Don't let me catch you after school."

"Who's messing with you?" I ask.

"Huh? Nobody's picking on me. It's just —" Sophia holds her hands up, water runs down her wrists. "It's just that they're out of paper towels, someone should tell them."

"They'll figure it out," I say, considering what's really up with her. So I ask, "You good? You'd tell me if you weren't, right?"

Sophia nods, but doesn't follow me to the door.

"You really need paper towels?" I ask, and she nods a second time. "Fine." I run all the way to the other bathroom, grab a handful of towels, and run all the way back. "Here." And then I ask again if she's okay for real, she tells me that yes, she's fine and wishes I'd stop asking because it's starting to weird her out, thank you. Then, she waits for me to open the door as if she's the queen of England and passes without further explanation. Outside, when the wind shifts our way, Sophia calms down and admits that she freaked out about her social studies test.

"I did awful," she says.

"Of course you didn't," I assure her, but heck if I know. I tell Sophia all about my great library find. And as soon as we part ways, I get the book from my backpack and slowly cruise home, reading Billie's story. I skim through the pages and catch phrases like ". . . moved around due to poverty . . . income paid for her addictions . . . fragile relationship with her father . . ." I stop right in the middle of the sidewalk. Dang.

THIRTEEN

Friday evening, Dad drops me and Mama off at Grandma's to borrow her car. Grandma hardly drives her Cadillac anymore, claims her eyes aren't what they used to be. It's a good thing, too, because apparently riding the bus all the way from Farmington Hills is not only wearing Mama out, but expensive. Did I mention that I have to stay overnight, too? Yep, Mama's working all weekend, Dad has weird new hours, and neither will let me stay home alone.

Now, you know my grandma is preachy, right? That's why the next morning I'm already up before she has a chance to rant about how only lazy people sleep in.

But I don't go to the kitchen for breakfast. I can't help myself from moseying to the big picture window in the living room, hoping Mama'll pull up any moment. Grandma's living room is cluttered with porcelain angels and a bunch of other breakable knickknacks. Next to the grandfather clock stands a huge six-shelf case that's a shrine of ancient photographs. There're pictures of young Grandma and Grandpa's wedding, her standing with her mama and dad, and more of Grandma and Grandpa way before he died, and Grandma and her sisters. The photographs look so old that those folks could've sang "The Drinking Gourd" for real. So I'm thinking there's got to be some passed-down story like the one Mrs. Hill shared. I'd ask, but Grandma might tell me one about baby Jesus and Bethlehem for the rest of the afternoon.

Mama's baby pictures — at least ten! — sit safe and protected in gold frames. She looks like a little white baby, all posed in pretty, frilly dresses. Grandma has three small pictures of me. One is of me crying on Santa's lap, another from kindergarten, and the last one of me, Mama, and Dad — that one doesn't have a frame. I wipe off the dust and slide them near the front.

Grandma comes bursting in just as I finish. "Here you are," she says. She then examines the photographs, and shifts the ones I'd moved back to where they'd been. She picks up one of Mama's baby pictures. "People would stop me on the street and tell me how beautiful your mama was. She was a good baby too . . . hardly ever cried."

"My dad says I've got Mama's smile." I beam proudly.

"Hmph . . . that's what he says?" She says this as if it's not true, but I know Daddy wouldn't have admitted it if it wasn't.

I decide to ask Grandma about our history. She eagerly begins telling me — again — who was baptized in an actual river, and the ages when each kin strode down the aisle to meet Jesus. But I know all that — I want the history she *hasn't* told me. So I point to a picture that she always skips over. "What about her?" Could she have been the one to sing old spirituals?

Grandma can barely glance at that one. But she does say, "That's my sister, Elizabeth. She's not with us anymore." Then she clears her throat. "You hungry? I could use more coffee."

I don't answer, and quickly try again. "My music teacher told us about her great-great-great granddad who was a slave. Did we have slaves in our family?"

Grandma gives a sniff. "No, we did not come from slavery," Grandma says, enunciating each word. "Our roots are filled with senators, architects, lawyers, and even ministers. Now, I can't speak for your father's side, but we come from hardworking people. My papa and grandpapa before him owned their own land down in North Carolina." Grandma takes a seat on the couch, and I sit beside her. I want to ask how they got the land in the first place, 'cause in social studies we're only taught that Blacks weren't allowed to own property — and then the lesson jumps all the way to Rosa Parks not getting off that bus. So what Grandma's saying doesn't add up. I'm also curious about Dad's side. Daddy's mama died when I was a baby, so I ask Grandma if she knows much about her.

"Of course I do. You don't think I'd let

my daughter marry someone without knowing their family, do you?" She rocks herself up out of the couch and goes to the kitchen. I'm right on her heels asking, "What was she like?"

"What was she like? Hmph, country and unrefined." Grandma pours coffee into her cup.

Did my other grandma fry catfish on Friday nights? Or tell funny stories about Dad and his brother? Would she have fussed at me about looking like her son? Or wrapped her arms around me and tell me that she loved me just the way I am?

"Your father looks like her." Grandma opens the kitchen curtain. A brown bird quickly flies away from the ledge. "She didn't care for my Sharon. Claimed we acted uppity . . . because we were 'yellow.' " Grandma snatches the curtain closed. "What kind of nonsense is that?"

I can tell right then that Grandma's the one who didn't like Daddy's mama. Based on how often Grandma puts Dad down, I'm realizing that *she* was the one acting stuck-up. And if that's true, then maybe Grandma wasn't feeling Dad because she didn't get along with his mother? Whoa.

"Grandma?" I start, deliberating about asking this question, but I need to know. "Why don't you like my dad? Is it because his mama called y'all yellow and stuff?"

Grandma gives me a sharp look. "What makes you think I don't like your daddy? I've never told you such a thing."

Should I be totally honest? Why not. "It's just that sometimes the way you talk about him makes me feel like you don't." I sit at the table, hoping she'll sit, too, and be truthful.

"Well, Genesis, some things are just . . . complicated." Grandma eyes me, as if judging how much I know.

"What is?"

"I shouldn't be talking to you about this, not without your mother, anyhow." Grandma taps the windowsill. Is she nervous? Irritated? Finally she sighs and says, "But this conversation has been coming for a while now. I guess it's about time for you to know some things."

"What things?" My heart starts beating like crazy. She sounds like she's about to reveal some major secret.

"That picture you asked about . . ." Grandma starts easing into the chair across from me.

"Your sister?"

"Yes. Lord, I haven't told this story in years." Grandma struggles with her next thought. "My daddy, you see, was a good man . . . a proud man. Everything he learned was passed on from *his* papa." She clears her throat, continuing. "Now, my daddy used to tell us how his papa would get so frustrated with the other Blacks in his county, Nash County. He said they bowed, scraped, and share-cropped for seed just to end up owing everything to white folks. But not my grandpa . . . he didn't till no land or work in any mill. He was smarter than that."

I'm listening real close, picturing Dad working hard and sweating harder at the plant, and then of Troy's dad all finely dressed, sitting at a computer. So I interrupt. "Why'd he get mad at 'em? I mean, somebody had to sharecrop, right? Why'd they be dumb for that?"

Grandma looks stumped for a beat, then says, "I'm not saying they were dumb, I'm saying they weren't . . . motivated. There were better jobs." Grandma takes another sip of coffee. "My grandpa, he knew enough not to break his back. He sold insurance, moved the family to Durham, and worked at North Carolina Mutual . . . a Black insurance company."

I'm not sure what any of this has to do with Grandma not liking Dad, so I remind her of my question.

"You see, Genesis, the folks my grandpa sold insurance to, those folks working in the mills and doing the hard manual labor were Black men. And, the poor sharecroppers? *Black* men. If he was able to get ahead, why couldn't they? Then he realized something — most of these men weren't just regular brown- or light-skin men, but . . ." Grandma stops herself.

My face must look as confused as I feel because then Grandma glances around, lowers her voice. "My grandpa understood that the only way we were going to stay ahead, as a family, was if we marry up."

"Whaaa? Marry up?"

"Look hard at those pictures, child. You

188

can see how attractive our family is. And every one of us had respectable jobs." Grandma inspects a small nick on her coffee cup, then says softly, "Elizabeth, she was the most appealing of all four of us girls. Papa never said it, but we all knew she was his favorite. And she knew the family expectation, but what does she do?"

Grandma barrels on, not expecting an answer. "I remember the day she came back home from the university. She was so happy, her new beau by her side. You could see it in her eyes."

Now Grandma's gaze shifts from inspecting the cup to eyeing me. "Papa took one look at him," she says, "went to the kitchen and got a brown paper bag. He stepped up to Elizabeth's beau, held the bag next to his face, and dropped it right there in Elizabeth's lap. Then he marched out the house without saying a word. She knew what that meant. And she cried and cried, but Papa was resolute. He wasn't about to break with family tradition . . . not for Elizabeth, not for love, not for nothing."

A bag to the face? Wait — I'm trying to

work it out — no! Nope, nope, nope, it's too . . . terrible . . . to consider. But Grandma's face says yes, consider. Consider that a brown paper bag was the determining factor to decide who to love, who to let into the family, who had the right color skin.

My hand goes to my mouth, my thoughts fraying.

"Genesis?"

How can Grandma be *proud* of that? Be proud of any of this?

"I can tell what you're thinking," Grandma is saying.

No, no, no, she can't. I don't even know what I'm thinking besides — *my* great-grandfather put a bag up to his daughter's boyfriend's face! But things are starting to make sense. All the times I've stared at Grandma's photographs, in the back of my mind I kind of noticed that everybody was light skin. And I wasn't truly bothered that Grandma only had three pictures of me — and just one of Dad — Mom's not great about taking pictures. But I get it now. We don't fit the mold to be in her shiny gold frames. How did I not realize this before? I feel so — stupid.

Grandma tries again. "It's shocking to hear, I know. But I'm not telling you this to confuse you or get you angry." Grandma reaches across the table for my hand. I don't reach back. "Understand that my grandpapa was a forward thinker. Our lineage is full of doctors and professors and successful businessmen. It's not luck, Genesis."

It *is* luck, my entire insides are screaming. Luck to be born the right color, the right shade of light. Luck to be able to shove a bag next to someone's head, knowing no one will ever shove one next to yours. Luck to only use lemons for spots on your hands and not your entire body. Grandma's luck. Great-grandpa's luck. But me? Dad? And I ask her, flat-out. "Would he have turned my dad away?"

Grandma's gray eyes go soft. She rubs that stupid nick on her mug. Finally, slowly, she tells me how she pulled out a brown bag for Dad. "I pleaded and prayed, but . . . your mother — she didn't care anything about tradition and sacrifice." Grandma dabs the corner of one eye.

Is this what Grandma meant when she reminded Mama that Dad wasn't the type of man for her to marry? Impossible. Grandma calls my name again, and I realize I've scooched my chair back, farther away from her. "You don't believe that, do you?"

"Oh, Genesis." She reaches out to me again. "You must understand — it was never anything personal. It's just . . . look around. Who's getting arrested? Who gets the worst jobs? Don't you see, honey? My papa didn't make the rules; he just understood them."

I hate, hate, hate to admit that she might be right. Yet my mind is racing because . . . because I'm reminded of the times girls said, "I thought you were mean," just because I'm dark. Or even when kids called me ghetto and dumb. I hear it all the time. And who's to blame? Mama for loving Dad? Dad for his strong genes?

"Truth is, I've come to realize that Elizabeth, who like your mama, married her man anyway, well, her husband was one of the good ones. He took wonderful care of her and . . . and was a smart business-man. But no one could've predicted that, not even my papa."

The good ones. One of the good "dark" ones.

I'm suddenly struck by another terrible thought: If this marrying-up business is what Grandma's family has always done, Mama clearly married "down" by marry-ing Daddy. So Grandma can't help but to look on *me* with shame. The same way Dad looks at me when he's drunk.

Wait — so . . . so did *Dad* try to marry up himself? And it didn't work, because look at *me.* And now I know — I don't guess or think — I know for sure what sends him to bars and casinos. Me.

I jump up from the table. "I'm going to take a shower."

Grandma's face relaxes. *Of course* it does. I'm leaving the room!

My brain is buzzing like mad. What if I inherited all Dad's ways? What if no one recognizes that I'm . . . one of the *good* ones?

And you know what? Sayings like

"Beauty isn't everything" and "Beauty's on the inside" or "Be Black and proud" are lies. Flat-out lies. If someone ever offers me one of those stupid lines, I promise I'll scream loud enough to make the walls of Jericho tumble down, because beauty *is* everything. I'll tell you what beauty ain't. It ain't some organ hidden on the inside — no one cares about how good your heart is. And another thing, being Black like me ain't nothing to be proud about.

I can't stop fuming over Grandma's revelation even after I'm done with my chores. I'm still boiling as I finish up my homework. Her theory can't still be true nowadays, can it? Take . . . Troy! He's dark, and he could seriously be a senator, mathematician, or something. But according to Grandma, he's one of the "hood" ones, until proven otherwise, like . . . my dad?

The questions keep flooding in. If I'm the spitting image of Dad, does that mean he hates the way *he* looks too? And you know what suddenly comes to me? This is why I shouldn't feel bad for trying to make friends with light-skin girls.

'Cause if I'm with them — well, then it means they think I'm okay, and then everybody would think I'm okay, and eventually I'll blend in to be one of them . . . kinda. Whoa. I think my brain is going to explode.

Grandma sidles up beside me and tugs on my clothes. "Stand up straight." I gape at her — but then she quickly says, "Grandma doesn't mean any harm with her fussing. Can't you see Grandma loves you?"

Good question.

FOURTEEN

As soon as Grandma falls asleep, I search the kitchen drawers for a paper bag. Ain't no reason to raise it to my face; my hand fails the test — as I knew it would. What am I, like three, four . . . five shades darker? Stupid, ugly bag.

Immediately I grab two lemons, three yogurt cups, and a scouring pad. Well, how else am I supposed to exfoliate? It's an extra-strength trial type of night.

I plant myself in the center of the bedroom and wait for the voices. Even welcome them. Dad. Grandma. Grandma's papa. Regina. Chyna. Porsche. Terrance.

Who you think's gonna love you . . . ?

Every single night I've prayed for God to make me beautiful — make me light.

And every morning I wake up exactly the same.

Look at you . . . thick lips, big nose, nappy hair, and blacker than black. . . .

I start with my left arm and rub with the scouring pad. Light at first. The voices get louder, and I press harder.

100 Reasons Why We Hate Genesis . . .

The bristly wool scratches lines into my skin, feels like I'm being scraped with razor blades. But I still scrub. I scrub the blackest parts of me. I scrub the tenderest parts, and the invisible ones too. Now my face. I start on my chin and I go for it. But oh God, it hurts . . . it hurts beyond any pain I've felt before. And I can't do it — the one place on me that everyone sees. I just can't, and I get mad for not having guts. So I take it out on my knees and knuckles and elbows. And I scrub the blue-black-purple. The bluck. The blurple. All of it.

Now the lemon. The juice seeps into the cuts, feels like a swarm of hornets stinging me. If only I can get the juice deep enough under my skin, maybe, just maybe it'll work. I bite down hard on my lip, forcing screams to stay in my throat.

My fingers are trembling, but I scoop out the yogurt. And, hey, hey, it smothers the burn. It almost feels . . . good. This'll all be worth it when the change finally happens. And when it does, Grandma won't only marvel about her old relatives. Dad'll be proud that it looks like he spit me out, and Mama really wouldn't want to ever trade me in for anything in the world.

Tiny sensations suddenly begin to pop all over my body like electric shocks. *Don't scratch,* I warn myself. But slight stings turn to major prickles, and suddenly it feels as if my body's exploding with blisters and — Arghhhh! I dart to the bathroom, twist on the shower, and let the water gush over me, washing the burns and my stupid, stupid hope, down the drain.

Everything hurts. My arms and legs throb with even the slightest move. Grandma's already called for me to get up twice now, and I do, slowly. And when I take off my pajamas — OH. MY. GOD. My arms, legs, and thighs have random streaks of scrapes across them. My elbows, knees, knuckles, and ankles look like they've been in a knock-down-drag-out fight. Most of it is already starting to scab, but a few areas are raw, oozing blood. Ohmygosh, how am I gonna explain this? *I was running down the street, tripped and skidded over the concrete with my entire body, naked. A bunch of cats attacked me.* The more I think, the more I panic, and the more stupid the excuses get.

In the shower, I don't dare use soap. I let the water do its best with cleansing me. Toweling down is out of the question, so I gently pat myself dry. Real gently. Thank God Grandma's medicine cabinet is stocked for the apocalypse. There's Neosporin and an ointment called zinc oxide; both claim they're good for scratches. They're probably as old as me, but I put a little on my finger anyway and lightly dab my elbow. Yeouch! I keep going, layering both medicines, until white, greasy smears cover every scratch. *Oh no.* My chin has tiny scabs too — makes it look like I have a little goatee. I dab there, then risk the pain to rub it in good so Grandma doesn't notice. The lemons from yesterday are hidden at the bottom of the trash can. And that's where they're gonna stay, no way that "healing food" will be coming anywhere near my skin today.

And you know what's the worst? The really, really worst part? I'm still dark.

Grandma knocks on the bathroom door twice. First, to tell me to come eat. The second time griping, "What in the name of Mary is taking you so long? No one needs that much time to do *anything* in the bathroom." Can I just hide in here all day? Finally and carefully, I get dressed, making sure my clothes cover every inch of skin possible, even my wrists.

When I go to breakfast, Grandma goes on about my slouching. Yeah, whatever, 'cause right now my shoulders are too heavy to even attempt to straighten.

Then I get to thinking about how I maybe went a little overboard last night. What with everything Grandma said yesterday — and what she didn't — she's never said I reminded her of Mama — ever! Come to think of it, Grandma's never even invited her other siblings to visit when we're here, is she *that* ashamed of us? Or is she now an outcast because of Mama? Oh gosh, the questions won't stop!

This all makes me mad. Mad! So mad that I don't care if Grandma gets mad at me, and I pop the question, "You wish I looked more like my mama, don't you?"

Grandma actually freezes. For a split second, but I can see it. Then slowly her eyes meet mine. I wish I could say that Grandma comforts me with: *No, sweetheart, you're just as God made you, and I love everything He makes. . . .* Or even answer with one of the scriptures people use at church: *You're fearfully and wonderfully made.* Whatever that means. I wish I could say she said those things, but I can't. What she actually tells me is: "Life would be so much less complicated for you, if you did."

Dang.

No, *I love you even with your dark-chocolate self.* No, *That was the old way of thinking, but love is love.* No, *I want you to be the best you can be, and that's all.* No nothing?

So when the doorbell rings after I've washed the last breakfast dish, I'm all too relieved to go back home — even with the stupid boxes stuffed beside the stupid refrigerator reminding me that stupid Farmington Hills is only a temporary place.

As I'm going to the bedroom to get my bag, stopping by the bathroom to grab those ointments, I hear Mama thanking Grandma for taking care of me. Just as I come back into the living room, Grandma gives me a hug, and I'm surprised she doesn't feel how stiff my body is against hers. Does she even notice that I don't raise my arms to hug her back? If so, she doesn't say anything. Just clears her throat, shadows us to the door, and watches us. Grandma lets me leave her house with all these family secrets, and I don't know if I'm supposed to keep them secret too.

"Where's Dad? Wait, Grandma's letting you keep her car?" I ask, when I see Mom heading toward it.

"For a little while," Mama says, not answering my question about Dad.

Mama has the eyes of a hawk, I swear,

'cause she asks, "What's that on your chin?" She takes my chin in her hand and swivels my face to meet hers. "What happened?"

I hate to lie, but I say, "I was going into the basement to get the laundry basket, and I fell down the stairs . . . scraped myself all up." I show her my knuckles and wrists.

"Oh, Genesis, honey," Mama gasps. "You have to be more careful. I keep warning your grandmother that those wooden steps'll get too slippery. I'll stop and get something for that." Mama drives off, still avoiding my question about Dad, so I ask once again and she says, "He left with Chico, so I don't know, Gen." A minute later Mama adds, "I'm just glad you didn't hurt anything else."

"Me too," I tell her. But inside, I'm like, *If you only knew.*

FIFTEEN

My arms and legs are just like Kadijah's. Kadijah is this girl I knew when I was in the fourth grade. She got teased worse than me 'cause she had scaly, patchy skin all over, and she used to scratch and scratch till she bled. She said she had eczema. I look just like her with my scaly patches and dry skin, except for one thing. My scabs are uglier. They're purple black. And itch. I slather on the ointments again. All that for *nothing.* But at least Dad won't see me like this . . . he ain't come home.

Still, I don't know why I keep expecting a change to happen overnight. Just like I thought the lemons, the baking soda, the milk, and all that other stuff was going to work. I have to believe that God wouldn't want me to have a hard life. I mean, I haven't done anything that bad, and if He's so good, then why punish me?

All this heaviness is weighing me down in English class. There's no concentrating for me with these scabs itching so badly that I could jump out the window. Then I get a wild thought: What if Troy feels the same way as I do? And Yvette, too? Is that why she's hip-locked with Belinda? And, oh my gosh, could that be why Terrance is always tailgating Jason? *Enough already!*

"Nia Kincaid will be the first student to read her essay." Ms. Luctenburg's announcement catches my attention.

Nia saunters up to the front and brushes her dreadlocks out of her face. They're so knotted that I mindlessly wriggle free the tangles in the back of my own head, the "kitchen." I don't want anyone to accuse me of having nappy hair like that.

She levels her gaze at us and then begins without even looking at her paper. I look over at Sophia, hoping she reads my *Don't tell me she memorized her entire essay?* mind. But Sophia is totally tuned in to Nia. "Imagine being free to live without cumbersome concerns and decision-making. You will never have to worry about choosing the right career, marrying the perfect person, or keeping up with the latest trends." The class grunts and nods in agreement. Nia goes on, and soon I'm leaning forward, almost forgetting about my hairy-looking chin 'cause I'm too busy imagining that world, that world without competition or comparisons. Even Jason's edged to the tip of his seat. Nia finishes. When Ms. Luctenburg moves to the next reader, I'm still left in her world.

What's up with that girl? Of all the schools I've attended, I ain't never met a girl so . . . I don't know, different? And who's her crew? I should go right up to her and say something like, *Hey, I loved your essay.* Or, *Hey, how long did it take you to write that? Hey, you're interesting, we should be friends.* Yeah right. I won't just be the new girl, but a stalker, too.

■ ■ ■ ■

Sophia couldn't wait to tell Troy all about my "fall," so she practically dragged me to the library to meet him for tutoring. Nothing dramatic must happen at this school if me tumbling down some stairs makes headline news. It started after I changed into my PE uniform: first there were the bugged-out looks, then the pointing, and finally, the interrogation. My scabby skin seemed to throb more with each question. And Sophia grilled for every tiny detail, forcing me to spin a tale better than Dad can. And now Troy's probably expecting the deets too, and I can't even remember everything I told Sophia in the first place. "Tell him, Genesis, and don't leave out the part about your grandmother —"

"Seriously, Sophia? I could've killed myself," I say, leaving to find a table, hoping that that would be the end of it. I check to see if Troy's coming along too. He's not. They're both standing there. "What?"

"Why're you walking like that?" Troy asks, and I can tell he's not trying to be smart, he just wants to know.

"That's what I was trying to tell you before she bit my head off," Sophia says, low. She's lucky she lives out here in Farmington Hills; otherwise she'd catch a beatdown for blabbing people's business.

"I didn't bite your head off," I explain. "I'm just a little achy, that's all."

Troy slides his backpack from his shoulder, letting it hang in his hand. "Well, is somebody going to tell me what's up?"

Sophia smooths out her shirt repeatedly, not saying a word. "Fine," I start, "well, what happened was . . ."

Ever since I can remember, I've always wanted a best friend. Someone I could be real with. And with the way Troy is looking at me, as if he earnestly cares, I want to be honest. But learning how people — not necessarily Troy — can be two-faced, smiling one minute and then talking about you behind your back the next, it's just best not to fess up to anything that could be used against me later.

So, my story is plain and simple. "I fell

down the stairs."

"Oh, no wonder you're walking so stiff." Then he asks, "You okay?"

"I'm fine, just got scratched up really bad." I show him my wrists and knuckles. "But I'm tough," I joke.

"Yeah, I see." Troy hoists his book bag back onto his shoulder. "Ready?"

"That's it?" Sophia butts in.

That's it? Maybe Sophia's folks let her ask all the questions she wants, but my folks taught me better. When I get too curious, Mom and Dad would be like, *If you don't have nothing to do, then we'll find something for you.* Translation: *Go on, get outta my face and do something else.*

This gives me the idea to pull a Mom and Dad on Sophia by saying, "Do you have a book to read, or you need help finding one?" Bam! Instant question shut down.

Sophia keeps at it. "Don't you want to know how it happened?"

I'm about to point out that she's the only one giving me the third degree, but Troy's answer is enough. "No, I'm satisfied with knowing she's okay." And when he asks me again if I'm ready to get started, as if my scarred-up chin is no big deal, I'm thinking Troy's all right, a real good dude.

Even so, I ain't telling him nothing.

When I get to chorus, I hurry to my seat. After last week's episode, I'm liable to flip out if one more person asks about my knuckles or chin.

When Mrs. Hill tings her triangle my heart begins to race. If she makes us sing that drinking gourd song again, I swear I'll head straight to the bathroom and never leave till Harriet Tubman herself rises from the grave and drags me out.

"Today, class, we're going to . . ."

Is she looking right at me?

"Do something a little different."

Hallelujah!

"Now, everyone in this class can sing well, but what sets us apart?" Mrs. Hill doesn't wait for an answer. "The emotion we put into the song. Great singers bring a little of themselves to their music, and for today I want you to allow yourself to be vulnerable. Surrender to the moment."

"Mrs. Hill, I don't wanna run outta here crying," says Terrance with a smirk. *Jerk.*

"If that's what it takes, Terrance, then what's wrong with that?" Mrs. Hill holds a large picture out in front of her. "Take a good look at this collage. It's by an artist named Romare Bearden." In the picture, a group of musicians play instruments while a lady sings onstage. "Who can tell me what you might hear if we were actually there?" Kids state the obvious: horns, drums, and a piano. Mrs. Hill taps the picture, asking, "What about this woman here?"

"It looks like she's going to say, 'That's my song,' " Yvette calls out.

"Good. Now how would she say it?"

"That's my *song,*" Yvette says with sass. Mrs. Hill makes us repeat the phrase like Yvette had.

"What does the horn sound like? Let me hear the sound, not the words." Someone shouts, *"Toot-toot-toot."* Everyone cracks up. Before we know it, Mrs.

Hill has us toot-tooting and boom-bapping all over the place. We scat-a-tat like the jazz singer. We snap fingers like the audience members. We boom-bap like the drum player.

Mrs. Hill breaks the class into groups and assigns us each a phrase. My group gets, "I can dig it, man," which we start saying real cool, like beatniks, half laughing, half embarrassed. Yvette's group gets, "That's my *song.*" Jeez, why couldn't I be in her group? Once everyone's giggle-practiced a bit, Mrs. Hill holds up a skinny baton, and directs us as she plays with our volume, pitch, and different combinations of the sounds and words until we start to sound like a real band.

"Boom-boom-bap!"

"Skiddle-dee-bee-bap!"

"Tt-Tt-Tt!"

"I can dig it, man!"

"That's my song!"

"Tt-Tt-Tt! Skiddle-dee-bee-bap! Ahh-ahh-ahh-ahh! I can dig it, man! Boom-boom-bap! That's my song!"

Mrs. Hill silences one group, then layers in another one. We're grooving and moving. I catch Nia's eye and we smile, both feeling the same vibe. Mrs. Hill works us into a fury, and then brings us down, silencing us, group by group, until we hear only the *Tt-Tt-Tt* as it fades to a whisper, ending with a mellow *I can dig it, man!*

We're so pumped that it takes three dings from the triangle for Mrs. Hill to get everyone's attention.

"Did you all like that exercise?" Nods and yeses from the class. "I'm glad, because I want to announce that auditions for the annual talent showcase are two weeks away! Sign-up sheets will be posted in the hall."

Immediately a buzz goes around the room.

"I'm doing it this year, I have to!"

"Oh my gosh, oh my gosh, oh my gosh. I've waited all year for this."

"Whatever you do, please don't do that mime thing. It's awful."

Terrance jumps up and shouts to Jason, "Ohhh yeah! That trophy is ours, bruh!" Yvette huddles close to Belinda, whispering. Eloise sits erect, writing furiously in her notebook. Nia sits back with a mysterious grin on her face.

Whoa, these folk are seriously into the talent show! When class is over, I wait for everyone to leave and then approach Mrs. Hill. I keep my chin down — I've told my falling down the stairs story so many times today that I'll be struck by lightning if I lie one more time.

"Genesis. Good work today."

"Thanks. I, uh, wanted to give you back your CD. I've listened to it almost every day. I can probably sing the songs in my sleep!"

She beams. "Glad you liked it."

"I even checked out a book on her. Yeah, I couldn't put it down."

Mrs. Hill looks happily surprised. "You did? What're your thoughts?"

"Well . . ." I hadn't thought too deeply about it until now. "She had a hard life with her father not being there. Plus, she was dead poor . . . and, the work she had to do as a kid . . . it was crazy." I pause, thinking, and add, "Then again, she seemed like she had a lot of freedom."

"Freedom? Was it really freedom?" Mrs. Hill starts straightening the chairs back into a semicircle, and I follow behind, helping.

"Well, I guess not . . . not exactly," I say. "What I mean is that she could make choices on her own. But now that I think about it, she was forced into certain situations because nobody was looking out for her."

"She made some very strong choices to survive, is that what you mean?"

I nod. "Yeah, and she had to sing in front of grown-ups when she was, like, *my* age. Just to make money to live. To me, all of that set up her life, you know, with her being addicted to drugs and stuff."

"Perhaps so . . . Billie Holiday definitely had a lifetime of struggles, but even still, she made a huge contribution to music. No one could ever deny that."

"Yeah, and her singing sounds so . . . easy. It's like she used her voice to express what she was going through . . . like her story's right there under the words. It's hard to describe it."

"No, you're absolutely correct. She

instinctively knew how to use her voice like an instrument. She could play with melodies and rhythms and add her emotions." Mrs. Hill shakes her head as though in awe. "She was and will always be the only Lady Day. But —" Now she tilts her head, looks at me. "I bet with some help you could tap in to her style."

Oh no. No way. The memory of me singing alone during that visualization exercise still flushes me with raw embarrassment. Maybe Billie Holiday could do that, but I can't. "Me? Naw."

"Yes, you . . . just listen to the radio. Erykah Badu . . . Jill Scott . . . I bet you could point out any number of singers Miss Day has inspired." Mrs. Hill puts the last chair in place, goes over to her music library, and files the CD back in its spot. "Well, anyway, I hope you consider auditioning. Believe it or not, you have quite a gift."

"Thanks," I say, and scoot off. On the way to my locker, I tumble Mrs. Hill's words over in my mind. Me? Audition? Gift? Mrs. Hill is a certified music teacher. She would know if I could really sing . . . but still . . . me?

"Hey, Genesis." Yvette's waiting at my locker.

"Yeah?" Yvette knows where my locker is? And she's here waiting on me?

"This is Belinda." Belinda waves.

As if their names haven't been memorized since Yvette had my back against Terrance.

"So, you sing a lot?" Yvette tucks her stick-straight hair behind her ear. Relaxer, for sure.

"No." My antenna goes up. This had better not be some kind of roast setup about my incident a few days ago. Still, I tell myself to chill.

"Oh, I thought you did because you're always singing in class."

"You mean singing with the class?" In that case, we're both always singing. But I'm not about to correct her.

"Well, yeah," Yvette says right away. "I'd be too shy to sing — even with a class — if I was new. Would you, Belinda?"

"I wouldn't open my mouth." Belinda shakes her head, and her hair swishes across her shoulders.

"You auditioning for the talent show?" Yvette goes on.

I swallow hard. "I hadn't really thought about it."

"Oh. Well . . ." Something catches Yvette's attention. Out of the corner of my eye I see Sophia speeding down the hall, heading straight toward us. "We were wondering if you'd like to —"

"Hey!" Sophia waves at me.

Just as I'm about to raise my hand, Yvette sucks her teeth. "You don't know *her*, do you?"

"Her?" *Hurry up and ask. Would I like to what? Sing with you in the talent show? Walk home with you? Sit with you at lunch? ASK!!!*

Sophia calls my name. I wave, weakly.

"Never mind. It's getting ridiculously noisy around here. Come on, Belinda." Yvette and Belinda stroll away, huddling together, whispering.

Sophia reaches me, breathing hard. "Hey, what's up?"

"Nothing." Only two seconds ago I

could've possibly been whispering with *them.*

"What did *they* want?" Sophia asks, glancing back.

"They didn't say. Asked me about my singing, though." I get my books for homework out of my locker.

"Oh," Sophia says quietly as we head for the doors. "They didn't say anything about me, did they?"

"Naw, just if I knew you, that's all." Yet, even though they didn't technically say anything about her, there's a ping of guilt recalling *how* they asked if I knew her. Then it dawns on me that there must be a reason behind Sophia's question. I push the door open. "Why you ask?"

"It's just that —" Sophia hesitates until I remind her that I told her my most embarrassing story today. "Well, the one with the bangs was in a class of mine last year. She wasn't very, how should I put this? Nice," Sophia says, letting the words hang there as if she's waiting for me to ask her about it.

Here's the deal. If what happened was *bad* bad, then I can't be cool with Yvette and Belinda. That's the code. Everybody knows that you can't be friends with somebody who disses your friend — even if the dis was a long time ago. And I really want to be cool with Yvette and Belinda. But I have to have Sophia's back. *Arrghhhhh!*

"You know what? Forget it, I'm being silly."

"You sure?" I ask, crossing my fingers that she's absolutely sure. Sophia says she is and lets it drop — which means it can't be too bad. If it were too bad, she'd be like me, still reeling from when none of the girls — not even Tasha and their repossessed car — stood up for me when Regina called my folks bums. Called me Char. That kind of "too bad."

After a beat she says, "Hey, wanna come over for dinner sometime?"

"Like to eat and chill?"

"Well duh! But I have to warn you — if you come, you might think my family's crazy." We head across the street and down the sidewalk.

"I've gotta ask my mom first, but I'd like to meet a family that's crazier than mine," I say. Mama will just be happy that I have an invitation, I think.

"Ask if you can come this Saturday. We'll have so much fun," Sophia says as she breaks away toward her street. "And hey, stay away from stairs!"

"You got jokes," I say, stifling my laugh because my scars hurt when I do.

As I watch Sophia walk away, I think, *Yeah, I'd like to go to her house.* We can sit in her room and tell corny jokes. I can teach her how to play Uno and Spades, and she can teach me some Greek curse words. I'll ask about Yvette because now I *do* want to know. And I might even let her hear me sing 'cause that's what real friends do.

This fantasy is good enough to revel in for the rest of the day.

SIXTEEN

Our walkway looks like an artist created it. For real, it's a zig-zag pattern of whitewashed and brown bricks leading to the steps, which are big flat slabs in a shape that would be great for hopscotch — but I'm too old for that. Anyway, it's like I'm Dorothy easing down the road, but without all the yellow. I'm so lost in it till I get to the door and — no no no. A chill runs from one arm to the other. Please don't let that paper be what I think it is. No no no, please. I take down the note, unlock the door, and run straight to my room. I close the door even though no one's home. Then I tear open the envelope.

Emory,
I haven't been able to catch you at

work. It has been almost a month, and my office has yet to receive your first month's rent. Our records show that you only paid the security deposit. Let me know what's going on. Call me.

Todd

I place my hand on the wall to hold myself steady. This wall is the cleanest I've had in a bedroom. This bedroom is the biggest I've had in my life. And this letter means — I'm about to lose it.

I fold the note into as tiny a square as possible and stuff it way in the back of my sock drawer. Same drawer as my list. I pull it out. Me getting nearly all the way to #87, no problem, since I might have to add: Because her grandma's right, her dad's going to get them put out in front of all those white folks. *100 Reasons Why We Hate Genesis.* Hah. No doubt I can make it to one hundred more.

I store the list next to the note, shut the drawer, and practically wear the tread

off my shoes pacing around nervously —
I should do my homework, but I can't
focus on anything but that stupid note. I
should be putting more Neosporin on
my scratches, but can't because of that
note. My pacing leads me to the kitchen.
I search the pantry for something, but I
have no idea what I want. There's nothing in there to fill the hole growing in my
stomach. I don't expect to find anything
in the cabinets, but I look anyway. And
something at the top of the cabinet
catches the light. I drag over a chair, and
that's when I find them — three gleaming bottles — Absolut vodka, Hennessy,
and Crown Royal. Dad! Why?! I haul the
bottles down and unscrew the Crown
Royal. It stinks like medicine. How does
he even *like* this?

"I hate you," I say to the Crown Royal,
with its fancy crown-shaped bottle, so
much fancier than any place we've ever
stayed besides this one. Fancier than the
off-priced food boxes. Way fancier for
sure than my clothes. I take another sniff.
I gag and close it fast.

"I hate you. I hate you!" I say again and
again. And I swear, it's as if mist swirls

around the kitchen and I disappear and another Genesis emerges. This girl is full of unanswered questions and rage. I hover slightly above this other Genesis, watch her run to the sink, all three bottles in her arms. When she unscrews the caps, one by one, I want to stop her. I really do. When she holds up the bottles, one by one, I stretch out my arms. They don't reach. When she tips the bottles over the sink, one by one, I should hold her back. I *should.* But —

I can't.

I won't.

When the last bottle is empty, when the smell of booze fills the air, the other Genesis fades away and I can hardly breathe. What have I done? I bend over the sink, trying to summon the liquor back up the pipes. It's too late. Too late. Tears burst out before I can fight them back. Because only now do I consider the terrible things Dad'll do once he finds out.

■ ■ ■ ■

I hide the bottles in the backyard, under the deck. Then I run inside again and lock the door.

Stop. Think for a second. I sit at the kitchen table racking my brain for a way to get out of this mess. I can plead with Dad to understand, like he does with Mama.

He'll never listen.

Or, I could simply apologize.

But wait . . . what if I'm actually doing Dad a favor? He told us himself that drinking is a sickness. Why should we help him stay sick? It's just like how Billie Holiday's husband tried to help her. And if he asks me, I shouldn't be scared to tell him, "I only wanted to help."

Ughhhh. That'll never work. Unless . . . unless Dad looks at me and sees more than Mama's smile. The stupid lemons haven't worked, so how? How? *I'm dead. Think, think, think.* I pull at my roots, stretching my brain. And my fingers get caught in my hair. Wait, my hair! If Dad sees me with straight hair plus my best

"Mama smile," maybe he'll forget all about his vodka and Hennessy. Yeah, that might just work. I scurry to get the comb and hot comb. Then I section my hair in four parts, like Mama does. I set the stove to high, and place the hot comb in the middle of the burner. It gets so hot that smoke rises. Then I take the hot comb, grab a chunk of hair, and — I can't.

I can't do it. I can't get the hand that's holding the comb to move closer to my head. I'm too chicken of burning my hair all the way off. I cut off the stove and scream out in frustration.

"I'm dead. I'm dead. I'm dead," I repeat my own, warped mantra. I gotta remember to add to my list, reason #88: Because she's thirteen and too scared to press her own hair.

"Genesis," Mama calls from the front door. "I've got bags."

"Coming!" I rush to shut off the stove and put the hot comb back in the drawer and go out to meet Mama. "Hey," I say, taking a bag from her arms.

"Thanks, hon." I follow her to the kitchen, sniffing for vapors. If her nose is anything like Grandma's, she'll surely whiff out the scent of alcohol. "I'll make dinner, but I need to get these put up first." She starts unloading the bags.

"I'll do it," I offer quickly.

"Excuse me?"

"I got it. You must be tired. . . ."

"It's all yours." Mama pulls out a package of ground beef from one of the bags. "I was going to make meatloaf, but how about hamburgers instead?"

When she needs a spatula, it's already in my hand. When Mama goes for the seasonings, I get them. One by one, she sprinkles the meat with them. Mama sneezes into the crook of her arm.

"Bless you," I say, at her heels.

"Thanks . . . pepper got into my nose," she tells me, and goes toward the sink.

I hover at her side, watching to see if she smells anything odd. She must not, 'cause she dries her hands and goes back to cooking. After we've eaten, I scrape the scraps into the garbage disposal, then sit back down across from her, trying not to think about what I'd done.

Finally, Mama catches my eye. "What's

going on with you?"

"Nothing," I say, glancing at the cabinets. Stupid! I mean, she can't read minds, right? But I'm even more worried about the note, Todd's note, hiding in my drawer. Mama should know about it. But dang it, if I tell her, she'll flip out and move us back to Grandma's *tonight.* Especially since she's been eerily chill about Dad taking her money. And double especially since Dad's been MIA. These are arguments she'd usually hold over his head for weeks.

"Genesis?" Mama prods, "got something on your mind?"

I pull my sleeves down over my wrists. I've done this so many times today. Stupid exfoliation. Stupid brown bag. Mama's waiting, so what pops out is, "Guess Dad's missing dinner. His schedule, huh?"

I swear her shoulders rise. But she's wearing her poker face, so there's no telling how much worry she has inside. Still, I feel terrible for bringing it up, especially since the whole brown bag thing was on the tip of my tongue. But I can tell it's not a good time to be asking anything surrounding that topic. So I go to the fridge, get the Sprite, pour her a glass, and set it in front of her.

"Thanks." Mama drinks half of it and her shoulders settle a little. "How's your chin? Been putting something on it?"

"Yes," I say, forcing myself not to look to where the bottles had been. If I talk, Mama won't get more suspicious. So I'm gonna have to talk about what I hate talking about — school. I tell her about Mrs. Hill's vocal exercises, Troy and my tutoring, and how Sophia and all the other girls questioned my scars during PE. Of course, I wanna shut up. I wanna go in my room, turn on my music, and not think about anything. Not Dad's liquor down the drain, his brother, marrying up, my scabby body, Todd's note — I want to think about NOTHING.

Mama gives the glass of Sprite a swirl. "Gen, I know it's been hard for you. But I'm so glad that you're already making friends. I just hope this all works out."

Her tone makes me quiver. All these different emotions are building up in me, and I'm ready to explode. Seriously, I'm on the verge of confessing everything when I realize that she actually looks hopeful, and I just can't do it. I swallow it all back down my throat and agree, "It will."

Then, to make her feel even better, I tell her that Sophia asked me over for dinner this Saturday.

"So that's why you're being so helpful?" she says, taking a sip of pop.

I laugh 'cause she has no clue. Then she laughs, which makes me feel better too.

"I'm joking," Mama says, her voice suddenly bright. "Dinner sounds good, but maybe not this Saturday. I was hoping to rent *Lady Sings the Blues*. . . . Maybe next weekend, but I'll need to meet her folks."

"They're crazy, she says."

"Every family has some form of crazy, trust me." Mama yawns and closes her eyes. She still has a soft face, like in her kid pictures on Grandma's six-shelf case. I suspect it was screwy for her growing up with Grandma's rules. Once, when I complained that Grandma never lets me play outside when it's sunny, Mama told me that Grandma wouldn't let her play in the sun either. She never told me why, but now I figured it out. Grandma ain't want her — or me — to turn no darker than we already were. But still, that was cruel, 'cause even though there was no hope for me to ever match that stupid bag, Mama wouldn't've gotten nearly as brown.

"Yeah, I guess there is," I agree, because hidden behind *our* closed door is *all* kinds of crazy.

I wake up the next morning. Dad didn't kill me.

Dad didn't kill me because he didn't come home. Again. Mama's so mad that she looks like she could spit fire. So she keeps her mouth closed. Me? I'm glad I poured out his stupid liquor. That's what he deserves for going back on his promise.

SEVENTEEN

That afternoon after tutoring, I slip over to the computers, leaving Troy and Sophia reading at the back table, and do a little research about lemons. Last night I was lucky not having to face Dad, but I'm even more determined to find some way to make myself look as much like Mama as I can. Then maybe he'll stay home more. But it turns out that you're supposed to mix the lemon juice with honey and something called turmeric. *Tumeric?* Where in the heck will I get that? And what the heck *is* it?!

When I finally rejoin my peeps, Sophia's reading her same book, Troy's in his alternate universe, and I settle in with Billie Holiday's biography. But it doesn't take long before my mind drifts to other thoughts, like maybe I should've shown

Mama the note. And man, do I wish my scrapes would stop itching. Then there's Yvette — I've seen her twice, and she has yet to ask me what she wanted to yesterday.

"Genesis? You staring at me again?" Sophia asks, out of the blue.

Troy glances up from his Black Panther comic.

"Why do you always think I'm staring at you?"

Ever since Sophia's bathroom episode, she's been on edge and accusing people, i.e. me, of staring. Maybe somebody should tell Sophia that everything is not about her, and some of us have our own issues to deal with, like dads staying out all night at the casinos.

"I hate it when people watch me, that's all," Sophia grumbles, almost to her book.

"Girl, chill, I was staring off into space, thinking." I add, fast, "Thinking how I forgot to tell you that I can come for dinner." *Dinner is what your dad hasn't been to for the last two nights. Shut up, brain!*

"Really?" Sophia says, sitting up in the

floor recliner, suddenly switching moods.

"Hey, I like to eat too," Troy pipes up.

"Girls only, sorry," Sophia teases. Troy shrugs and goes back to his comic book. "I'll tell my mom. She'll probably start cooking the next minute."

"Yeah, but tell her to slow her roll; I can't come till the Saturday after." I try to cheer myself up by picturing me sitting at Sophia's table surrounded by her family — her *all-white* family. I've actually never been to dinner at a white person's house. Now I'm worried about that stupid paper bag test — not that Sophia's dad will put a bag to my face — but will they view me like Grandma's family would? This is not a good thought to be entertaining, so I change subjects. "Okay, so, this talent show . . . everybody's talking about it like it's a big deal."

Troy perks up. "It *is* a big deal. Bigger than football and basketball for a lot of people."

"That's because we have teams that suck at defense," Sophia says. "What? That's what my brother says," she adds when Troy groans, "Heyyyyy."

"Our teams are decent. And to answer

your question," Troy goes on, "the PTA rolls out a red carpet and decorates as if it's a music awards show."

"Yeah," Sophia agrees, all enthusiastic. "Plus, they have a bunch of noisemakers and paparazzi. All the drama queens hang out front hogging up the spotlight."

"What's the prize? A trophy?" I ask.

"Yeah, plus they get a write-up in the school paper and sometimes the *Farmington News*. They don't win money, but the PTA makes this huge gift basket. Last year they had an Xbox with games and stuff. I wish I won; my dad won't buy me a gaming system."

"Really? Who won last year?"

"This guy named Joel. He was amazing," Sophia raves. "He did some kind of balance slash juggling act. You would've thought he grew up in a circus. After he won, everybody treated him like he was a real celebrity."

"Yeah, he was good," Troy tells me. "Thinking about auditioning?"

"Me? Naw, I just keep hearing about it, that's all."

"You can come see me, then. I always

play my violin," says Troy.

"You play the violin?" *The violin.* I wonder if kids ever blasted him for playing that white people's instrument, but actually . . . I think it's kinda cool. Shoot, I wish Grandma could meet him, Troy being so good in math will punch a big fat hole in her grandpa's tradition theory. I ask, "How come you never mentioned the violin?"

"What do I say? 'Hi, I'm Troy. I'm a Virgo, and I play the violin.' " Sophia and I burst out laughing. A librarian shushes us. "Plus, I haven't won yet, and notice I said, 'yet.' "

Before we leave the library, I ask the librarian to make a copy of the cover of Billie Holiday's book. Normally, I don't take the time to hang up posters, but I want to decorate my walls with singers, sort of like Mrs. Hill's classroom — even though Todd's note is a big ol' clue that it won't stay up too long. I also check out a book about this other singer who's mentioned in Billie's biography: Ella Fitzgerald. Who knows, if I like her, then she'll go up on the wall too. If there's time.

■ ■ ■ ■

Wednesday night, I keep an eye on the front door while Mama and I catch an episode of *American Idol,* and even though it's good, it's hard to focus on it because . . . well, Dad. He's never been gone longer than two days, as far as I know. What if he comes home ready to drink his vodka? What if he goes off with his stupid teasing? Or empty his pockets with his winnings, argue with Mama, and plead for another chance. *If* he comes home. I need a distraction. So I brush Mama's hair. The more I brush, the more I relax. Mama finally relaxes too.

For a moment, my mind even wonders about — of all things — that guy Joel. He could've been a cornball, outcast, or a regular dude, but once he won the talent contest, kids treated him like a celebrity. *A celebrity.*

"Hello? Genesis? Hey, the brush hasn't gone through my hair in a minute." Mama leans her head back, looking at me upside down. "Wow, your chin is almost back to normal." She then asks, "So, what's up?"

"Sorry." I nudge her head back down and start brushing again. And I tell her all about the talent show.

"A talent show? Really?"

She pats the cushion next to her. "Are you trying out?"

"Uh-uh. I was hoping to go watch, that's all." I come from behind the couch and settle down beside her. Then we go on talking as if our lives are oh-so-great, ignoring the big elephant stomping around the room, or, more specifically *not* stomping around the room.

"You know," Mama says, picking up the remote, "I remember wanting to audition for a talent show. Modern dance was what I wanted to do."

"Why didn't you?"

"Scared."

Now I'm wishing I could tell Mama that I sorta want to audition, but I'm too scared to. Scared to sing in front of everybody, especially after the chorus incident. Scared my voice isn't good enough. And scared, yes, I have to admit — scared they'll call me Ape or Blackie. But I'm even scared to tell my mom *that*!

So I tell her nothing as we watch TV, each of us keeping one eye on the door.

Mama's phone rings, and she hops up to answer it. It's Tootsie, and that means a lengthy conversation. The idea of me possibly auditioning gets me excited, so I take this opportunity to slip into her room and borrow her foundation. I tie my shirt over my head and make a pony-tail. This shirt is my *real* crowning glory. Dang, I wish one of my songs was playing on the radio. Might as well load the player with the Ella Fitzgerald CD that I borrowed from Mrs. Hill. It doesn't take long for me to realize that even though the music's old, there's something . . . stylish, yeah that's the word, and rich about her voice. She's not as mellow and deep as Billie, but fun and upbeat. Ella sings about funny Valentines, Paris, and summertime. Happy stuff.

But like Billie, Ella gets me singing too. I don't know if Ella flips her hair, but I do. I whip my long hair, flick my scraped-up wrist, and let a hand rest on my hip. I wink and wave to my audience as they scream my name. My skin glows just like Regina's, Nia's, and Belinda's. I don't care about our family's history or Dad's issues. Nothing matters. Not *now*.

The clapping's thunderous, like a tornado blasting through Kansas. Its echo vibrates up my back, and I sweep into a bow of acknowledgment. Gratitude. I bow to the left, I bow to the right, and then everything goes into slow motion, because as I look up, there, in my doorway, stands Dad. A crooked smile snakes its way up the left side of his mouth.

Dad tilts his head to one side, appraising me, then says, "Well, well, well . . ." He calls out, "Sharon, you need to see this."

I could run to the bathroom, but he might block the door. The closet? He'll come there, too. Dad studies the black shirt draped on my head. I snatch it off.

"No, leave it. It's finally long, just like you want, right?"

So much for those doggone alcoholic meetings.

Only seconds ago I was gorgeous and amazing. Even glowing. *Glowing!* I wipe my face with my sleeve, leaving tan streaks across my shirt.

241

"Don't let me stop you. Go on with the show," Dad says with an ugly eagerness. Ella's joyful voice mockingly drones on and on in the background.

"You've got a lot of nerve —" Mama's eyes meet mine for a fraction of a second, and I drop my head.

"I know I was wrong . . . ," Dad says. "But look, your daughter's been performing in white face. Chubby Cheeks, go on, put that thing back on yo' head . . . show her. . . ."

Lord, please let me die right now. Let me pass out right here.

"Emory —" Mama's at a loss for words, but suddenly her eyes go steely. "You're . . . you're stinking drunk!"

Mama's fists are balled, and her face is flaming. And there's nothing he can say that'll convince her to let go of four days' worth of anger.

"You lied *again*! And you don't even call? You leave me worried and —" Mama holds up her hand, stopping Dad's next line. "Not. A. Word." Sometimes I wish she'd go *off* off, carry a baseball bat and smash stuff up like Beyoncé in her "Hold

Up" video. But no, she was raised a "lady," whatever the heck that means. Still, Mama's so composed, it's scary — so scary that not even Dad knows how to react.

"Wait," he finally says, already breaking out his pleading voice. He takes out his wallet, and pulls out a slip of paper. "See, I paid the rent." He holds up the receipt.

Even though I'm desperately wanting to disappear, my heart starts singing. He paid the rent! We can stay! Then my mind flashes to Todd's note. If he's paid the rent, then why did we get the notice? Maybe the note came before he paid! Of course, that's it. There's no need for me to even worry about it anymore. He came through. Dad really came through.

"So, Gen-Gen, what you practicin' fo'?" Dad turns to Mama, asking, "Can I at least hear the girl sing?"

Now I'm back to mad, so mad at Dad for — for dogging me out like this.

Mama scowls for about ten seconds, then pushes past him and goes straight to my dresser. "Genesis, pack a bag." But my feet won't budge. Part of me wants to stop her and plead that Dad . . . yes, he was gone, but he paid the rent. A part of me wants to remind her that she said she didn't ever wanna go dragging bags back to Grandma's like a failure. But the rest of me, the rest of me is so — confused. Until . . . until Dad starts back egging me to perform. And now I hope that Mama finds the note, then he'll be the one under the spotlight.

"Stop it, just stop it!" Mama suddenly yells at him. She yanks open my drawer and thrusts some pajamas into my hand. "Pack whatever you need," she orders, and storms to her room.

"Wait a minute, Sharon —" Dad says, his voice garbled. "This was my last chance to go all out . . . 'cause I'm gon' commit, fully commit, to that program," he ends with a bellow.

Ever since I was little, I've replayed in my head the times when we sang together — just him and me. I believed that something real was hidden somewhere deep under all the layers, the drunkenness. And yeah, mostly when I trust him, he says something mean, makes me want to hate him. But then there are those times . . . those times when he says the right words, letting me know that I'm his baby girl. "Dad?"

He turns and smiles, not a mean one. But a simple, drunk smile.

I waver, but force myself to boss up. I don't even know what to say, so I stutter, "I, uh . . . uh . . ." Gosh, why can't I ever find the right words to say?

Dad sways from side to side, saying, "What? Cat got your tongue?" Then he howls with laughter. "Get it?" He howls till tears run down his face. Howls until he has a coughing attack, and I hope he chokes to death. Finally, he wipes his mouth with the back of his hand, and stumbles out of my room.

That stupid joke wasn't even funny.

I wash the stupid makeup off my face. I use half the bar of soap. My eyes are burning. I wash till the tiny scabs on my chin peel off. I wash till my face feels raw. Dad's laughter keeps blowing through my chest like a Joe Louis punch. So I keep washing.

After forever, I shut off the water. See my hands. My black hands. My feet. My black feet. Black and dirty. Filthy. I hate it! Then I see it — there in the corner, a jug of bleach —

"Genesis!" Mama calls. "We're leaving. Now!"

EIGHTEEN

We're halfway down the front steps when Dad calls out, "You really gon' leave?" Like me, he's stunned that Mama's threats are finally coming true. "You going to yo' mama's," he snorts, stumbling again. He grabs hold of the railing, straightening himself. "You goin' there, knowing how she is. She's gon' put you down, then what?"

Mama opens the car door, not daring a single glance at him. Dad's usually as tall as a tree, but now he looks small. Yet nothing's small about his voice, especially as he shouts how Mama's breaking her vows, how her daddy would be ashamed, and that soon we'll be back. *And* now all these white folks are opening their doors, peeking out.

We ride in silence. The radio is on, but

I can't recall which songs have been play-ing. Dad's right. Grandma berates Mama — *always.* How does she stand it? Shoot, if I had some money, I'd have Mama drive us to a fancy hotel just to get away from everything. I really wish this, espe-cially when we park in front of Grand-ma's house and Mama breaks down. I mean, really breaks down. The car's not even turned off before she's banging on the steering wheel, fists pounding so hard I'm afraid it'll snap off. She lets out a sob so deep that it sounds like it's been trapped inside her forever.

That's when it occurs to me. Mama's stuck. Between Dad's issue of keeping us on the move, and Grandma scaring her with marriage vow scriptures, and Mama needing to prove to Grandma that she *didn't* make a mistake in marrying Daddy — and me. She can't do anything. Or go anywhere. Dang-ee.

My mama's tough. I can count on one hand how many times I've seen her cry. And all those times combined don't come close to this. I suspect that I'm not supposed to see this. It feels way too private. Mamas probably don't want their kids to see them lose it. But I'm not about to leave her alone, either. So I rub her back lightly.

Dad. If he only knew. But no, he's probably searching the cabinets for his stupid bottles of liquor right now, finding them missing. Good. At least I ain't there to hear about it. And I hope he's too drunk to remember.

"I'm okay," Mama says at last, wiping her face with her jacket sleeve, looking at me with red, watery eyes.

We both know Mama is not okay. And she should know that she doesn't need to make me feel better, not for being real. Not for finally putting her foot down.

After we ring Grandma's bell, she unlocks all the locks, cracks open the door, and starts right on in — just like last time. "Lord ah mercy, Sharon, y'all evicted already? For heaven's sake." Grandma keeps right on with her scolding, not knowing how long it took for Mama to get the courage to come in the first place. She keeps right on going, not even noticing how puffy Mama's eyes are.

I want to go straight to Mama's old room and rock myself to sleep. But

Mama looks so beaten down, and Grandma's badgering doesn't stop.

"Lord knows we raised you better . . ." On and on she drills, not caring what we've been through or understanding that we just can't do this. Not now.

And I don't mean to be rude or insolent when I interrupt, "Grandma?"

She turns to me, as if finally noticing I'm in the room. "What is it?" she says, annoyed.

"She's tired." I add, "We're tired."

It's only then that she looks at both of us, really takes us in and says, "I see. Why don't you both go on to bed."

We do, but neither of us sleeps. We wrestle with our own thoughts. Most likely, Mama's replaying every moment, maybe even questioning her leaving. Me? I'm questioning if I'll be able to go back to Farmington Oaks tomorrow and what Dad's face will look like after finding no vodka. I'm hoping Grandma doesn't rehash last week's conversation. I even wonder if Sophia and her family eat stuff like asparagus for dinner . . . what was it that Yvette wanted to ask me . . . Troy, he's such a good tutor . . . and dang . . . Mama got the car keys . . . and we were ghost . . . she pulled out the keys . . . and we . . . we . . .

Light streams through the curtains. Shoot, I don't even remember falling asleep. I roll over, expecting to feel Mama's back, but she's not there. I lie still, listening for her voice. Nothing. I get up and mosey to the kitchen, and Grandma's at the table with the phone in her hand.

"Where's my mom?" I ask, forcing back my agitation. It feels weird to be around Grandma after everything she told me last time I was here. "She didn't wake me up!" I glance at the clock; it's almost nine. "I don't have to go to school?"

"I don't suppose you can go walking in there this late without a parent, can you? And your mother, she must've left at the crack of dawn because I've been up since six." Grandma dials a number. "She's not answering her phone, either. What exactly happened last night?"

I offer Grandma a light version minus Dad's four day gambling binge, drinking, and teasing, no need to give her all the details.

"Hmph, that doesn't make sense. But at least she's making some decisions. I just wish she'd call me back."

Like always, Grandma assigns me chores: dusting and polishing. When I get to the picture frames of her old dead relatives, I barely touch her father and grandfather. The only one I dust well is her sister, Elizabeth. The rest of the day goes as if Mama didn't walk out on Dad for the first time: TV for Grandma, homework for me, and three calls from Dad intercepted by Grandma. I ain't trying to talk to him, I'm still too mad to hear his voice and too scared he'll ask about his liquor.

Mama comes back about six o'clock, and Grandma doesn't even hesitate before playing detective.

Grandma: Where have you been? I've been calling you every hour.

Mama: I needed to sort things out.

Grandma: You couldn't've done that here? You could've at least told me.

Mama: Sorry.

Grandma: Why'd you leave in the first place? The story Genesis told me doesn't make a lick of sense.

Mama:

Grandma: Tomorrow we're going to church, and I'm going to have the pastor pray over you. It'll do you some good.

Mama:

Was Grandma like this the whole time Mama was growing up? Geesh. She harasses Mama so much that Mama gets the keys and leaves the house again. Grandma calls out to ask where she's going this time, and Mama answers, "To breathe."

Friday morning Mama's gone again, so Grandma takes her nagging out on me. To get away from her grumblings, I go over my homework. Afterward, when she starts back complaining, I voluntarily busy myself with cleaning. Now I'm hiding out in the basement, pulling towels from the dryer. Mama must've finally come back, because as I'm hauling the laundry basket up the stairs, I hear Grandma saying, "Well, I'm not going to tell you I told you so because you already know that."

Should I run up the steps and stop Grandma's madness before Mama walks out for a third time — leaving me here?

Before I even decide, Grandma goes on. "No, I didn't mean that." She clears her throat and begins again. "What I'm trying to say is . . . when I see you hurt . . . I hurt."

"Ma," Mama says, trying to interrupt.

"Hear me out, Sharon." Grandma continues, "It's clear as to why you've been avoiding me." Then — whoa! — Grandma goes all the way to Jerusalem and back to admit that she's made some mistakes, and that maybe she shouldn't speak every thought on her mind because if *her* parents were so down on *her,* then she'd think twice about visiting too.

"What I'm trying to say is — you've got to do what's best for you and Genesis. I'll understand if you need to, you know, go back . . ." Grandma's voice breaks.

I'm sneaking up the steps, straining to hear the rest of Grandma's speech, but with this darn laundry basket in my hands, I trip and drop it.

"Genesis?" Grandma calls out. "You

fall down them stairs again?"

"No, ma'am," I say, then louder: "I'm all right." I crouch there, waiting to see if Mama'll come check on me. Instead, I hear her softly say, "Thanks, Ma."

Something's wrong with me. I should feel good about this, but I don't. It's not like I don't want to go back home, to our beautiful home. But what about the five years of trying to help Dad get better? Or the "Go to Alcoholics Anonymous or *otherwise*"? Dad hasn't done *anything* to deserve us coming back. Heck, he should have to do more than beg and make promises. He should — he should act like he *wants* us home. Is that even possible?

When I finish picking up the spilled laundry and step into the kitchen, Grandma's face is shiny and Mama's eyes aren't as tired looking. I try not to stare. But I'm sorta amazed. After all this time — the preaching and family traditions — Grandma has had a change of heart. Well, shoot, anything's possible, then. So maybe, just maybe, after these last few days, Dad's changed too.

■ ■ ■ ■

Boy, was I wrong.

When we get home Sunday evening, the first thing Dad says when Mama goes to put her bag back in their bedroom is not about his missing liquor, but, "Well, that didn't last long." And the second thing he says is, "Been practicing for your show, Chubby Cheeks?"

Wishing my eyes could shoot lasers, I glare at him, then storm to my bedroom. My shirt — my stupid, ugly shirt — is still on the floor. It's exactly where I left it, covered in streaks of makeup. It's there, taking me right back to Wednesday night. I snatch it up in both hands and pull, but it won't tear. I yank again and again, but nothing. I dig out my scissors. And slash. I slash it in two, and I slash it again, and then rip it apart with my hands. Slash and rip. Slash and rip till there's nothing left but shreds. For years I've had this shirt, and now I gather the scraps and dump them in the bathroom trash can. No more pretending. No more swinging my hair and flicking my wrists. And no more imagining me singing alongside *Dad.*

But just then, I catch my reflection in the mirror. And the voice — Dad's voice — has been waiting.

Naw, she ain't nothin' like me. . . .

"Shut up."

You were supposed to come out looking like her.

"Shut up, *please.*"

Who you think's gonna love you with the way you look . . .

He's right. He's right. He's right!

And I hate him for it.

And I hate that I've tried everything — and nothing works. What. Does. It. Take?!

There, in the corner, is the bleach.

The label warns dangerous. But the label also promises to whiten. Brighter than bright. Disinfects ugly, black mold, too. Turns everything sparkling white. I fill the tub with water so hot that steam rises. I uncap the bleach. The smell is strong, but I pour a tiny bit in the tub. Then a little bit more. And then I undress with a prayer: *Lord, let this water lighten me.*

Wait — what if it burns? I slowly, carefully stick my hand in and wave it through the water. I count to ten, and then twenty. No burn.

I step one foot into the hot water. And then the other.

Reason #75: Because she's tired of trying to be friends with the pretty light-skinned girls.

I hold the sides of the tub, and ease myself in.

Reason #63: Because she doesn't have straight hair.

I ease back and let the bleach soak into my pores.

Reason #84: Because she can't stop adding to this list.

I slink farther down to drown everything out, but not too deep — can't get my hair wet. And I try not to care, but I do. I try not to hurt, but I am. I try not to feel, but I can. And so I say, "Forget it," and squeeze my eyes tighter than tight before dunking my head under the water. When my lungs are about to explode, I burst out of the water. It had to be, what, seven, eight minutes of being in the tub. And I'm still black. The stupid bleach doesn't burn; it doesn't even offer a tingle of change. Not even where my scabs are. And now my hair needs re-straightening!

There's a knock on the door. Then quietly, "Gen?" I don't answer. "Genesis?" Mom says in her *answer-me* voice.

"Yes?"

"You okay?"

"Yeah."

"Okay," Mama says.

I wrap myself in a towel, and wrap another around my head. It's as if Mama gives me time to dress because as soon as I get my pajamas on she's cracking open my door. "Hey." She comes and sits on the edge of my bed, looks up at Billie Holiday.

"You added a picture? To your wall?" Mama asks. "It looks nice up there." She pauses, as if she isn't sure what to say. "I still have to check for that movie. Keep forgetting . . ." is what comes next. Almost a minute goes by before she comes out and asks, "Do you want to talk?"

I glance toward the door. "Where is he?"

"Your dad? He's . . . he's in our bedroom. You don't have to worry about him." Mama rubs my back and asks once more, "Anything else you wanna talk about . . . like the night we left?"

Eventually I'll have to explain why my face was covered in her makeup. "No," I say, but then quickly change my mind. "Yeah. Why we come back this soon?"

"Because —" Mama pauses, and I wonder if *she* even knows why. Then she says, "Honestly, I'm just not there yet, to completely walk away." Huh. Seems to me Mama was mighty close to her breaking point last Wednesday when she was beating up the steering wheel.

Even so, her answer is one that I can accept. Because truthfully, I'm not ready for us to move away from Dad either. Not that I'm not done with his drama, because I am. But we can't go because — and it's killing me to admit this — but if we leave for good, then I'll never truly be *his* baby girl . . . he'll always see me as . . . *nothin' but Chubby Cheeks* from the basement! And I ain't no Chubby

Cheeks, get what I'm sayin'?

"You think those meetings really gon' help?" They haven't done a thing yet. Then I catch myself because heck, even Grandma's coming around.

Mama twirls her hair, thinking. "Your father, his pain is deep rooted from when he was a kid. I'm not saying this to —" Mama gazes off now, her eyes troubled. "I just don't understand why he gets so mean toward you."

That's easy. "Because he hates me."

Mom looks shocked. "He doesn't hate you!"

"Yes he does, and you know it. You were right there in that basement when he said I was nothin' like him. You hear him talk, *all the time* about how I don't look like you. Even Grandma notices. Shoot, I don't blame him."

Mama's lower lip is trembling. I don't want her tears, 'cause she already knows the truth. But then she surprises me. She collects herself and says, "When you were born, you were this tiny, light-brown ball of joy. And your dad . . . he was so proud . . . except when my mama said

261

things like, 'See how dark her ear tips are and those cuticles, that's how dark she's going to be.' " Mama half smiles, remembering. "That made me happy because I didn't mind having a chocolate baby. I didn't want you to be picked on for being light like I was."

"Wait, *you* got teased?"

"All the time. People called me 'stuck-up' and 'Lite-Brite,' and a whole bunch of other names. I've never told your grandmother, but I was in a couple of fights. 'Course, she loved when people told her I looked white. I hated it 'cause at school it was, 'Oh, you think you're cute,' and 'You think you're better than everybody, I'mma beat you up.' I got all that."

Dang, that's what I — oh no! — thought about Nia.

"And my hair was even longer than it is now. My mother never let me cut it — she was proud of it. But it wasn't *her* head being yanked all the time. I got so many threats from other girls. One time I got so tired of the threats that I chopped it off. To my ears! I got a good beating for that." Mama dabs at her eyes, but now I can't tell if it's because she's laughing or crying. "Every day she reminded me that I was better than most Blacks. Not because I was smart or kindhearted, but because I was light-skinned. *Light-skinned.* Can you believe it? She'd say, 'Sharon, you could marry —' "

"Mama, that's it. Don't you get it?" I say, it's all clicking together now. "I'm not light like you — that's why he hates me."

"What? No," Mama says, fast.

"Yeah, it is. And it's all because of Grandma and that stupid brown bag."

"Brown bag?"

"Grandma . . . she told me about the brown bag and how she pulled it out with Dad," I say, fiddling with my fingers.

"Did she." Mama waves her hand as if waving the bad thoughts away. "It's not the bag, baby. Your daddy, he loves you. It just seems the older you got, the angrier he grew. When you were about eight or nine, it's like a light dimmed in him. He used to tell me how his own mother treated him, calling him 'no good' and 'trifling' and 'black this and that.' So I thought he'd be the opposite, knowing the hurt that meanness causes. . . ." She trails off, thinking.

Maybe that's why Dad doesn't talk about his mama. *No good. Triflin'. Black this and that.* His own mama didn't even think he was one of the good ones? "So why did his mom dog him out?"

"Don't know for sure. But my guess is that because *his* father abandoned them, all the anger and bitterness she held for him, well, she took it out on your father. And I know it seems like I'm always making excuses for him, but . . . he's had a bad childhood. And maybe I feel guilty, especially for allowing stuff like the brown bag to happen. I didn't even realize I was stuck in the habit of defending him, or rather defending the man I chose to marry. I felt like, if I didn't defend him, then my mother would be convinced she was right in the first place, see?" Mama stands up and stretches. "And still, still I keep waiting for him to come back around to being your proud daddy."

"Yeah," I say, "me too." Then I can't help but ask, "Do *you* believe it? The family tradition?" I want to ask if she regrets marrying Dad, but hold back.

"The brown bag is . . . such an old way of thinking. A *wrong* way of thinking. I know it's history, and I really am ashamed it's our history, but you can't believe in that. You just can't."

Yet, and yet, Mama's always complaining about doing my hair, calling it "that head" or "tangly mess." She believes it at least a little. It peeks out when she describes someone dark complexioned and adds: "But he or she's still good looking." Mama may not mean it; in fact, I know she doesn't, but it's there, under the surface. That's why tonight, now, I let her make me pretty the best way she knows how, by washing my hair. She doesn't even ask why my hair's wet in the first place. She blow-dries it even though that's my job, and we don't have a meltdown. Mama presses my tangled hair without a word about how thick it is. Even though she's drained, she still straightens it. And me? I'm too grateful to care that a thousand-degree hot comb is millimeters away from my scalp.

That night, when my head falls on the

pillow — smelling of BB SuperGro — I have a fitful dream of Dad in a clown's mask, cutting off my long, straight hair. But then there's something else. A familiar smell. A favorite smell. The smell of Dad's famous shrimp. A real smell. It wakes me up. Yet I don't move. It beckons me to come, but I don't budge. Dad is tempting me with a plateful of apologies. I know this for sure because I hold my breath, lie very still, and I can just hear it . . . the groan of the hardwood under his feet. He stands outside my door.

I roll over and pretend to be asleep.

NINETEEN

When chorus is over on Monday, I help Mrs. Hill by neatly stacking all the sheet music. She is giving Nia advice. "Go ahead and be daring. That's who you are, and you have to be true to yourself, right?"

I want to join them, but I'm not one to stick my nose into someone else's business uninvited. Still, I can't help but ease my way over and nod at the right times, as if I'd been included in the conversation from the get-go.

Nia says, "I'm trying to figure out if I'm dooming myself with an original piece." Then, to my surprise, she turns to me. "What do you think?"

"Me? Well, sure . . ." I hesitate.

"So you agree with Mrs. Hill, then?" For the life of me, I can't recall what

Mrs. Hill just said. "You wouldn't tune out an original song, especially when everyone else is doing top tens?" Nia presses.

"No, I'd listen." They both look at me so intently that my brain freezes, until Mrs. Hill nods for me to continue. "Like, your essay was amazing. No one else wrote so deeply about a book, or read theirs the way you did. If your music's the same way, then you'll win. For sure."

Nia studies me, lifts her chin in acknowledgment. "Thanks."

Mrs. Hill agrees. "I keep encouraging Nia to stop playing it safe. Don't sell herself short." She turns to Nia. "You're so gifted," she says. "And you, Genesis, have a voice alive with raw emotion. I encourage you, too, not to disappear behind your fears. You girls don't know what you have. If I was your age" — Mrs. Hill snaps her fingers — "I'd strut on that stage and turn that place out."

"Okay, I hear you, Mrs. Hill. I needed that." Nia grabs her binder and waves good-bye.

"Did you need something, Miss Genesis?"

"Yes, I wanted to give you back your CD." I don't tell her that I can't listen to it anymore, that Ella's voice is now forever drowned out by Dad's mocking claps.

Mrs. Hill takes the CD. "How did you like Ms. Fitzgerald?"

"She has a great voice, but half the time she, like, doesn't even use words."

Mrs. Hill laughs. "That, my child, is called scatting. Like we did in class the other week. It sounds like nonsense words, but it's a technique that some singers — good singers — do to make their voices sound like instruments. Here, let me show you." Mrs. Hill guides me to her piano.

"You sing, Mrs. Hill?"

She raises one eyebrow saucily. "I've done some singing in my day. Do you have time for a few scatting exercises?" I tell her yes, so she sits, plunks at various keys, and has me mimic the sound. "Good, but a little less staccato. And one more thing, good singers have good posture. When you collapse your sternum, you can't get breath from your diaphragm."

Grandma's words snaps at me, *Pull your shoulders up, stop hunching.* Yet, Mrs. Hill's calm pushes me past this moment. "Stand with your feet shoulder width apart. Good. We artists feel everything. We're very vulnerable beings, and sometimes we collapse our bodies without even knowing. It makes us feel safe. We have to fight that. Now, repeat after me." Mrs. Hill starts be-bop-de-bop-ing. I echo her. Let me tell you, it ain't easy, but scatting is kinda fun!

"Now, going back to Ms. Ella Fitzgerald. Scatting is usually improvised. It takes confidence — there's no room for doubting yourself. So maybe give her another listen." She closes the piano. "And like I told you before, *you* have a gift. You should really consider auditioning."

"I'll think about it," I tell her. And then I ask, "Do you take this much time with everybody?"

"Come on out, class, she's on to me," Mrs. Hill calls out behind her. After a moment she shrugs and says, "I guess just you," and quickly adds, "and, maybe a few others."

Why me? I ask, but only in my head. So — she really thinks I'm good enough for the talent show?

People always talk about believing wholeheartedly. I've believed a lot of things in my life, even prayed hard about them too. But hardly any of those wishes ever came true. So, what if I make it into the talent show and believe with all my heart that I'll win, and say somebody else believes with all their heart that they'll win too. Which one of us will take home the prize?

Tuesday's lunch is chicken fingers. Not chicken nuggets — chicken fingers. And they're good. But I have to scarf them down because today Mr. Benjamin announced a math test on Friday, and Troy has to help me work a miracle. Yvette and Belinda are a few tables over, sitting with some other girls. I try not to stare; it'll make me seem too thirsty. But I'm imagining me on the other side of Belinda, leisurely sipping my juice as we joke and laugh. As soon as I've finished eating, I stack my tray and hustle to the library.

Up the hall a bit is Troy, with two other

guys. Because of all our moving, I've learned to pick up on body language. The taller guy tags Troy in the chest. I step up my pace, but by the time I reach them the guys take off.

"Hey," I say. "What's up?"

"Nothing," Troy says, but he sounds annoyed.

"Friends?" I say, nodding in the direction the guys went.

"No, I wouldn't call them that." Troy opens the door to the library. "You ready? Got a lot to cover for the test."

"Yeah, that thing," I say, bumming because one, Friday's test, and two, Troy technically didn't answer my question. He's hiding something, for sure, but I don't press him.

We find an empty table, and Troy pulls his textbook and some paper from his bag. He turns to the work pages at the end of the chapter and has me solve them on my own while he watches. Which, let me tell you, is nerve-racking. Every time I finish a problem, I glance over to see if it's right, but his game face is tighter than Mama's. When I'm done, he circles the ones that I got wrong and goes over my mistakes.

"I'm gonna bomb it. I just know it," I say, frustrated, now totally getting Sophia's major freak-out about her test.

"You're not going to bomb it," Troy assures me. "This is about C work already. Study for the next few days and by Friday you'll kill the test, trust me." He's packing up his books, and looks, I don't know, uneasy? I bet it's because of those guys from the hall, and I just have to ask again.

"So," I start, "those guys I saw you with. What's up with them?"

Troy flashes me a look. "What do you mean?"

"They didn't look legit, you know." I want to be there for him, but don't want to pry too much. So I throw my hands up in an *I'mma-back-off* sort of way. "I'll leave it alone if you want."

"Naw, it's fine. They just want some notes," Troy says, waving away any concerns I might have. Or so he thinks, because I know and he knows darn well that those dudes wanted more than notes. I know their type; they want to pass without doing the work. But if Troy's not ready to talk about it — like I'd been about "falling down the stairs" — then I'm straight with just knowing he's okay.

After school, Sophia and I hang out on the bleachers to catch a few minutes of softball practice. I tell her that I can't stay too long because even though nothing much happens out here in suburbia, Mama'll have a fit if she beats me home and doesn't know where I am. And when she starts to balk, I remind her that I can't be making my mama mad since she's letting me come over Saturday.

"Being a pitcher is hard, a lot of pressure," Sophia mutters. Her eyes are now on the pitcher who just took her place on the mound. "Being at bat, that's tough too."

"You play?" What all is Sophia into besides reading, I suddenly wonder.

"Not anymore," she says, nodding hard as the pitcher fires a perfect pitch. Before I can pose another question, she's telling me that she played as a kid, but things got too hectic. "So my mother said we should scale back on some of my extra-curriculars."

"I never have any extras," I start to say, but then I remember Mrs. Hill. "But you know what? My chorus teacher thinks I should audition for the show."

Sophia turns to me. "Seriously? Are you going to do it?" She breaks into a genuinely happy smile.

"I'm not sure." I debate delving into it, but talking about it might help me figure out if I do want to do it, or not. "Here's the thing, Sophe, I'm not really down for putting myself out there like that. I just feel like, I don't know, I'll get ripped apart or something."

She nods. "Yeah, like when I played softball. If the team lost, there was someone always wanting to point a finger. I wish those fingers didn't bother me," she says, squinting back out at the field.

"Yeah, those stinkin' pointer fingers," I say, wondering how it was that some people were not able to care about them. And why weren't we two of them?

■ ■ ■ ■

The rest of the week, Dad's been coming home every night. Mama's leaving must've scared him straight because he ain't even been drunk. Good thing, too, because I'm already pulling at my hair, worrying about math. On Wednesday, Sophia tries to prep me for Saturday's dinner at her house, but my mind is on solving equations without solutions. Thursday, I miss our library time because Troy took pity on me and gave me an extra tutoring session. And Friday — well, it's lucky that I have any hair left.

My number two pencil is between my fingers, ready. I glance over at Troy, and he mouths, *You got this.* I cross my fingers, wishing us both good luck. Once Mr. Benjamin gives us permission to begin, I'm off. Pretty soon I'm whizzing through the test, determining x, y, z, simplifying fractions, and wondering why I was even nervous in the first place. And then there's this question: *Find the missing number so the equation has no solution.* Whaaa? Isn't the point to have a solution? This has got to be a trick question. Skip. I'm back rocking and rolling, and solving equations using diagrams. And wouldn't you know it, Mr. B. sneaks in a word problem. Yes, a word problem!

One of your friends is heading north for a holiday and the other friend is heading south. If their destinations are 1,029 miles apart and one car is traveling at forty-five miles per hour and the other car is traveling at fifty-three miles per hour, how many hours before the two cars pass each other?

This makes no sense at all. Like seriously, if Sophia leaves heading north for, say, Christmas, she ain't gonna make it. Hello — have you seen our winters? And let's say Troy's going south? How would I know if he's going forty-five miles per hour or fifty-three? And they're both going for a holiday vacation? Score! So, Sophia's traveling north, Troy south — wait just a minute, if she's going north and he's going south, how in the heck are they supposed to cross paths?

Mr. Benjamin calls time. I wait until after everyone turns in their tests before approaching him. Mr. B. asks how I think I did and I answer, "Fine."

"If you have a few minutes, can you

grade it?" I ask, adding a sweet "please." Mr. B. checks his watch and informs me that he has only a few minutes to spare. I stand at my desk as he pulls out an ink pen and furiously begins marking and scribbling. *That's a lot of scribbles.* I might as well pack up and go to the lower class. Finally, Mr. B. waves me up front, and I swear his face is as dark as the Grim Reaper's.

Mr. B. hands me my paper. I knew it. Just knew it. A doggone 76 percent. Wait. Seventy-six? I passed. I passed! I really passed!

"Thank you!" I say, holding up my test. "Thank you," I say, kissing it. "Thank you," I just about scream, as I fly out of the room.

"Genesis?" Troy's propped up against the lockers, waiting. "Is everything okay?"

"I PASSED!" And he hugs me. Me and my big green 76 percent.

TWENTY

On Saturday, Mama escorts me over to Sophia's. On her street, the houses are even bigger than on mine. One thing about these Farmington Hills folks, they sure do like to keep their curtains open. You can see all through their houses. It's like they're not even afraid of thieves scoping out places to rob.

I hook my arm around Mama's, both of us still feeling real proud about my math test *and* . . . drum roll please . . . that she ordered a college catalog. We pass fresh cut lawns and neatly trimmed bushes, and she points to different flowers that are blooming. "And those are ferns, but I want to plant some of those blue ones, periwinkles. Aren't they pretty?" Out here folks hire landscapers. They're always in some yard cutting and mulching. By some miracle, if we were to actually stay here, Mama'll need a whole lot of planting time just to keep up.

Mama reads the numbers on the mailboxes. "What's the address again?"

"93488."

"The even side is over there. So, eighty-four, six . . . this must be her house here."

"Whoa!" It's big, real big. There're four tall white columns lined across the front porch. Potted trees that twist up like the tops of soft ice-cream cones sit on each side of the front double door.

"Do I look okay?" I say, stepping in front of her.

"Yes, you look great. Wait, is Sophia a boy?" she teases.

I elbow her, grinning, as we climb the steps and ring the bell. The doors are glass, with intricate flower designs etched in them.

"You call me if you want to leave before nine." Mama squeezes my arm, as if she's sending me off to my first day of kindergarten.

The door opens. A woman with dark

hair and glasses greets us. "Well, hello!" She has the exact same brown eyes as Sophia, so it must be her mother. "Come in, come in. Sophia!"

We step into the foyer, onto a red rug with black swirls and gold leaves. A pot that holds umbrellas sits in the corner and a big WELCOME TO OUR HOME sign hangs on the wall. "Sophia's told us all about you. You must be Mrs. Anderson. I'm Elissa." Mama tells Mrs. Papageorgiou to call her Sharon, which she does. Mrs. Papageorgiou leads us through a second set of doors and into a huge living room. Shimmery gold curtains are suspended from the ceiling all the way down to the ground. The couches and chairs are white, their legs etched with ornate antique-ish designs. They even have long mirrors framed like pictures and medium-size chandeliers — six to be exact.

Fancy.

Mama must be in shock too, because all she manages to do is smile.

"Sophia!" Mrs. Papageorgiou calls out again. "I hope you brought your appetite, Genesis." It's then that I smell spices. I can't put my finger on which. All I know is that it smells good.

Sophia comes running into the room and thumps my shoulder. "Hey, you!"

Mrs. Papageorgiou introduces Sophia to Mama, offering, "Would you like to join us for dinner? There's plenty."

Mama's telling her, "No, thank you," and Mrs. Papageorgiou informs Mama that she, herself, will personally bring me safely back home. Sophia takes my arm, and I give Mama one last wave before I'm whisked away.

"This is going to be so much fun," Sophia exclaims.

She guides me through rooms, introducing me to her father, three of her brothers, three younger cousins, and two uncles. Everyone talks so fast that I can hardly understand them. The kitchen is a frenzy of food preparation: pots clang, steam rises, and spoons stir. Several women, who Sophia points out as her aunts and grandmother, chop, stir, and taste, fingers full of food while laughing and talking.

"Hey, everybody," Sophia announces.

"This is my friend Genesis." There's a chorus of waves, nods, and hi's.

"Who?" Her grandmother leans forward in her chair where she's rolling meat into little balls. "What did she say?"

"I said," Sophia repeats, louder, "this is my friend Genesis."

"Genesis? Like in the Bible?"

"Yes, Mom, that's what she said," says Mrs. Papageorgiou, who's joined us. Then she addresses me, saying, "You might be thinking this is a lot of food, but in our family, we show our love by feeding you."

"It's true," Sophia says. "She'll keep offering, but at one point you'll have to say 'I know you love me, but no' or you'll bust. She doesn't realize her love leads to high cholesterol."

"Sophia!" says Mrs. Papageorgiou, play-smacking her.

Sophia grabs my elbow and leads me around the gleaming marble island. It would blow Dad's mind compared to ours. Sophia says, "We call our aunts 'Thea.' Just call my grandmother 'Yiayia,' that'll be fine." Then Sophia stops in front of the kitchen cabinets, which aren't really cabinets at all but a wall with glass doors, the dishes displayed like pieces of art. "Here, take these." She hands me several plates, not just regular plates, but breakable ones with elegant designs, the kind that Grandma keeps in her china cabinet and never uses. Then she pulls out glasses and I follow her to the dining room. She sets the glasses down on a long, polished wooden table. Next, I put down the plates.

"No, that's not how it goes," Sophia says, correcting me. "The plates have to be exactly in the center, just like this, and glasses to the right. You have to measure it with your hand." Sophia determines the distance, slides the glass a millimeter, and studies it again.

"Sorry. I didn't realize it was that serious. We don't follow any particular dining rules at my house." I feel kind of embarrassed.

"No worries, it just has to be a certain way." Sophia goes and gets a box of silverware. Silverware in a box? Each piece has its own little holder. Yikes! Sophia notices my look. "Yeah, my yiayia's nutty about the silverware — it's from Greece and hand-forged. So they have to be handled gently and placed perfectly." She now starts removing the utensils piece by piece, laying them down just so, then readjusting them, too.

Mrs. Papageorgiou breezes in with a tray of food. "Sophia, it doesn't matter, remember?"

"But —" Sophia starts, but then the theas swoop in, each also bearing a tray, and proceed to load so much food onto the table that it looks like Thanksgiving. The holidays at my house *never* have this much food, or people. Sophia and I go back and forth for more plates and glasses. The theas rotate in and out with serving tools and more trays, and pretty soon the aromas summon all the relatives into the dining room. The food smells so good that I worry I might actually drool.

Sophia slides out a chair. "Sit near me. I always sit near my baba — my dad." Mr. Papageorgiou parades in with the uncles, goes straight to Sophia, and kisses her forehead. He has a mustache like Dad, but he looks friendly, like a TV dad.

I can't remember the last time Dad kissed me on my forehead.

We all squeeze into chairs at the dining room table, and once everyone's settled, Sophia's baba prays — in Greek. Then Yiayia says another grace — in Greek. As heads are bowed, I notice all the whiteness surrounding me. A month ago, I'd never even been around white people, except in passing at the mall. I sit on my hands, suddenly afraid to reach for the same spoon as someone else in case they notice the difference too. Yiayia finishes the prayer, and they all draw an invisible cross from their head to their chests and across. Amen.

"Genesis, try the souvlaki, which is chicken on a stick," suggests Mr. Papageorgiou. "My wife makes the best." Mrs. Papageorgiou's cheeks flush happily as she tells me that that's why he married her.

Sophia points out all the dishes — I only recognize olives and feta cheese. "These green things are grape leaves stuffed with beef and rice, dolmades," she explains. "There's lamb, too. Here, try some." She holds the serving fork out to me, but I hesitate. *I wish the bleach bath lightened me.* "C'mon, try some — it's good."

Slowly I take the fork, waiting for all eyes to turn my way. They don't. Everybody's busy filling their own plates. So I relax and take some lamb and then go for it like everyone else, making sure to take some of Mrs. Papageorgiou's souvlaki. Sophia piles up her plate too. Except she's extremely careful about making sure the food doesn't touch. When an olive rolls toward a meatball, she quickly flicks it back over to the other olives. And guess what? Mr. Papageorgiou has set up his plate the same way, nothing touching.

Conversations erupt across the table. "Then she goes in the market and says . . ." "Ha! Is that so?" "It is so! When we were growing up in the village, things were very different!" They talk in both English and Greek. They wave their forks, slap the table, and fill their plates with more food. Then Sophia asks her yiayia to tell me the story about the goats chasing her every time she went to milk them, which she does, and everyone starts interjecting their two cents, slowing down the story for me to hear the best parts.

We laugh and eat. And Mr. Papageorgiou was right, the souvlaki is delicious. Even the spinach wrapped in a flaky pastry called spa . . . spa . . . I whisper to Sophia and ask for the name again of these tasty things. "Spanakopita," she says. Like everyone else, I go for seconds, while Sophia's still on the first round, eating one thing at a time. Really, really slowly.

When dinner's over, Sophia shows me her bedroom. "I get my own room because I'm the only girl," she says, swinging her door open.

"Wow, everything's so —"

"So what?" Sophia asks quickly.

"Neat. Mine's a disaster!" Butterflies dangle from the ceiling. There's a shelf full of stuffed animals, probably kept from since she was a kid. Everything's perfectly placed. "How long have you lived here? Your whole life?"

"Yeah," Sophia says, as if that's a stupid question.

Her younger cousins, two little boys

and a girl, run in. "Hey, get out of here!" Sophia shouts. "Don't touch my things." They jump on her, wrestle with her, and twist her hair. They eye me curiously as well, probably wondering if it's safe to jump on me, too.

"Okay, out now." As he leaves, one of the boys deliberately shoves the notebooks on her desk so the perfectly aligned pile slides to one side. "Hey, I told you about touching my stuff!" Sophia yells.

"Fat head!" the boy yells back, and they all run out of the room.

"Finally." Sophia locks her door. Then she centers her rug and brushes out the wrinkles on her bed.

"Now I see why you go to the library," I say with a laugh. "Wish I had a lock on my door too."

"Privacy's the best." Sophia restacks her notebooks.

"Yep, the best," I agree. "You've got a cool room. What're all these trophies? I didn't know you did anything besides read and, well, play softball." I go to her shelf for a closer look.

"You think I only sit on my butt with a

book in my hand?" Sophia laughs. "My mom used to enroll me in everything. Classical piano, fencing, tap, gymnastics, you name it. There's a lot of pressure being the only girl."

I take it all in. Must be real nice to take classes like fencing and gymnastics. All I ever got to do was play kickball, checkers, and make art at some youth program. Must be cool to win a trophy with your name on it. "But, hey, you get your own room."

"Yeah, how about that trade-off?" She laughs again. "It's probably not a big deal to you because you've never had to share — you being an only child."

There's no way I'm admitting to sharing rooms with my mama, and sometimes with *both* Mama and Dad. So I shift the conversation. "Hey, I just thought of something — you can audition for the talent show too! You can play the piano while Troy plays his violin."

"No way. That's not my thing, either."

I pick up a picture that's sitting on her nightstand. Sophia's with her dad at a carnival. She holds a bag of cotton candy, and he's squeezing her like he's trying to get all her juice out. They both have gigantic smiles.

"Uhm, so — it makes me nervous when people touch my stuff." Sophia says it nicely, but she also takes the photo and places it back neatly.

Okay. A little weird. But I say sorry. "I wasn't going to break it."

"Sophia?" Mrs. Papageorgiou calls through the door. Sophia goes and unlocks it, and Mrs. P. pokes her head in. "You girls need anything?"

"No, Mom."

"Is it all right if I take a quick snap of you two?" Mrs. P. asks next, and Sophia opens the door fully, then we stand next to each other posing and cheesing. "Got it . . . cute," Mrs. P. says, showing us the picture on her phone.

"Okay, Mom. Byyyyyyye . . . ," Sophia says, going back to her door. Then Mrs. P. starts whispering in Greek. Sophia whispers back. And back and forth they whisper till Sophia says, "You're making me anxious." All the whispering makes me nervous too. Are they talking about me? After her mom leaves, Sophia locks the door again. Her hands are shaking.

"What was that about?" I ask.

"Nothing." Then she says, a little more at ease, "You know how mothers are . . . always checking in. Wanna watch TV?"

"Sure." We settle into the big, comfy floor pillows — ooh, I wish I had these in my room. Sophia turns on the TV, searches through the channels slowly. I mean s-l-o-w-l-y. Even Grandma's faster than her. She goes through all the stations, starting at channel three. *Click, click, click,* goes back to the last channel, *click.* Finally I say, "How 'bout Nickelodeon? It doesn't matter."

Usually Sophia's sharp and quick witted, but I don't recognize her today. Am *I* making her uncomfortable? 'Cause now I'm getting uncomfortable. I can't figure it out — we're totally chill at school. And all this awkwardness builds up until my mouth can't do anything but shoot out, "I never had any friends before." Sophia's eyes are on me and I continue. "We've moved a lot, like, a real lot. And I've . . . I've never been invited over anybody's house, either. So what I'm trying to say is that I was kind of scared when you asked me, 'cause I didn't know what your family would think of me."

Sophia looks at me like I have two heads. "What? I told you my family would love you."

"Yeah, but I was still worried. So then I thought, 'Sophia's my friend, might even be my best friend, so it doesn't matter.' "

Sophia throws a pillow at me.

"Best friend, huh?" she says.

"That's if you want."

"That's if *you* want."

"Yeah, sure," I say. "So, if we're going to be best friends, we should make it official."

Sophia sits straight up. "I'm not smashing your spit in my hand, if that's what you mean."

"Eww, gross." I sit up too. "That only happens in old movies."

"Well, I'm not cutting myself to be blood sisters, either."

"Eww, grosser. That only happens in *old* old movies," I say. "How 'bout we just tell each other a secret or something?"

"Secrets?" Sophia frowns. "I don't know."

"Then you come up with an idea."

After a few seconds Sophia says, "I've got nothing. Okay. Secrets. You go first."

"Me?"

"It was *your* idea."

All of a sudden I wish I'd kept my big ol' mouth closed. My secrets — she can't know my secrets. "Hmm. Sure you don't wanna do the spitting thing?"

"Here, I'll go first." Sophia glances at the door. "I go to the library during lunch because I hate for people to watch me eat."

"That's it? That's not bad."

"That's not all. Kids used to make fun of me."

"Just because you don't like your food to touch?"

"Not just that. Genesis, I've seen you watching me in the library, so please don't pretend like you haven't noticed . . . ," Sophia says, sounding nervous.

"What? That you like to read your pages twice? Maybe it's a good book."

"Are you being funny?"

"No," I say, "honest."

She glances at the door again, then says, "Okay. So. Here's the story. I have obsessive-compulsive disorder, OCD. You saw me in action that day in the bathroom. And I don't have friends because I got tired of their teasing, especially behind my back. Weirdo, Freak, you name it, they called me it. I hate being like this. So there you have it."

Sophia watches me like she's waiting for me to unlock her door and run for the hills. But, why *would* I? I just take my turn. The words rush out of my mouth in a wild, twisted tumble that I can't even believe is coming from *me.* "I've never had friends because I'm too ugly, and I hate that I'm so black and my hair's not straight and kids tease me all the time too, and I've been called Gorilla, Eggplant, Aunt Jemima, and a whole bunch of other stuff. And I sing in the mirror with a shirt over my head, pretending to be light-skinned with good hair and —" I catch myself, stunned. Stunned at what I just revealed.

"What's 'good hair'?" Sophia asks, as if

that were the only secret she heard.

I do my best to explain this to someone like her — especially without using the word *nappy* — a word that makes me flinch. Sophia nods like she gets it and then asks innocently, "Can I touch it — your hair?"

"No!" I cry, automatically ducking my head, even though she's not near enough to reach it. Everybody I know knows better than to put their hands in somebody else's head — shoot, we learned that as kids. No way am I going to sit here and let Sophia feel how kinky my kitchen is. "Why you even ask that?" I say.

Sophia's entire face turns pink. "I've never touched . . . hair like yours before."

Hair like mine? *Oh, I get it.*

Sophia looks hopeful, as if I'll change my mind, so I quickly say, "I'd rather not."

OCD. I don't really know anything about it, have only really heard that term when kids get all clean obsessed about their lockers, sneakers, rooms, and stuff. Every now and then someone'll say something like, *My locker partner is so messy, she's making me OCD,* or *Some-one stepped on his sneakers, now he's act-ing totally OCD.* But it's a real thing, I know. And Sophia has it — and yes, I do watch her sometimes — and it's like she can't control herself. It now clicks . . . the basketball inspecting, shoe tying, page flipping, lens wiping, hand washing — and no paper towels. That's intense.

The voices from the television fill a long silence.

Finally I say, "And for the record, I would never call you weird."

"Good." Silence again. Then Sophia says, "And for the record, I'd never think of you as ugly."

Well, glad that's settled.

We sit back in our big floor pillows, content. A thought comes to me. Maybe I am good enough to audition on Mon-day. If I can hang out at Sophia's and not one person looks at me funny, then maybe I can get onstage and not worry about some stupid name calling — aside from Terrance. I can get a song together by tomorrow night, but dang, it's . . . it's too late to sign up.

■ ■ ■

It only takes two minutes after Mrs. Papageorgiou drops me off for my good vibes to turn sour. Mama cautions me that Dad's upset about some missing liquor, accused her of pouring it out — which she wished she had — but not to worry because he probably doesn't recall drinking it, and now that he's in AA he shouldn't have it anyway. The bottles. Dang, I forgot about them. Maybe I should go out back, get them from underneath the deck, and show her what I'd done. Or at least *tell* her.

And I try to, I really do, but my mouth goes pasty, as if it's sealed with glue. Because beyond *that,* that I did it, she needs to understand *why* I did it.

"Ma?"

"Yes, honey?"

I part my lips to say more, but the truth gets stuck in my throat.

TWENTY-ONE

"Don't make us late," Sophia says, speed walking ahead of me. "We promised him we'd be there." She opens the door of the auditorium, opens the door to chaos. Students are practicing dance moves in the aisles, massive instruments take up two seats at a time, groups of kids harmonize on and off pitch all over the place. "He said he'll be down front — come on."

Troy waves from a seat up by the stage. We weave through the tangles of nervous bodies and overconfident posers. "Thanks for coming," he says, tightening the strings on his violin.

He looks really impressive with the violin in his hands. I take the seat closer to him.

Mrs. Hill stands at the microphone.

"Good afternoon." Hardly anyone notices. "Good afternoon, ladies and gentlemen," she says again, louder this time. The clatter and clangs cease. "Thank you for your attention. Welcome to the auditions for our annual talent showcase. We'll begin in the order of the sign-up sheet. Thank you and good luck." Cheers echo through the auditorium. Mrs. Hill steps back to the microphone. "One more thing . . . two rules: One, no booing. Two, you boo, you're out. Only clap to show our talent your support."

"You're not nervous, are you?" Sophia asks Troy.

"A little," Troy admits.

"You've made it every year. At least you know you'll get in," Sophia says earnestly.

"Gee, thanks for the pep talk."

I chime in, "Don't listen to her. When you're onstage, just imagine yourself in a different galaxy and get into your zone."

Troy nudges me with his knee. "Thanks . . . that's much better than Sophia's words of inspiration," he jokes.

Across the auditorium, I spy Jason. He's with Terrance, and the way he keeps balling and unballing his fist tells me that he's nervous too.

In the first twenty minutes, we see an a cappella ensemble, two hip-hop and one modern dance group, an all-girl singing group, a Justin Bieber look-alike, and an Eminem wannabe who wouldn't last a minute on 8 Mile. The auditions start to drag when a soloist sings in French and a magician does super corny tricks.

Then Yvette struts onstage with Belinda and another girl. They stand in a V formation with Yvette front and center. She doesn't wait for Mrs. Hill to tell them to begin, just counts off "Five-six-seven-eight!" The music starts and, in unison, they all begin to sway. Troy nudges me a second time and says something, but I can't tear my eyes away. They're moving in a sexy, graceful way that I can only fantasize doing when I'm alone in my room. The crowd cheers for them just like they do for me in my imaginary world. It's like . . . it's like they are me, or rather, I'm them . . . my eyes go wide. Was that . . . was that — singing — that they'd wanted to talk to me about?

"Genesis." Nudge number three.

"Huh?"

"What do you think?" Troy asks.

I glance at him, then turn back to Yvette's group, saying, "They're amazing. Real amazing."

"Yeah, they won second place last year; *they* thought they should've won first."

"Yep," Sophia agrees. "And they were real mad about it too."

Troy adds, "They've got a real good chance of winning it this time," as the three sashay off the stage. Aww, song's over.

"Number twelve?" announces Mrs. Hill. "Number twelve? Going once . . . twice . . ."

Jason jumps up. "That's us!" He runs onstage, Terrance right behind him. When the music blasts on, they march back and forth, back and forth, and finally start rapping. They grip the microphones so close to their mouths that I can hardly make out what they're saying. Apparently, everybody else understands perfectly because some of the kids shout "Whoa!" "Hit 'em hard!" "That's blazin'!" When they come off the stage, other guys give them fist bumps, as if they've already won. Personally, Jason and Terrance did too much jumping around, and the lyrics I could make out were, well, weak. *My rhymes are tighter than Saran Wrap.* Really?

Next, Nia Kincaid walks — no, strides — onstage holding an acoustic guitar by its neck. She adjusts the microphone's height, then clears her throat. "I'd like to perform a cover of 'Here' by Alessia Cara," she tells us, so calm. Hey, I thought she was gonna sing an original song. And hey, how's she so chill? She nestles the guitar under one arm and begins to strum. Her voice is neo-soul-jazzy smooth. We're all tuned in — especially Jason, who's leaning forward with his mouth hanging open — probably thinking the same thing: That girl is *bad* — good bad. I know it's true, 'cause even Sophia says, "She's great."

"Yeah," I agree. If you ask me, she's almost as good as Yvette and them.

Troy is nodding too. "Yeah, she's got it. Well, I'm next. Wish me luck."

Troy's already onstage when Mrs. Hill

announces his number. He tucks his violin under his chin, with the bow in place. "Go, Troy!" Sophia screams, which must embarrass him because he gives a false start and some kids laugh. I want to cover my eyes and not witness the reason he never wins. Kids whisper and call him "nerd." Thank God Mrs. Hill told us we can't boo. Troy's arms are in position again, and once the bow hair strikes the strings — he plays . . . classical music! Don't get me wrong, it sounds great — better than great — but not winning-a-talent-show-in-middle-school great. When he's done, both Sophia and I are the only ones who stand and cheer. We quickly stop when Mrs. Hill peers into the audience.

Troy trots back to us. "How'd I do?"

My mouth's sealed shut; I just nod and smile like I'm stunned speechless. But Sophia all but screams, "You were amazing!" Of course she does, she used to play classical piano, and all.

Mrs. Hill is back at the mic. "What an enormous amount of talent in this school." She scopes the audience, and I swear she zooms in on me when she adds, "That concludes our auditions for this afternoon . . . unless . . ." Mrs. Hill stalls.

Dang — I should've signed up. 'Cause like, what if? What if I did make it into the show? And . . . what if — what if *Dad* sees me? Would it make him proud? Would it? Dad used to love singing with me —

As if reading my mind Mrs. Hill continues, "Unless someone didn't get the opportunity to sign up and wants this last chance."

What if he gets so proud that he'll never want to miss a rent payment again? That he'll automatically go cold turkey with his drinking?

"Going once . . ."

Maybe I'm being totally unrealistic. . . .

"Going twice . . ."

But dang it, what if? *What if?* I push through the crowded aisle. People are already packing up and moving toward the door.

"Hey, where're you going?" Sophia calls after me, but I can't answer because I'm moving too fast, else I'll chicken out.

I climb the stairs and step out to the microphone. The lights — whoa, they're blinding!

"Miss Genesis, I was hoping you'd come up." Mrs. Hill's voice is a layer of calm. "Do you have music?" *Relax. I can do this.*

I shake my head. I know everyone's staring at me.

"What're you going to sing?" Mrs. Hill encourages.

I can't think of a single Beyoncé or Rihanna song! But one of Dad's favorite Motown songs come to mind, one that we've sung together hundreds of times in my imagination. " 'Ain't No Mountain High Enough,' " I say.

Mrs. Hill nods. "Go ahead."

I'm at the microphone, unable to move. There's no breath in my body to even sing with. Mrs. Hill taught me to have good posture, so I stand up straight, take in a deep breath, open my mouth, and nothing.

Giggles.

Is it first, *ain't no valley low* or *ain't no mountain high*? I can feel my forehead breaking into a sweat as bad as Dad's. I search every corner of my brain, but the words aren't anywhere.

Laughter.

"Miss Genesis," says Mrs. Hill. "How're you today?"

I shrug. I've no idea how I am today, was yesterday, or even five minutes ago.

"When did you first hear the song?" asks Mrs. Hill.

From Dad. We were at Belle Isle and it came on the radio. He sang it, and he sounded so good. I promised to remember the words so we could sing it together. And I did. And, oh, oh thank you thank you, the words come back to me now. I close my eyes, and let the song out, let it free. When I'm done, the entire auditorium is silent.

"Good job, Genesis. Good job," Mrs. Hill murmurs, just for me. Her eyes — they're glistening.

I hurry back to my friends. My sight's blurry and my hearing's warped, as if I'm swimming underwater. Hands grab at me, but I keep moving. I don't stop until I reach Sophia.

"Why didn't you tell me you could sing?!" Sophia demands, her voice joyous. "We're supposed to be best friends!"

"*You* were awesome!" Troy is exclaiming at the same time. "Where've you been hiding *that*?"

Jason slinks by, grinning like the Cheshire cat.

Yvette and Belinda both snake their way over too. I want to blurt out how fab their audition was, and how perfectly poised Yvette was onstage. Why can't I be poised like that when I sing and shake? But no, I get sweaty Dad brow.

"Oh my gosh, Genesis, you were so stinking good!" Belinda finger combs her already perfect sandy-brown hair and adds, "I thought you said you weren't auditioning?"

"I didn't say that," I say, still coming down from all that crazy energy. But my mind's clear enough to remember the day they asked me about it. "I said, 'I hadn't thought about it.' "

"But you decided to do it," Yvette presses. Sophia steps away to the side, and Troy is now somewhere laughing it up with the wannabe rapper.

"Yeah, I guess so," I say, hoping she doesn't think I lied to her. We're both hashtag team dark-skinned, right? Why else would she have stood up for me that day? "It was a last-minute decision, like, right before I went up there." Then I add, "Y'all were awesome too."

Yvette thanks me and gives me the strangest look. She never did tell me what she wanted to two weeks ago. What was it? Now she's wishing me good luck before maneuvering back through the masses.

Yeah, good luck. For real, now that I've auditioned, to even think that winning is a possibility is as crazy as me actually believing that God'll turn me beautiful. But not quite crazy enough for me to give up hope. Because if the angels do decide to smile upon this pitiful child and let me win, then for one moment I can believe Dad'll smile too. And that moment might turn into weeks as Dad retells the story over and over to his friends how his "baby girl stole the show." That moment might last for months as he laughs and hands the rent check to Todd.

Sophia's back at my side, and the look on her face tells me that there's definitely a beef between her and Yvette.

"Genesis." It's Nia. "Very powerful audition." My "thank you" gets caught in my throat, and my response sounds like a frog's gurgle. She saunters away before I can tell her how dope her own audition was.

Everybody's asking me questions, and I want to respond, but can't. I can't believe it. I did it. I, Genesis Anderson, stepped out onto that stage and sang. Out loud. In public. Alone.

TWENTY-TWO

It takes forever for Wednesday to get here. My mind can't contain itself. Ms. Luctenburg catches me daydreaming twice and threatens to send me to detention. Coach makes me repeat my sit-up drills three times because "I'm not trying hard enough." Mr. Benjamin mentions that I'm not demonstrating my potential. I'm too busy wondering if I made the show. Then there's Mama secretly studying her college catalog. And I still haven't told her that I poured out Dad's liquor. So really, how can I concentrate?

Finally, I try to relax with Sophia in our peaceful corner. I should be reading Ms. Luctenburg's novel study, *The Outsiders,* but Ella Fitzgerald's biography is holding my attention. Like Billie Holiday, she had to struggle at a young age. When she was fifteen, her mother died, and Ella was placed in what was called a "colored orphanage asylum" — which sounds really close to a mental hospital, but it wasn't; it was a reform school, but still! — and which, she ran away from. And, oh my gosh, she went to an amateur night talent show — and just like me — she was nervous; everybody stared and was ready to boo — although Mrs. Hill doesn't play that booing mess. Just as I'm getting to the part where she used to sing a lot, but not in the mirror with a shirt on her head — Troy sneaks up on us.

"Guess what?"

"Hey! What?" Sophia and I say one after the other.

"They just posted the results!"

"Really?" He nods, grinning wide. "Let's do this," I say, wanting to know, but sorta scared to find out.

Troy holds out his hand to pull me up. "You coming, Sophe?"

"Of course," she says, closing her book. We wait for her to stand up and brush the wrinkles out of her clothes. There aren't any wrinkles, but we wait patiently.

A horde of students are mobbed around the wall under the TOGETHER WE STOMP OUT BULLYING sign. Some come away with fist pumps, others look stunned, and not in a good way. I grab Troy's hand, and he squeezes. The closer we get, the tighter I must squeeze because he whispers, "Don't break my hand! It'll be okay."

I grab Sophia's hand, too, as we maneuver our way through the crowd. She lets go and backs away. "Hey, you coming?"

"No, I'll hang back here." Then she mouths, *Crowds.* She doesn't do those well, either, I guess.

Troy and I continue pushing forward. Elbows jab ribs. Heels squash toes. Chests press against backs. We forge on, sliding and ducking till we make it to the front. Troy runs his finger down the row of names and turns to me, his face ecstatic. He brings me in for a bear hug, shouting, "You made it! We both did!"

I made the cut? Me, Genesis Anderson, made the cut! I hold a thumb up over the crowd to Sophia, then I break out into a quick two-step hallelujah dance. Troy laughs, then leaves to ham it up with a few of his other friends who made it too.

"Congratulations," Sophia exclaims, once I make my way back to her, after scanning the list myself, just to be 1000 percent sure.

"Thanks," I say, still in disbelief. I'm so relieved I could float. I made the cut.

Sophia and I part for our next classes. And right then I spot Nia a few feet away, adjusting her messenger bag. I'm right up on her before she notices me. "Congratulations on making it into the talent show," I say, wanting to add more, but what?

"Thanks. You too," she says, already on the move to chorus, no doubt.

I string along. Gosh, this is so stalker-ish, but my feet keep striding. I think of something else to say. "Hey, your audition song, was that the idea you were talking to Mrs. Hill about?"

"Kind of," she says, shifting her shoulders to slip past kids. "I planned on doing an original song, not an arrangement. But I wasn't ready, you know?"

"Yeah, but I liked it. Kind of reminded

me of old-school Lauryn Hill." Man, Nia's fast, my feet are on double duty just to keep up.

"I get that a lot. But I'm still on the fence about busting out my own thing, just wanna do it right." A few kids yell out congratulations; Nia thanks them without slowing down.

"I hear you," I agree, then tell her, "I'm still trying to figure out my style too."

Nia pulls a loc from underneath her bag's strap. With that hair, how does she possibly think that she can be anything other than neo-soul? What singer has locs, besides the reggae ones? Then I really stop short as something occurs to me — I sound judgy! Like, like — too much like Grandma's stupid tradition! Nope I'm not going there. Nia can be who she wants.

As she turns into the classroom, I'm right behind her when I hear: "Hey, Genesis!"

Yvette's coming up the hall, Belinda by her side. I wait for them by the door, and when they reach me we exchange congratulations. They're *congratulating* me — and I gotta admit — it makes me feel extra hype.

Jason and Terrance bounce up — they're really trying hard with their stroll — and Terrance hugs and congratulates Yvette and Belinda, but not me. Jason lavishes his praise to *all* of us before going into the classroom.

My private celebration fizzles out when Yvette motions in Nia's direction and warns, "Don't hang around her, she's so stuck-up it's stinking ridiculous."

"Why you say that?" Being "stuck-up" ranks high on the list of worst names to be called. And "stuck-up" is what my mama was called.

Yvette pulls me away from the view of the class. "You never see her talking to anybody, do you?"

"She's a strange one," volunteers Belinda in a hushed tone as kids dip into the classroom.

I take a step and peek into the room at Nia, who's now flipping through her notebook.

" 'Strange'?" Yvette scoffs. "How 'bout 'freak'?" I flinch. Sophia's been called a freak. Wonder if she'll call me a freak too, if she ever finds out I rub myself with lemons and soaked in bleach? "I'm joking, Genesis," she says flippantly, "but seriously, I heard her hair stinks. She probably doesn't wash it. Gross."

Actually, Nia smells like gardenias, or jasmine.

"You can wash locs," Belinda counters. "They're kind of cool."

"If you're one of them fake bohemian types," says Yvette.

"Or a rapper," I say, easing into their groove. I kinda feel like I'm selling out Nia, but it was Yvette who had my back against Terrance, I reason.

"Exactly," Yvette says, nodding like crazy. "I know the value of a good hairstyle; my mother pays a ridiculous amount of money to have this weave flown in from India. Looks real, doesn't it?" Yvette pulls at her strands. "So, Belinda, get you some of those nasty things if you want. You won't be hanging out with me." Then Yvette looks right at me. "No offense."

"What? I don't have locs." I pat my hair down.

"I know, but . . . how can I say this?" Yvette frowns. "I can smell your cooked hair."

My hand flies to my head again. My hair smells? Cooked?

Just then, Mrs. Hill comes up and greets us. We all say, "Hi, Mrs. Hill" in unison. Class is about to start, and it's the perfect time for me to roll in too, when Belinda asks how I feel about making the show.

"Good, I guess."

"You feel good now," says Yvette knowingly. "When it's time for the actual show, that's when you start to worry. Standing in front of a whole auditorium full of strangers who're expecting perfection, waiting for you to mess up and stuff. . . . It's so stinking stressful that last year I lost ten pounds. I don't know why I do this to myself." She shakes her head at the memory.

"I hadn't thought about that." Not exactly in those terms, anyway.

"It's not *that* bad for me," she goes on. "I'm in a group. But you? You're all by yourself. I wouldn't have the guts to be onstage all by myself. Would you, Be-linda?"

"No way!" Belinda gasps. "Plus all those bright lights, they're awful."

"The lights, yeah, they're the worst," I agree.

"Ladies, I know everyone's excited," interjects Mrs. Hill, "but it's time to get started."

"Excited" isn't the word for how rau-cous the class is. You'd think the entire class made the talent show. Everyone is up chatting in groups as music plays in the background.

"But it can't be that bad, right?" I whisper. "Troy told me it was fun."

"Troy?" Yvette laughs. "What does he know? Seriously, last year he used to drone on about *Star Trek.* Like really, my dad watched that lame show *twenty years ago.*"

Star Trek may not be a show that I'd purposely watch, but dang, part of me is definitely not feeling how Yvette is clown-ing my friend. I should speak up, but Mrs. Hill dings her triangle. On the way to her seat Yvette whispers one last thing:

"But really, I'd rather die than perform all alone."

TWENTY-THREE

Why?

Why is there another white paper attached to our front door? Dad has a promotion. He's been going to AA meetings. He showed us the paid rent receipt! Okay, maybe I'm jumping to conclusions. It might be an invitation from our neighbors. All sorts of community meetings and dinners probably be happening out here. It could even be an advertisement from the landscapers, or — it could be exactly what I thought it was.

I snatch the envelope off the door. And no, it's not addressed to me, but I rip it open anyway. Ugh. Ugh-ugh-ugh. The last note was on, like, a regular piece of paper, but this one is all official-looking.

From the office of Todd Moreno

Dear Emory Anderson:

Your May rent has not been received as of the date of this notice. As a result and according to your lease, a late charge has been added to your total balance. You currently owe $1,589.00. This entire balance must be paid immediately. This is a serious matter and your urgent attention is required. Failure to act promptly will lead to eviction proceedings.

Just when things were getting better. I *knew* this was coming. I knew it. Why do we trust Dad for one hot minute, why?

Think. Don't get mad — *think.*

What if we explained to Todd — but, explain what? That Dad'll pay?

What if we can convince him to give us more time? At least till after the talent show.

Yes, that might work. It has to. I unlock the door and slip inside. Maybe Mama could talk to him. No, that'll lead us straight to Grandma's. Who else? Think, Genesis. Not Dad, and definitely not

Grandma — *dang.* Not me either. I can't talk to a landlord. I'm a kid! That's stupid, 'cause like, how would I even get all the way to Dad's job? Without money?

I run to my room and dive facedown on my bed. Where to now? A new neighborhood. Another school. I'm not moving again. I'm not! And you know what else? I'm tired of no one doing anything about it!

Shoot. Lying here won't help. It's gotta be me, I reason. So I get up and go to Mama's room. I search her coat pockets, jiggle Dad's pants, then check their drawers and under the bed. In the living room, AA pamphlets still lay on the table, as if proving that Dad is making good on his promise. *Whatever.* I dig between the couch cushions and in Mama's other purses until I scrape up enough change for bus fare — there and back. I should leave a note, but no. The sooner I get there, the sooner I'll get back.

At the bus stop, I keep my head down, scared of Mama or Dad somehow spotting me. I'm not afraid to go to the city by myself; shoot, I've been riding public buses for forever — even to go to school.

But wait, how do I even get to Dad's job? I know he works on Woodward Avenue, and I remember the stores around it. Mama calls them landmarks. If I can just make it to 7 Mile — one of the stops Mom and I used to catch the bus from to get to Dad's job — I'm sure I'll recognize the route to his work. I study the map just like Mama taught me, but I can't figure out where to transfer. When the bus comes, I climb in and ask the driver which bus'll get me to 7 Mile and then connect to Woodward Avenue. He tries to explain, but I must look confused because he finally says, "Just sit behind me, and I'll let you know." Which is very nice of him. People get on and off, and I watch them on the sly. Mama always taught me, *You've got to have eyes in the back of your head.*

The driver informs me it's time to transfer, and which number bus to take. I thank him, get off, and focus my thoughts on what to sing for the talent show, and *not* what I'm about to do. I wait, getting peeved at Yvette for dissin' someone as nice as Nia and Troy — and Sophia, for that matter. I'm still waiting, now in panic mode. What if the bus driver told me the wrong bus? What the heck I'm gonna say to Todd? Fifteen minutes later, the bus chugs up the street, and then I'm asking that driver if he knows the stop for Mumford Manufacturing Company. He frowns, irritated, as if being kind would hurt him. Then he says, "You've got about eight or nine stops to go." I thank him, then find a seat next to an older lady and begin counting stops.

Todd's note is folded up, safe in my jean's front pocket. I pull it out and study it. Mama believes Dad sabotages himself because he's afraid. What can be scary about paying the rent? It has to be more than that. The way I look at it, me scrubbing my skin and putting yogurt on my body ain't about me just wanting to be pretty. So Dad's gambling ain't just about him trying to win money.

The Woodward Avenue street sign catches my eye. Dang it! I almost miss my stop. I leap up and reach over the old lady — "Excuse me" — to ring the bell. Once I'm off the bus, I put on a poker face. A big, open lot sits in front of the plant and a barbed wire fence surrounds the property. I wander around the place searching for a main entrance, then see a crowd waiting at a food truck. The aroma of Philly cheesesteaks drifts in the air. I ignore the tiger clawing in my stomach as I search the faces for Dad's.

Alongside the building are openings huge enough for eighteen-wheelers to back up into. Dad used to work in press stamping or something like that, but I have no idea what department Todd works in. A Black man wearing a uniform is posted by the fence. I glance around for Dad before approaching to ask if he knows Todd Moreno. He shrugs, points to a white man, and says, "Ask Freddy, he's in charge." Freddy stands at one of the truck openings, staring down at a clipboard in his hand. As if it's perfectly normal for me to be here, I cruise over to him and in my most mature voice say, "Excuse me?"

"Yeah?" he says harshly, and then looks up from his clipboard and sees me. "What're you doing around here?"

"Uhm . . . I'm looking for Todd Moreno."

326

"Todd Moreno?" He taps his clipboard, thinking. "Todd Moreno in stamping?" I nod, guessing he's right. "Whaddaya want with him?"

"I have a message for him, that's all."

"Hold on, he might've gone for the day. Who's asking?" He lifts the walkie-talkie to his mouth.

"Uhm . . . Gen-nie," I say.

The man calls for Todd. My palms are sweaty. I scan the place, expecting Dad to step up at any minute. Would he come from inside or the loading dock? A voice clicks back, "He already left for the day."

"There you have it. Wanna leave the message?"

"No, thanks," I say.

He shrugs as if it makes him no never mind.

This could've been disastrous. I turn to leave, but I stop myself. *Hold on,* I didn't travel over an hour for nothing, did I? *Yes,* the scared part of me screams, hoping to jet from this place with a swiftness. But the part of me that talks big and bad about what I should've done after it's too late — well, that part of me turns back to Freddy and asks, "Excuse me, do you know Emory Anderson? I think he's in stamping too?"

Freddy looks at me, impatient. I get to tapping my foot because he's staring me down. Just as I'm about to fly out of there, Freddy says, "I know him. Why ya' asking?"

My throat tightens. I swallow and say, "Uhm . . ." I cannot think of one single story to tell this guy — especially with him glaring at me. The only thing I come up with is the lamest, corniest lie on earth: "We heard he got a job promotion and wanted to know his new hours so we could surprise him with a party."

We? Who the heck is *we*? Freddy cannot possibly believe this story. Especially since he bursts out laughing. When he finally catches his breath, he says, "Well, Gennie, you tell your people that Emory will never get a promotion here. He doesn't even work here anymore." Then he laughs again.

All the brain cells in my head start to pinball, knocking around the question: Did I hear him right?

Freddy calls over to someone else.

"Hey, Harry, listen to this, will ya?"

Yeah, I heard him right, so I hightail it to the gate as fast as I can without actually running. I pass the Philly cheesesteak truck, the smell now turning my stomach.

"Hey!" A man in the food truck line calls out to me. "Hey, remember me? Chico."

I stop in my tracks.

Chico.

"It's been a while, but you still look just like your old man. What's your name, again? Wait, don't tell me." He snaps his fingers and says, "Jordan? No . . . Janice? No . . ."

I turn and hoof it out the gate.

"Hey wait, you looking for your dad?" Chico calls.

I don't turn back. And I don't stop moving till I reach the bus stop.

"Where have you been? I've been worried half to death!" Mama hits me with a barrage of questions and doesn't take a single breath before launching into the next. I couldn't answer them, anyway. I don't even recall getting on or off the buses home. All I know is that I'm too numb to consider her anger and fear. Too stunned to create a story to tell her. An easy lie falls from my lips. "I was working on a project with Sophia."

"It's after seven o'clock. What project was so important that you couldn't pick up the phone?" I hang my head as Mama continues, "Don't act like crime doesn't happen out here."

The only thing to say besides "sorry" is the truth: *No, I didn't think to call because I just found out Dad doesn't have a job! He's been leaving the house every day, pretending to go to work. Forget not getting a job promotion, Dad's NOT GETTING PAID AT ALL. He's probably even lying about going to the meetings, too.* But I'm not laying all that down yet — I gotta think.

"Don't let another 'project' stop you from calling or coming straight home, you hear?" Mama continues to rant, her voice ringing throughout the house.

When Mama's done, I quietly close my door. I dig the eviction notice out from my pocket. Dad's nothing but a *LIAR*, talking about promises and job promotions. I should tell Mama and get this whole moving thing over with now. It'll be way better than having our stuff sitting on the curb. I can't get over it — DAD HAS NO JOB! Since when? If it weren't for that note and me having the courage to go speak to Todd, then we would never have known till it was too late.

I can't unthink this, no matter how many times I try to push it out of my head. I get the Ella Fitzgerald CD from my bag, find a song to match my mood, and relief comes in the form of *woo-woo-woo-woo-woo-woo*'s as Ella tells me to "Cry Me a River." And now I will, thank you very much! But Ella doesn't let me. She doesn't sound at all sorry for me, and pretty soon I stop feeling sorry for myself too.

Ella can sing a sad song with a jubilant twist, and she secretly switches your mood. She's smart and tricky like that.

Tonight I did something pretty dumb. But part of me feels kinda proud because

I did something. *And* I made the talent show.

I did something. Twice in one week.

Take *that,* Dad.

And Dad . . . well, he ain't here. Nine o'clock. Ten. Ten thirty. He's still not home. And now my thinking is ramped up again. Where does he go all day, with no job to go to? What is he doing? How is he getting money? Is he even trying to get the rent money before Mama finds out? What else is he lying about?

TWENTY-FOUR

Sophia and I walk together to Ms. Luctenburg's class, or rather I lag behind her. She asks if I'm okay, and I tell her I'm tired. Which is partly true. I fell asleep late trying to wait up for Dad. I can't stop thinking: *What in the heck does he do all day?* At my seat, a note rests on my desk. *A note.* My mind flashes back to Chyna and Porsche. I slyly glance around for the culprit. Only Jason watches me. He nods his curly head toward the paper. I pick it up and open it.

Hey, new girl, your audition was banging. How about singing a hook for me?

The words tumble around and around in my brain. Sing a hook? For him? I look back and he widens his eyes, anticipating a response. From me. I read the note a second time. Me, sing a hook for him?

Ms. Luctenburg enters the room before I'm able to write an answer back. As usual, she gets right to the point. "Our discussion question today will explore whether there is a difference between the Greasers and the Socs." Hands spring up and kids talk, but they all say the same thing. "Ponyboy thinks the Socs' girls are classier." "Cherry says money and values." "Ponyboy thinks the Socs are all right, driving Mustangs." Everybody shares ideas from Ponyboy's and Cherry's observations. To me it's all the same: Greasers versus Socs, rich versus poor, dark versus light, Grandma versus Dad.

I dare raise my hand, and she calls on me. "Well, the book says that Ponyboy thinks the main difference is money, but I think the two groups are different because they separate themselves, well, by their opinions. The Socs all look at the Greasers and think they're better than them based on how the Greasers all look and what they've heard about them. The Greasers look at the Socs and say, 'They think they're all that.' No one stops to think for themselves. No one sees the individual persons. They make a judgment based on the outside, without even getting to know one another."

"Ms. Luctenburg?" Sophia raises her hand. "To piggyback off what Genesis said, each group thinks the same way: Look at a person, form a conclusion, and the conclusion is based on comparing them to yourself. I think both Ponyboy and Cherry knew they were the same, basically. Well, Cherry was just afraid to stand up and admit it or convince her friends."

Ms. Luctenburg twists her mouth and says, "Good argument, ladies. Anyone else?"

I give Sophia the *Go-head I see you* look.

When Mrs. Luctenburg releases us, I grab my bag and bolt for the door.

"Hey, Genesis." It's Jason.

I move out of the way as everybody pushes out of the classroom. "Yeah?"

"You read my note," he says with a smile. "So, whaddaya say? We could use you to sing our hook."

Sophia eyes me, and I give her the one-minute hand signal. "What kind of hook?"

"Well, you're from The D . . . and you know what they say about Detroit, you feel me?"

No, I don't know, unless he means no-one-survives-the-hood-without-at-least-a-gunshot-wound or something lame like that. I've seen enough touristy I SURVIVED DETROIT T-shirts to assume what people think.

"It's just real from where you from, and your voice is . . . dope, know what I'm sayin'? Only you can bring the hook that I need, you feel me?"

Even though Jason is flavoring in way too many *you feel me*s for a thirty-second convo — just for a moment I forget about Dad and his no job, and I picture myself onstage, singing while he raps. It's exactly like my singing daydreams, except Dad's no longer the man with me — Jason is. "Sure," I say breathlessly — yeah, I'm that sad — "I'll do the hook."

■ ■ ■ ■

"Sorry I'm late, it's fish taco day, and that line was crazy," I say to Sophia when I get to the library. She's browsing the nonfiction books. She snags one and scrutinizes the cover, ignoring me. We're having our first friend argument over the silliest thing — me singing for Jason. When I showed her the note in the hall, after Jason left, Sophia read it four times, and her response was "I didn't know y'all were friends." Duh, we don't have to be for me to sing.

"Come on, Sophe," I say. "It's just one little hook. Do you know how small a hook is? Like five or six words." It's annoying that I have to go through this with her, when there are bigger issues going on — like Dad not having a job, or us getting evicted at the end of the month, and how to tell Mama before it's too late.

Sophia places the book back exactly where she got it. "Don't you think it's odd that all of a sudden he's writing you notes?" Okay, it's sweet that Sophia is being protective of me. And I get that she's not too trusting of other kids —

heck, I'm not either. Even I questioned whether Jason was playing some kind of prank. Sophia practically rolls her eyes at me. "You didn't hear yourself sing on that stage. I hate to say it, but he might be using you for your talent."

"Well, thanks for bursting my bubble," I say, and head for our usual spot. I sink down on the floor pillow, deflated, 'cause why not me? Can't this one time a boy see something about me that is boss? And on the other hand, I *do* wonder, "Why me?" Jason could've gone to Yvette, Belinda, or Nia, even.

This is where I have to stop myself. And I really do try to. But I can't help but measure myself to other girls — and I'm just being real — but when I rate myself to Belinda and Nia, I ain't no stunner. And there's no need to rehash my life and replay some of the things I've done lately, 'cause then I'll get down. What I do know is this — I shouldn't even have to wonder why Jason asked me, and there shouldn't be doubt in Sophia's mind either. And I *wouldn't* wonder, if I were like Nia . . . like Mama. So that tells me one thing —

"Hey, I'll be right back," I tell Sophia.

"Where're you going?"

"Gotta check something on the computers." What I've been doing hasn't been working, not fast enough. And, truth truth, I don't know what else I can try. So I google "how to lighten," and "skin" instantly pops up. The sites offer the same old suggestions: lemons, baking soda, milk, yogurt, honey, etcetera. Just as I'm about to blow smoke out of my ears, I stumble on bleaching creams. Bleaching *creams*? I click on "images." Whoa. I can hardly believe my eyes. Just about everyone's done it! How did I not know about this? The websites show women all the way in Jamaica, Africa, India, and Korea, all using bleaching creams. Hundreds and hundreds of women, no, maybe thousands, all feel the same as me: #70: She can't stand being this black.

"Hey, what're you up to?" Troy stands behind me. "I wanted to show you this cool comic —"

"I'm coming." I close the tabs, but the stupid computer's slow, slow, slow.

"What's that?" He leans over my shoulder, and I can feel my skin flushing darker.

"Nothing." My coal-black knuckles stand out as I grip the mouse. Troy looks at me, and I know he's seen it. "I was just messing around." I laugh, trying to play it off.

"Yeah, sure," Troy says, backing away, leaving.

There's disappointment in his eyes, and I want to call out, explain. But then I get all fired up. I shouldn't have to explain myself to him. Troy has no right to judge; his family is perfect, his dad pays the rent. He's read all those books, but doesn't know *my* reality. I reopen the tab and quickly copy the 1-800 number.

And as soon as I get home, I slip into Mama's room, dig around in her drawer and find her emergency credit card. For a moment I feel awful, like I'm just like Dad when he took money from her purse. But I shake the guilt away as I find the 1-800 number in my notebook and dial.

The next day in the locker room, Yvette and Belinda approach me just as I'm pulling up my shorts. Can you say, awkward? But still, shorts up or down, I really want to know what *they* want.

Yvette sidles up to me. "Belinda and I were talking, and we both agree that we're ridiculously worried about you being onstage all by yourself, with this being your first talent show and all."

"Yeah, it's not like you even planned for it," says Belinda, eyes wide with concern.

"Anyway, we've decided that you should join our group. Isn't that so stinking great?"

Really? I think, not exactly sure how I should react or what I even think of this.

"Really?" I say, 'cause should I be excited or not?

"Yeah, because if we were new to a school, it would make us feel ridiculously comfortable if someone did a huge favor like that for us." Yvette rubs my arm, and I immediately tingle from this foreign, girly gesture.

"I have to admit, I am kinda nervous," I say uneasily. At the same time, my head is exploding: *They want me to join their group! And they're so good!*

"We got your back, girl," Yvette says. It's true, even when she didn't know me. "And one more thing. I feel badly about the other day."

"The other day?"

Belinda smiles hopefully. "Yeah. Yvette sort of mentioned your hair. I told her that was foul."

"My bad." Yvette shakes her perfect bangs out of her eyes. "So let me help you. I could do your hair for you. I'm good at it."

"For real?" Dang. Maybe I've mis-judged them.

"My mother buys a ridiculous amount of hair stuff, it'll be no problem."

Mama would never approve of a re-laxer. "I don't know."

"You'll want it done for the show. It's like, in two weeks," says Yvette.

There's a tiny voice pestering me: What

if they're asking me to join them for the same reason that Sophia believes Jason is asking me to sing? But that pesky voice is fading fast because me shaking and slaying onstage with Yvette and Belinda — is a dream coming true — and there's no way Dad wouldn't be proud of me. But now that he doesn't have a job, will it still matter? Then I think, no, it matters even more!

Yvette takes out her cell phone. "You know what, text me and let me know. What's your number?" Then she glances over my shoulder and frowns. Sophia's hanging around the gym doors, waiting. "Well, you can give it to me later," Yvette says fast, tucking the phone away in her short's waistband. "See you on the track." Yvette and Belinda merge with the other girls, passing Sophia at the door.

Sophia doesn't ask what they wanted, and I'm staying tight-lipped about it. That is, until I figure out what I'm going to do. Join them? Or not?

TWENTY-FIVE

When Mama comes home I take a break from *The Outsiders.* And boy, does she look whipped. I can imagine what she'd look like if I broke Dad's news to her. Or my own — me pouring out that liquor. There's no way I can drop either bomb, just look at her. So, I tell her to take it easy, that we can eat leftovers or cereal. She says that sounds about perfect, and lays her head back on the couch and closes her eyes. She does perk up a little when I tell her about auditioning *and* making the talent show. I go back over to my homework spot by the big picture window, but end up gazing at the orange red of the sun bleeding across the sky. Not a second later, Dad rolls up the driveway like a madman. "Dad's home," I announce. Home from *where* is my question. Such a fraud. He sits in the car — that's supposed to be parked at the Mumford Manufacturing Company.

"He must've gotten off early," Mama says, pushing herself up from the couch. She's beside me, watching too. He notices us. And it doesn't take a psychic to read that he's in a mood.

"I'm gonna go finish my homework," I say, picking up my books and escaping to my room.

"Go 'head, it won't take long to make cereal," Mama jokes.

I keep my door open a smidge. When Dad comes in, I recognize his tone even before I register the words — it's the rock stuck in his throat voice. Not a drunk voice, but a mad voice. When I hear Mama ask, "How do you know?" and Dad responds, "Chico," that's when my stomach clenches.

I have two choices. One: Wait for Dad to come for me. Or two: Go out on my own. Neither sounds good, but I know what I have to do — even though every muscle in my legs are resisting it. Slowly I step into the living room. They don't notice me — how can they not feel the electric pulses sparking from my body?

"Wait, wait, wait," Mama is saying. "Let me get this straight. You're telling me she caught the bus all the way to your job? That's simply impossible, Em." She's staring at my father as if he's said I flew to the moon.

I try to speak. I have to. *Say it!* I swallow real hard and say, "No, Mama. I did it."

Mama spins toward me. "What? How? Why on earth — ?" With each word she charges a step forward. I back up, suddenly afraid.

Dad: To get me fired, that's why.

Mom: How'd you get all the way out there?

Dad: What the hell were you doing snooping around my job?

Mom: How do you even know the route?

Dad: It doesn't matter how she knew.

Lord, please let the floor crack open so I can fall through and disappear forever.

Mom: What were you thinking?

Dad: She wasn't thinking. I tell you

346

what she was doing. . . .

Mom: This happen when you came home late that day?

One lie out.

It takes all my energy, but I force myself to say, "I wasn't snooping." My voice is shaky. "I . . . I wasn't trying to get you fired." I want so badly to call Dad out on his secret, but I don't have the nerve.

"Then what were you doing?" Dad demands, towering over me.

I struggle to meet his eyes. I give up.

"I *said,* 'What were you doing?' " His nostrils flare.

"I was trying to save us. Trying to save you."

"What? What the hell does that mean?" Dad's voice is so loud that the crystals on the chandelier shake. "Save me? Sharon, she's talkin' crazy. You hear her?"

"Emory, calm it down!" Mama cries out. "Genesis, what do you mean?"

When people say they break out in a sweat when they're scared, it's true. I'm proof. But somehow, I calm myself.

"We're gonna get evicted again. If we

get evicted again, you said you're gonna leave. If we leave, then we'll live with Grandma. So I . . . I took the bus and, I don't know. I thought if I could just speak to the landlord and convince him to . . ." My voice cracks, but I don't stop. I tell her about Todd's notes, and yes, it was wrong for me to hide them, but they are what made me go to Dad's job. "I'm tired of coming home and our stuff's on the lawn waiting for crackheads to steal it! I'm tired of staying in people's basements! Why can't you just pay the rent? Just stop gambling and pay the rent?"

We all stand in a triangle, letting the words settle. "Wait, wait, wait wait wait!" Mama squeezes out through gritted teeth, "You haven't paid the rent? You mean to tell me —"

"No, it's not what you're making it out to be. . . . I mean, yeah," Dad stutters, getting tripped up on his tale. "Listen, I'll tell you everything, but . . . but we gotta deal with Genesis."

"Don't tell me what we gotta do. I *know* what we've got to do — and paying the rent is one! So, don't think we're not gon' talk about it." Mama turns to me and with that same strong voice she says, "And Genesis Anderson. You had no business going to your father's work, traveling across town like that. You should've come to me, let me handle it." I want to say, *And then what?* She's only threatened to leave too many times already — and two weeks ago when we did leave — we were right back before he even had a chance to be sorry.

Dad doesn't say anything at all. And stupid, stupid me, I'm still hoping. Hoping he'll say the magic words, "Everything'll be all right."

Something flashes in his eyes and now it is *he* who can't meet *my* gaze. Even though I've broken into a full sweat, I go on, "Why don't you just tell the truth, Dad?" I take two steps forward, praying that he takes two too.

But he doesn't. He doesn't even raise his head. He swipes his hand down his face and breathes out, "Naw, I got nothin' to say."

Nothing to say? Nothing? Mama's now looking at me like *I'm* the guilty one. Yes, it was wrong of me to go to Dad's job. And yeah, it was stupid of me to lie about it. But she doesn't even care why I went. And now, her eyes bear down on me, and I can't take it. Doesn't she see I was only trying to solve our problems? Doesn't she see how tired I am of having to move and make new friends over and over again? So tired of keeping secrets — Dad's secrets, hers, and mine.

Well, I'm done with that. I'm not even aware of what I'm about to say, the words just tumble out. "And it was me who poured out Dad's booze."

"I should've known," Dad groans.

Mama cocks her head, as if trying to decode what I just said. "You?" Then her face goes furious. "You let me go through all that with your father and didn't say *a word*? Not one word?!?"

"I'm sorry," I whisper. "I thought that if I got rid of it, then he'd stop —"

"I don't want to hear it!" Mama yells. "Can't anyone tell the truth in this house?!"

The truth? And then I can't stop. If not for me, then for Mama. She's dreaming of planting periwinkles and going back to school, and she's clueless that Dad's about to snatch those dreams away. Again. She deserves the truth.

And Dad. He's so mad, steam might as well be spouting from his ears. He's going on about me being punished and needing to take responsibility. But him? When he gets in trouble, nothing happens. And I've covered for him. I didn't say one word about him smoking inside the house, did I? Or about the notices from Todd. Stupid. Stupid. Stupid. But Dad doesn't deserve me keeping his secrets. Not any longer.

"But, Mama?"

Mama's looking wild. "Better not say nothin' that'll get you in more trouble," Dad warns.

More trouble? I know he's right; what I want to say will be trouble for us all. But Mama's right too — it's time for the *truth*.

"Mama." I try to be strong, I really do. So I blurt, "Dad doesn't have a job. I found out when I went up there."

Dad's eyes narrow. "Genesis, shut up now," he orders.

It takes all of twenty seconds for the news to register in Mama's brain. Then she goes ballistic, swings toward Dad. "You don't have a JOB?"

"Baby, listen —"

"You don't HAVE A JOB?"

"It's not what you think —"

"YOU DON'T HAVE A JOB?!" Mama screams, and I swear she's about to throw something. "Where in the — what have you — when were you —" Mama can't even get one question finished before another barrels up.

Dad tries begging, but Mama's not hearing it. "They gave that promotion to somebody else — somebody I trained! What did you expect me to do?" Dad's excuses keep coming, until finally, he grabs his jacket and says, "I ain't gotta go through this."

Mama and I stay where we stand until the engine's roar fades. And without saying a word, Mama wraps her arms around me. Then *everything* — from this last month — hits me. Me pouring out the liquor, hiding Todd's notes, Dad's secrets, his sadness about Charlie's death, Grandma's sister, the brown bag, the lemons, the yogurt, and the bleach. So many secrets. So many. And I let go.

■ ■ ■ ■

Ever notice how crying wears you out? Like really, if you've ever cried hard and long, afterward all you wanna do is sleep. Maybe that's why babies are always sleeping. And on Saturday that was me, like a baby, knocked out. Mama was dragging around drained too. And you can about guess that after walking out, Dad didn't make an appearance for the rest of the weekend. You know what's a trip? You'd think Mama would've drilled me with more questions, rehashing every single detail. But no, it was a lot of quiet in the house. Like, thinking quiet. No, a kinda scary quiet. The kinda quiet that made me keep questioning . . . What did I do? What's gonna happen now?

Needless to say, Monday morning I'm too distracted to volunteer to read my paragraph on what the author is emphasizing, yet Ms. Luctenburg calls on me. Then in PE, I'm too wiped to do push-ups, and I'm forced to tune out Coach's barks to dig deeper. And by the time I get to math, well, you already know there's no chance of me untangling an algorithm when my own mind is gnarled in tangles.

And what's also not on my mind is Yvette's and Belinda's offer. I'm reminded of it when I see them at their lockers. When they first asked, I was so hype imagining Dad seeing me onstage with them. Who knows if that'll even happen now? *Stop it, brain!* Gosh, do I sound hopeless or what? Yvette and Belinda are laughing, smearing on lip gloss, and looking like nothing but rays of hope. Shoot, this might be my one chance ever to rock a stage with a crew. So I shove my funky mood aside, go straight up to them, and say, "I'm in."

"Cool!" Belinda smiles big.

"Yeah, cool," Yvette says, busy puckering her lips, snapping a selfie.

And heck, why not go all in and do it big, right? So I ask, "Will you still do my hair?"

"Well, yeah! We can't have you in our group looking janky." Yvette laughs at her own joke, which doesn't sound like a real joke. "It's going to be so stinking cute!"

And you know what? I'm starting to

feel a little bit excited again. I won't have a shirt draped over my head — I'll be *performing,* in a hot dress, hair swaying down my back, and fans screaming our names. Well, maybe not *that.* But close enough. Which is way better than nothing.

When I meet up with Sophia after school, I gently break the news to her. Sure enough, she thinks they're using me, just like Jason. But what she doesn't get is that with them, *I'm* guaranteed to win.

Sophia grasps my arm, stopping me in the middle of the sidewalk. "Did you even stop to think about it first?" She unzips her jacket.

"It's just so much going on, Sophe. And me learning a song and creating a routine, in, like, barely a week, well, it's just too much."

Sophia zips up her jacket.

"I wasn't even going to audition in the first place," I remind her.

We continue on. She unzips her jacket.

"Plus, it's scary up there on that stage, with all the lights," I say, regurgitating

Belinda's words.

She zips her jacket.

"Since I'm new they're going to like, ease me into it, you know."

"Funny . . . ," Sophia says at last. "I thought you were from big bad Detroit."

"I am. But it's not like I was going to win, anyway."

"You don't know that." She unzips.

"Yes, I do. You saw them; they were super good." She zips. Then unzips. "Would you please stop with the zipping?"

She stops. Her fingers hang loosely on the zipper. "I didn't know it bothered you so much."

"It doesn't. I didn't mean it like that, Sophe." My nerves are jangling. I calm myself before saying, "Call me stupid, but I thought you'd be excited for me." Then I make my appeal to her. "Sophe, remember when we shared those secrets? And I told you the one about me singing in the mirror, with a shirt on my head?" Sophia nods. "Me, on the stage, looking beautiful and winning? That's all I've ever wanted. But if it's going to make you mad at me, then . . . then I'll have to think twice about it, I guess."

Sophia zips her jacket up to her chin and stuffs her hands into her pockets. "If you're joining them just to win, then yes, go ahead, join them. But I have to say, it's people like Troy that you should learn from. He does it even though he knows he won't win."

"Which is kind of silly," I say jokingly.

She raises one eyebrow. "Genesis, it's not always about winning. You know that."

She's right. It's not always about winning, and yes, I know that. But Sophia can say that because she has a dad who takes her to carnivals, wants to sit beside her at dinner, kisses her forehead, and pays the rent. So I look her straight in the eye. "Right now, for me, it's only about winning."

TWENTY-SIX

The oddest thing is happening at our house. Mama is in the front yard, planting flowers. We're most likely getting evicted — and Mama's planting flowers. I'm convinced she's lost her mind.

"Hey," I say, standing over her. "Uhm . . . the flowers look good."

"Always wanted to plant periwinkles. Might as well do it now." She pats the dirt around the stems. "Flowers, they don't have to worry about a thing. They only need water, sun, pruning, sometimes a little talking to, and they'll bloom so pretty." She stands to face me. "You shouldn't have worries either. Our grown-up mess has been your mess way too long. . . . You didn't sign up for this . . . out here trying to be the parent, rescuing us. My baby girl, trying to rescue us!" Mama exhales. "How'd it get this bad?" She brushes her gloves off on her scrubs.

I'm too stunned to utter a syllable. I finally say, "We're moving, ain't we?"

She nods, vacantly. "Funny how you become what you fight so hard not to be." Mama kneels back down to her flowers. "I never wanted to be one of those women who put their 'man' before their child. And you know, all this time I thought I was better than these types of women. I thought I was choosing *family.* Come to find out, I'm no different."

Mama just, wow, put it out there. 'Cause yes, I've been mad as heck for her seeming to always take Dad back so easily. I'm guilty of that too, to be honest. But truth, it means a lot to me that she's had these thoughts swirling in her head. And just to clear my conscience totally, I apologize again. Because I *am* sorry. For lying. For hiding the late notices. For catching the bus to Dad's job. Just sorry for a whole lot of things.

Mama apologizes too, for not listening to me. And that I should be a kid, and let her be the grown-up, even though that means she'll have to delay going back to school. "It'll work out," she says, digging a small hole. She points the trowel at me when the holes are a few inches deep. "You know, you've got guts, Genesis, getting on that bus like that. I had no clue you were that brave. . . . Guess you're not a little girl anymore." Mama squints up at me. "And I realize something . . . it's time *I* stop being afraid."

Dad comes waltzing in after Mama and I already started eating dinner. We both look shocked when he asks, "What you cook?" as if he hadn't been gone for nearly three days, as if this past weekend wasn't out of control.

"Beef stew," Mama says, but she doesn't rise to fix him a bowl.

I don't know what to say, so I don't say anything. I keep my eyes on my food.

Dad goes to the sink, washes his hands, humming his mystery song, and I don't care to even try to figure it out. He sets his bowl and spoon on the table and goes back for a glass of water. He sits, and out of the corner of my eyes I catch him watching us. I shift my spoon around in my stew, waiting. Because someone can't take off for three days and come back without something happening. I wonder who's going to go first — Mom or Dad.

The beef stew isn't spicy, but Dad's forehead is sweaty. "Damn it, I can't eat when it's this quiet. Let's get last Friday night straight. Genesis —"

"Uh-uh, don't you open a fresh wound 'less you've got a Band-Aid," Mama cuts him off. "And there's no reason to swear, either. If you wanna talk, talk, but don't swear."

Clearly now speechless, he fills his gaping mouth with a spoonful of stew. Then he says, in between chews, "I'm just sayin', it's quieter than a graveyard in here. I come in, nobody asks how I'm doing or nothing." He wipes his forehead with his napkin.

Finally, Mama says dryly, "Fine. How you doing?"

"Just dandy," Dad says in a voice that says the opposite.

Then Mama lays in. "So, you been going to those meetings or been lying about that, too?"

Dad's grip on his spoon tightens. "Those meetings ain't for me."

"What do you mean those meetings 'ain't for you'? Who the hell do you think they're for, Emory?" Mama's no-swearing manners have left the table.

"It's for people who — how many times do I have to tell you, I don't have a problem! Now, would you get off my back about it?" Dad's really sweating now.

"Are you serious, Emory?" She sets down her spoon, hard. "Every month we have to rob Peter to pay Paul! We've been put out four times! And now you don't even have a job! How can you say you don't have a problem?"

"Okay, I messed up! But I *don't* have a problem!" Dad shoves back from the table. The bowls jump. "It ain't like I haven't been trying. . . . You won't even give me credit for getting this house!"

"We ain't got *this* house anymore," I mumble.

"Every time I turn around you nagging me about something." Dad pulls a pack of cigarettes from his shirt pocket, slides one out, and goes through the ritual of tapping the end to shift the tobacco. He lights it, knowing that Mama's asked him a hundred times to not smoke inside. "I'm telling you those meetings ain't for me, and I don't wanna hear no more about it." He puts a final period on the conversation when he takes a long drag from the cigarette and blows out the smoke.

"Fine." Mama picks up her bowl, gets up from the table. Dad doesn't hear Mama's final period on the end of that word, but I do. She scrapes her food into the garbage disposal and turns it on. It's not the grinding that sends chills through me, but Mama's disposition. She kisses me on my forehead and tells me to clean the kitchen. Then she goes to take a shower. Dad doesn't even go after her. He splits to watch TV. After I wash the last dish, wipe the counter, table, and stove, only then do I slip out to the back porch to sit on the top step. I want to be alone, but I'm afraid Dad'll sneak up on me in my room again.

Mama said she wished for a patio set for the summer. *Wished.* Grandma's back porch ain't too bad, I guess. Besides, it's too quiet out here in stupid Farmington Hills anyway. No shouting, music, or honking. Nothing. Farmington Hills is missing all the friendly gossiping from the neighbors' porches. The "What up, doe?" from the old men playing dominoes. There aren't even any corner stores selling Better Made chips and Faygos out here. No Lou's Deli serving thick corned beef sandwiches. Yeah, I'll be okay going back to Detroit.

I gaze at the sky. It seems like there're a whole lot more stars out here than in the city. After a while, the back door opens. Then the flick of Dad's lighter. Then the stink of his cigarette.

"I was gonna pay the rent," Dad mutters.

Ha. More lies. Does he *ever* not lie? Earlier, Mama called me brave, but am I? If I were brave, I'd speak up. But it's not in me to do so. Now my other self starts arguing. Brave. *I am.* So now I do use my voice. "Dad," I start. "I want to . . . but I just don't believe you. Not anymore."

Dad throws on his charm, as if he

weren't a roaring tiger last Friday. "Aw, don't say that. 'Cause this time —"

"Will you stop with the promises! I'm tired of 'em. We're tired of 'em!" I say, throwing up my hands. They're shaking, and I can't get them to stop. Dad doesn't attempt to sway me with more words. Does that mean he's actually *listening*? After a minute I ask, "Why don't you have a job, anyway?"

He takes so long to answer that I figure he's ignoring me, not listening after all. Then Dad puffs, blows, and says, "After all those years, now they talk like I wasn't good enough for the position. Used words like 'unreliable' and 'irresponsible.' At the end of the day, I know the deal. It's got nothing to do with me showing up late every now and then. It's all about politics."

I almost get caught up in Dad's anger, taking his side once again. And yet, being late, that's being irresponsible, right? And he really hasn't answered me, so I finally face him. "But why don't you have a job still?"

Dad stubs out his cigarette and immediately lights another. I swear people'll think we lit the fireplace, with all his smoking.

"I told them to kiss my . . . well, you know." He puts his cigarette on the edge of the wood railing and pulls out something from his back pocket. A bottle. I know the shape all too well. Crown Royal. He unscrews the cap and takes a long swig, then picks his cigarette back up.

"You're not gonna stop drinking, are you?"

"Now, don't you start," Dad says exhaustedly. He tips the bottle to his lips and swallows. A lot.

I won't start. Not about that. Another question's been lurking inside me, begging to know for five years now. It's time to ask. Right now. "Dad? Why you choose alcohol . . . over me?"

Dad doesn't say a word, doesn't even look at me. But he's heard me, I'm sure of it.

I stand up now, pressing, "Is it because I don't look like Mama? Is that why?" He's still not answering, but he hears 'cause I'm talking louder now. "You drink 'cause of me. Don't you? You drink 'cause you hate me?"

"I don't!" Dad raises his voice, a little too loud for Farmington Hills. Lowering it, he continues, "It's not that I hate you . . . but . . ." He starts to raise the bottle again but stops, and finally recaps it. "But it woulda been a lot easier. . . ."

Easier? For what? To love me? Look at me? But he doesn't finish. You wanna know the crazy part? I should be telling him about the talent show, and how I've been listening to Billie Holiday and Ella Fitzgerald. He should be giving me advice whether to sing Jason's hook. He should be making me feel like how Sophia's dad makes her feel. But no, he just keeps right on smoking, and I go right ahead and tell myself I don't care. Why can't I *not* care?

I can't be out here another minute, not without breaking down. But I stop myself, because even though the tough inside me is crumbling — truth: I'm brave. I sang alone — onstage — and that means something, and doggone it, Dad needs to know that his daughter will be singing again. After all, he's why I auditioned in the first place.

"Dad?"

"Genesis, I don't know what else to —"

"I was just gonna invite you to my talent show," I say, rushing the words. I tell him the date and that I hope he comes. He doesn't say anything, and now I'm right back to wondering what would've been a lot easier. I turn to go and when my hand's on the door handle, Dad stops me.

"Genesis." The softness in his voice makes me wait, hoping, stupidly hoping, that he says he'll proudly come. I wait as he takes a drag from the cigarette, flicks it in the air, and says, "I am trying."

TWENTY-SEVEN

The very next afternoon, a tan package sticks out from our mailbox. It's addressed to Mama, but the return address reads LUSCIOUSLY WHITE. *Lusciously White?* Oh, my cream! Dang, I'm lucky Mama hadn't gotten the mail before me. *Luck.* That word just zinged me. Reminds me of Grandma talking about her family, marrying up, and how it wasn't *luck* that made them lucky. It sure wasn't luck that made her hold that bag up to Dad's face or got him choking his words, *It woulda been a lot easier.* All that luck . . . yeah, that luck is exactly why this cream is now in my hands.

Even still, I've gotta admit that my stomach is doing that squeezing thing that it does — but for a good reason, 'cause as soon as I get in my room, I tear off the tape and slide out the box. It's, oh my gosh, pink and shiny, with cursive gold-embossed letters. *Gold-embossed letters* — now how can I stay mad? They're so pretty; I can't stop tracing them over and over again with my fingertip. When I open the box, I'm extremely careful not to damage it even a tiny bit. A small, folded piece of paper sits neatly on top of the jar, like a welcome letter. I carefully open it. Inside are testimonials, with before and after pictures. And at the bottom of the paper it reads: GUARANTEED RESULTS IN FIVE DAYS. *Five days.* You mean, I could look like Mama in five days?!

I lift out the jar. It's white with a shiny, gold lid. I hold it in my palm, but my hands are clammy. I place the jar down and wipe them on my jeans. Then slowly, slowly, I twist off the top, and there it is. Good-bye, ugly; and hello, beautiful! I'm about to dip my pointer finger in the cream, but my heart is beating so fast. Questions bombard my mind, and they scare me. Will this really work? What if, like, my face breaks out or something? Would my life really become less complicated? I picture the look on Troy's face when he saw me reading about this stuff. And just like that, I'm not sure if I can do this.

I stare at the swirl of white cream for a long, long time. Even that swirl of cream at the top of the jar is perfect. Perfect. Oh, I want to be perfect. I dip in my finger, put a little on my cheek and rub it in. I put a dab on the other. It slides on smooth like satin. It feels cool, soothing like moisturizer. Dip, dab, and rub. I can't control myself, and soon I've slathered my face, hands, and neck. Then I pray the prayer I've prayed for so long: *God make me beautiful, make me light, and give me pretty hair.*

After dinner Mama suggests we take an evening stroll. We haven't done anything like this in quite a while, so it feels kind of strange. We stop at the corner, wait for a car to cruise by before crossing the street. We pass huge houses with drapes wide open. Flat-screen TVs and artwork can be seen through some of the windows. People are out jogging and some walking dogs. And once I finally loosen up, Mama drops the bomb on me. "We'll need to start packing."

Packing? I knew it was coming, *I knew it.* But what about my friends? What about me finally getting math? What about Mrs. Hill and our special times after school? What about . . . what about the talent show? Dad has to see me sing —

"Mama, we can't move."

"Genesis, I know you and Sophia are becoming fast friends." Then she slows her pace. "Believe me, it's ripping my heart apart to know that we can't stay. . . ."

My staying isn't only about Sophia. It's about so much more. Never would I have imagined that I'd get the nerve to audition for a talent show — but I did. And it's made people pay attention to me — Mrs. Hill, Yvette, Belinda, Nia, Jason. It's as if I'm . . . popular. And bottom line — I've got to do that show next Friday. When these last words spill from my mouth, Mama says, "Okay."

It must be hard for Mama to stay. Dad's not making it easy at all. Part of me feels guilty to ask her for anything, especially since she's given up so much for so long — her dreams of being a dancer, a journalist, going back to college, and now staying in a house that she can't have.

"When do we have to move?"

"Before they put us out," Mama jokes. A gut-punching joke, but I ease out a chuckle for her. "No, seriously, they'll have to file the eviction papers at court and stuff, but I need to save money. So that means we'll move in with . . . Grandma." Mama lets out a loud sigh.

"Think we can stay till . . . the end of the school year, at least? *Please?*"

Mama says she'll try to make that happen, but no promises, especially with Dad not having a job. I thank her over and over again and add a reassuring "We got this, Mom!" And that's when I do something that's been long overdue, right there on the sidewalk, in front of somebody's house with their curtains all open: I hug her.

Twenty-Eight

This Saturday morning, Yvette calls rehearsal at her place. I can tell Sophia's still bothered by my joining the group, but says she understands, so I don't feel too bad about going. Before getting dressed, I study my face for a change. Nothing. I'm on my fifth day already and *nothing.* I apply a layer of cream and prepare to leave. I'm super hype, not just about practice, but because today — Yvette's doing my hair.

Mama lets me go by myself to Yvette's — well, only after walking me nearly to her doorstep — because come on, I can't be strolling up Yvette's sidewalk with my mother! She made me promise to call when I get inside. But I almost forget because Yvette's house is fancy and *huhuge,* huger than Sophia's, but she doesn't show me around. She leads me straight to her room, which is large and light purple and has a bathroom attached. You can go through the bathroom and cross into a whole other room.

"Come on, let's get started. Belinda, you ready?" Yvette calls out.

Belinda springs up from a pink-and-white striped cushioned chair. "Yep."

Yvette presses on her iPod, which is docked on a station next to her bed. "This is the song we're gonna sing," she informs me. I haven't heard it before. It's a pop song that's probably only played on white stations; it's definitely not something that would ever be on FM 98's R&B rotation. Yvette assigns the vocals and has already made up the moves! Just like in the auditions, she's front and center, only now with Belinda and *me* slightly behind her. When I ask about the other girl, the one who'd been with them when they'd auditioned, Yvette waves her hand dismissively and says, "Don't worry about her." It isn't until we finish one run-through that I realize that Yvette's doing all the lead vocals, Belinda has a few, and I have one line.

One line?

"Hold on," I say. "Are the vocal assignments set in stone?"

"Yes," Yvette says decisively. "We thought it'd be better to keep it simple, especially since we now have less than one week to teach you the song and dance steps."

"Yeah, it might be too much if you had to do all kinds of memorizing, don't you think?" Belinda adds, her eyes baby doll wide.

I start to protest, but have second thoughts. I better not pick an argument with the person who'll be putting chemicals on my head in a few minutes.

"So are we ready? Let's run through it again." Yvette claps her hands, and we swing our arms out to the sides, twerk during the bridge, and a few other moves that are easy enough for me to pick up. Yvette drills us on our marks and harmony, as if we're just her background vocalists. But I don't say anything. She's doing my hair.

When she's decided we're done, Yvette leads us to the bathroom. She has me sit on the toilet seat lid and begins to base my hairline with Vaseline to protect my skin. "You're going to love it once it's done. Trust me." Yvette opens a black jar with a brown label. "This stuff's ridiculously amazing," she says, all confidence. Starting at the back of my head, she plunks a ball of cream on one area and works it through my hair with the comb.

"I cannot believe people still press their hair. It's so . . . ancient," Yvette is now saying, adding more cream.

"I know, right?" I agree. Mama did it over a week ago, so I pray she won't notice any change. Yvette works her way to the top of my head. "It's starting to tingle," I tell her.

"Tingle is good. That's how you know it's working. Now hold still, we've only got fifteen minutes to get this through your hair — well, less than that now."

I breathe in my nose and out my mouth real slow. I count to ten. Then to fifteen. Then to fifty. This "tingle" is worse than getting nicked by a hot comb. By the time she reaches the front of my head, I can't concentrate on anything except the fire in my follicles. "It's burning . . . in

377

the back and around the edges."

"You've been scratching your scalp, that's why. You should know better," Yvette scolds, and continues combing.

"Just hold on," Belinda urges calmly, "you're nearly done."

I struggle to stay seated another minute, then one more. Then Yvette runs a comb through my hair and the teeth feel like they're scraping my scalp open. It's hot. So hot that I can't take it anymore. I leap up.

"It's on fire," I cry out. I push Belinda out the way, stick my head in the tub, and turn on the faucet. Cold water runs over my head, and Belinda helps wash out the cream. Then something miraculous occurs — as she washes, I notice . . . the slight touch of her fingertips! My hair's so thick that Mama has to scrub *hard* for me to feel her touch on my scalp. And . . . the weight of my head also seems lighter. How can that be? There's something else, too — wet strands stick to the sides of my face, just like white people's hair does when they get out of water! After I pat my head with the towel, Yvette gently combs it out, and

378

the comb doesn't get caught. There's no torturous yanking and pulling at all. Next, she dries it and won't let me look.

"See, I told you," Yvette exclaims at last, finally turning me toward the mirror. "You'll have to watch for scabs, but your scalp'll stop being sensitive in a day or two. Trust me, I've made the mistake of scratching before a relaxer one too many times."

"Wow, Genesis," Belinda is saying at the same time, and I see truth in her green eyes.

I get up to look. My hair! It falls down on my shoulders, smooth as silk. I give my head the slightest of shakes, and my hair moves with it! My fingers glide through the strands. It's never done this, even with a fresh press. I shake my head again as if this is some kind of trick. "It's so . . . light," I exclaim.

"Want me to flat iron it?" Yvette asks.

I do, but I tell her no. Mama would surely notice.

"It's so stinking cute that it's ridiculous," Belinda coos, flipping my hair playfully.

"Yes." I agree. "It *is* so stinking cute."

"You know what would really be stinking cute?" Yvette asks rhetorically. "If you add extensions."

"Extensions? No, not me."

"Oh my gosh, yes!" Yvette points to my head. "You could add a piece here and one right here to hang down your back."

Mama would go off bad enough if she knew I got a relaxer, so there's no way I can walk in the door with a *weave*. Shoot, I still gotta walk in the house with my funky ponytail.

Yvette claps her hands together. "I just had a thought. What if we give you a makeover?"

"No." I take a step back. "I'm not feeling that."

"Yeah, let's do it." Belinda runs to get a kit, and before I know it I'm back sitting on the toilet lid, the two of them powdering and dabbing my face. They have me dreaming all kinds of what-ifs. What if I really do turn out beautiful? What if I can get hazel-colored contacts, or green, like Belinda's? What if Mama loves my hair and lets me keep my relaxer and add extensions?

"You look so freaking cute," Yvette announces. I get up and face the bathroom mirror. I am very freaking cute.

"Oh my gosh," I gush. "Ya'll are so ridiculously amazing. I don't even recognize myself."

"See?" Yvette raises an eyebrow, cocky. "Stick with us, it only gets better." I blink, almost in disbelief. These girls took time to make me pretty. They smile with me in the mirror, hugging me. Then I think of Sophia. I can't imagine how they could possibly be mean to her. I want to ask, but I can't ruin this moment. At last, I have friends — pretty and popular friends. Could Sophia be wrong? I mean, why would Yvette take time to make me look like this if she's trying to use me? When Yvette twirls my hair around her finger and says, "Don't you love it?" I nod because I do. In this moment, I forget that I only have one line in a verse. In this moment, I love my friends and I really do, finally, ridiculously, love my hair.

On Sunday, Yvette fusses about my messy hair after all the work she put in. Ain't no way I can tell her that I have to wear it like this to hide from Mama. She moved on and had us rehearsing dance steps. Even though it was fun, all the twerking made my back and thighs sore. Still, once I'm back home, I hobble up to the mirror to see if today's the day that God has answered my prayers. I study my face, craning my neck this way and that way. And yes, I see them! Tiny light spots, barely noticeable. After washing up, I massage on more cream. And as I brush my hair, stroking it over and over — my light, bouncy hair that sways with every move — I can feel the small scabs from the relaxer burning my scalp. I muss it up just a little, but it doesn't matter, look at me!

When I get to school, the first thing I do is sneak off to the restroom to comb my hair again. It's so straight, even the edges. Then, I search my face for more changes. Hopefully someone'll notice the difference. No one does, not even Sophia.

Not even the nosey girls in PE. So I determine that the changes are either my imagination or desperately high hopes, and I stop focusing on them. But then at tutoring, Troy does something strange. He moves his desk to sit across from me instead of beside me. And he stares. And stares.

"What?" I say. "I can't solve for *m* if you're going to sit there looking at me like that."

"You bought that stuff, didn't you?"

"What stuff?" I play dumb.

"The stuff that was on the computer. . . . You said, 'It's not what it looks like,' remember?"

I'm about to deny it, but as I raise my finger in protest I spot some light splotches on my hand. Barely noticeable. I extend both hands in front of me. How could I not have seen this before?

"So, I'm right?"

"I . . . I . . . wasn't actually going to get it," I stammer. "It kind of just happened." Troy gives me a look. Should I explain myself to him? Would he understand? I test the waters with a joke. "But it's not like I got butt implants." He doesn't laugh.

My heart is sinking. He's the first and only boy who's been my friend, and I don't want to mess that up. "Okay, okay. I don't know how to say it, but . . . I just want to be pretty."

"You don't think you already are?"

I want to tell him that there's nothing pretty about being black like me, but he should already know that.

"*I* thought you were," he goes on, "but that . . . that's not about being pretty. You're taking it to another level."

What does he even know about being pretty? "Well," I start, not really knowing how to respond, "sorry to disappoint you, but . . . there's nothing wrong with try-ing to improve myself. Shoot, girls do it all the time with weaves and fake con-tacts." Troy sits stone-faced, as if I'm not making sense, so I go on. "Blackie. Ape. Those are just a few names I've been called, Troy. And I'm tired of it. Tired of being told to work twice as hard and be twice as good. When people look at me they think 'ghetto.' You're as dark as me, but, well, maybe you don't know what it's like 'cause you're here, living in a fancy bubble."

Troy's tapping his pencil against the table, fast and hard. "A fancy bubble? Really, Genesis? Don't think I don't get the speeches too, and don't think I've never been called names: Black Nerd, Chocolate Einstein. People look at me and expect me to be this great baller or rapper or dancer —" He closes his book, shoves it into his backpack. "But what you're doing, that's not a solution. You're still gonna be Black. You'll still be called names. And you'll still have to be twice as good."

I stand up to disagree. "No, 'cause I'll be light. That's a whole different set of rules." Then I ask him, "For real Troy, how many Black superheroes you see in your comics — well, besides Black Panther?" I gather my notebooks, too, adding, "And you know how I know you live in a bubble? 'Cause you're playing *classical* violin at a talent show."

I make it down the hall and slam into the girl's restroom. I can't believe I was so mean to Troy. *Classical violin, really, Genesis?* My heart's racing. I inspect my face and instantly feel better. My skin appears smoother, and yes, there are tiny, light circles. How did he even notice that? Then I grin because Troy noticed the difference, and that means — thank you, God; thank you, God — my skin's lightening! It's really, finally happening.

Right before chorus, I make up a legit reason to stop Jason. What I really want is to see if he notices I'm lighter too. "Hey," I say, flipping my hair out of my face. "When do we rehearse?"

"Rehearse?" Jason asks. Terrance comes up and smacks his back, like guys do.

"Yeah, I've got to know where to stand, what to wear, stuff like that." Jason looks blank. "For the show?" I prompt.

Terrance starts grinning. "You didn't tell her, Jay?"

"Tell me what?" I squint at Terrance. I want so badly to smack that smirk off his face.

"Well," Jason says, "you're only laying the hooks on a track, along with the beat."

"Huh? You mean just recording them?"

I say, confused.

"Oh snap!" Terrance yelps. "You thought you were gonna be onstage with us?" And he bursts out laughing.

"I thought I heard an animal howl." Yvette comes out of the classroom and drapes her arm over my shoulders. "What's so funny?"

"Nothing," I say, feeling dazed by my own *STUPIDITY*! Sophia was right!

"Your girl thought she was gonna be onstage with me and my boy," Terrance informs her.

"What? Are you fraternizing with the enemy, Genesis?" Yvette smiles, smooth. She plays with my hair, saying, "She's in our group, sorry, boys."

"Oh, so *you* recruited her. I see you, Yvette," says Terrance. "Making moves like a chess player."

Chess player? What does *that* mean? I can hardly think, or think beyond how, once again, I am so stupid. I AM SO STUPID! Like I was going to prance on-stage alongside Jason. There's no way I'm going let myself be played by him and that jerk. So I say, loud and clear, "You know what, Jason, I won't be singing for y'all." I shove past them into the class-room.

Behind me, the jerk keeps mouthing off. "She loco if she thought she was gon' be onstage with us. Look at her!"

Stupid boy didn't even notice my skin. Or hair. My thoughts, however, aren't enough to drown out Terrence's yapping as he, Jason, and Yvette saunter into the room.

"Yvette," he's saying, "what happened to your other singer —" Quick, quick, I fake busy. What *did* happen to her? Yvette's voice goes low when she an-swers, and I can't be sure, but it sounds like — *do whatever it takes to win.* Then snickering, and not just from Terrance. But by the time I swivel Yvette's way, she's composed, glances from me to the guys, then back to me, and rolls her eyes as if to say that she, too, thinks Terrance is a jerk.

Mrs. Hill announces that we'll start preparing songs for the graduation cere-mony. Cheers from the eighth-graders go up. My focus remains on Mrs. Hill, because despite Yvette's eye roll, I *don't* know what happened to the other singer in her group and can only guess the meaning of "whatever it takes." And no way am I looking in Jason's direction. Does he feel the same as Terrance?

Before class is over, Mrs. Hill reminds us that our song title for the talent showcase must be turned in for the program by Wednesday. After everyone's gone, Mrs. Hill informs me that she noticed I was "somewhere else" in class. What do I tell her? The truth? No. "Anxious for the talent show?" she asks.

"Yeah," I say. But all I want to do is escape it all. Listen to Billie or Ella and go somewhere else in my head. But I gave back the Ella CD. I'd had it for more than two weeks. Maybe she'll lend me another? I ask, and for once something goes right — Mrs. Hill leads me to her collection.

"You'll find both my old and new gems mixed in here."

These must be all those old singers and musicians that Mrs. Hill identifies us as. Like when she said I was a Billie Holiday, it was a good thing. Billie Holiday opened my ears and showed me that there's a way to ooze out pain. Even though she didn't peg me as Ella Fitzgerald, Ella reminded me to bring out the positive amid the hurt. But now I search on my own, not sure what I need. I play a few bits from several CDs. Nothing speaks to me. I try a few more. Nothing. I'm just about to give up, when I pop one last CD into the machine and hear the first strums of a guitar, and then a smoky, mellow voice cries out, *"Something told me . . ."*

I restart it and listen. I press repeat and listen again. I do it one more time — in disbelief. This is it! Dad's mystery song, the one he always hums. I push the headphones tight against my ears, gulping the song down, trying to figure if it's the words that move Dad or her voice. It's another song about a broken heart, but the way she sings it, man . . . I feel it deep in my belly. I finally found it — then I think with a laugh, no, Etta James found me.

Twenty-Nine

Even though Mama told me to be a kid, my brain doesn't want to stop trying to figure out what Dad might be doing all day. Thought bubbles hover above my head as I smear the cream onto my face and hands. And suddenly I'm struck by a terrible thought. What if I'm doing all this and Dad *still* doesn't consider me beautiful? What then?

Perhaps if I read more books, then I'd see things differently . . . see things like Troy. Eagle-eye Troy. I still can't get over what I said to him. I know, I know, he was only trying to help. *I'll fix it,* I promise myself.

And that's where I end my thoughts for now, 'cause Etta James is blowing through the speakers with her soul. As much as I tease Dad for singing old

Motown songs, I never thought I'd be listening to ol'-school blues. Track two plays: "I'd Rather Be Blind." When Etta James hits the first three notes, I immediately feel the hurt in her deep, raspy voice. Struggle, too. I restart it and sing along, restarting the song over and over until I determine how she moves her voice, until I can pull up my own bad memories that help me match her strength. I can't of course, not nearly as well as Etta, but I put everything into it, eyes closed, being blind.

Overnight, my light spots have grown — definitely noticeable. My fingers are really light around my fingertips and there're a few dots on my hands. On my chin, where my scrapes were, is a little spot. Two on my left cheek about the size of a fingernail, and three on my right. A few smaller dots are on my forehead, too. When I put my arm next to my face, I swear my skin shade has gotten a teensy bit lighter; shoot, it's not much, but I'll take it. Mama will surely zoom in on the changes, so I stall in the bathroom — half the time admiring my face and combing my hair, and the other half getting ready for school — until I know she's left for work.

Here's the thing about friendships: sometimes you gotta admit that you were wrong . . . and they were right. And in my case, Sophia was right again. That's why I immediately need to explain to her what I've decided. When Coach tells us to run four laps on the track, I jog alongside her, arranging the sentences in my mind. Because even when I told myself I was using Yvette and Belinda as much as they were using me, I realize it's just like #86: Because she let them call her Charcoal, Eggplant, and Blackie. And here's Sophia, who's never wanted anything from me, except friendship.

I gotta own this. So I flat-out say, "Sophia, you were right about Jason."

"What makes you say that?" She curves off to the side of the track.

"I kinda knew it, but I . . . got caught up in a fantasy, you know?" We stop and catch our breath. "There's one more thing. I'm quitting the group."

Sophia looks at me now, so closely that

she *has* to see my spots. But she keeps mum. She keeps mum because I am her friend. And I need to let *her* know that *she* is my friend. Yeah, I get all dazzled by the popular girls, but I think, maybe, a little, I'm learning to see beyond them. To seeing who my friends really are. So I ask Sophia directly, "What did Yvette do to you?"

Sophia's fingers now twist and untwist the bottom of her T-shirt. She glances toward Coach, who's screaming as usual. She's got her T-shirt twisted so high her stomach shows. Coach blows her whistle, waves at us to get running.

"I know I should've asked you way before now, but — I was afraid to know." There, I admitted it. Sophia's twisting her T-shirt so hard I worry it's going to rip right off, so I go on. "I didn't *want* to know. I thought that if I didn't know, then I could get to know them and they'd get to know me on their own. And I didn't want it to mess up my friendship with them . . . or . . . what I wanted to believe was a friendship."

Sophia's face has gone red, and she no longer meets my eyes. I almost regret fessing up, but hiding it was wearing me out.

"Papageorgiou and Anderson, if you don't get those feet moving I will hold you here after school and run you like racehorses!" Coach looks ballistic.

Sophia pivots and faces the track. Slowly she takes off, and so do I.

"Aren't you going to say something?" I ask, really, really needing her to say something, anything. Sophia's friendship is one of the only things that makes sense in my life right now. We pass Coach again, and she warns us to not let moss grow under our feet or she'll keep us after school every day for a week. "What did they do to you, Sophe?"

We slow down, but our feet keep shuffling. I'm sweating now, but for once there's no need for me to worry about my hair kinking up.

Sophia begins, "When I first got diagnosed, I was really upset about it. I tried my best to hide it. But kids would, like, make fun of me when I'd move my desk — you know . . . linoleum squares? Lining up?"

I nodded — I could fully imagine

Sophia needing to get her desk exactly along the lines of the linoleum square flooring. She was watching me carefully — I could tell *she* could tell I got it, because she continued.

"One day, Yvette saw me crying in the bathroom and was really nice to me. I'd never told anyone about my OCD, but I thought I could trust her . . . then, like, the very next day, everyone started mimicking me." Sophia looks me straight in the eye. A *pay-attention* look. "She even made up a cartoon called 'Fear the Walking Freak.' Guess who the main character was?"

"Dang, Sophe. That's beyond foul," I pant. Now I want to get on the stage more than *ever.* Not only in hopes that Dad'll be in the audience, and that Mama'll know that I'm even more courageous than she thinks. But for this — this might sound selfish, but — I want to beat the sequins off Yvette and Belinda. "You all right?"

"Yep, I'm over it." We speed up till we get past Coach. "So what's up with the makeup? Is this part of the demands of the group or something?"

I shake my head. "So, uhm, remember my secret?"

Sophia grins. "Which one?"

"Funny! The one where I told you what I didn't like about myself?"

"Yeah."

"Well . . ." I glance around, making sure no other girls are around before continuing. "This ain't makeup."

Yvette and Belinda pass us on the track. They wave at me, but I refuse to raise a hand to them. They keep going, clueless to my angry rebellion.

Sophia ignores them and sticks to the issue. "Then what is it?"

I spill the full story about me researching skin bleaching online, how Troy found out, how I ordered it and now Troy's acting funky because yes, I did flip out on him. I end with, "I can't believe you even noticed them."

"Well, yeah, I noticed. And . . . wow . . . I can't believe you did that." Sophia purses her lips, thinking, then says, "How're you going to explain to your mom and dad that all of a sudden you're —"

"I haven't figured that part out yet."
My left calf is killing me. "I'm debating
whether to tell people that I have the
same thing Michael Jackson had."

"Vitiligo?" Sophia says. "I don't know,
Genesis, claiming a condition that you
don't have . . . you might jinx yourself. I
wouldn't if I were you."

Geesh. Even though she took away my
one reasonable answer, she's got a point.
Plus, if I've learned one thing this week,
it is to listen to Sophia's advice.

It's time to talk to Troy. Once again, I
don't have a clue as to what to say, but
I've gotta say something. When I meet
him in the library, I drop my notebook
down on the table.

"You definitely know how to hold a
grudge, don't you?" Okay, not the best
start.

"You definitely know how to insult your
friends, don't you?" Well, at least he said
"friends." That's promising.

"Me flippin' out on you wasn't cool.
And I'm sorry," I apologize. "You taking
it the way you did, well, I didn't see that

coming."

"It kind of just happens when it comes to people I care about."

I dare to smile — he didn't say "used to," he said he does! "But I don't get it, Troy. That didn't have anything to do with you."

Troy slides back from the table, shifting in his chair. "Yeah, you *don't* get it. You were cool . . . just the way you were. You weren't wearing fake hair down your back or trying to be a made-up superstar, somebody you weren't. You were *you,* without all the extra."

"Hold on, you're mad at me because I'm not what you wanted me to be?"

"No, I'm not mad. It's just that you started switching up. It's like you're falling in line with all the other girls." Troy takes a moment, then says, "Remember me telling you that my folks made me read *Malcolm X*? And I said it taught me to think for myself? It's like, you're believing the hype without asking questions."

"Well, I didn't read any of those books," I say defensively. "So you saying that you never felt like how I feel?"

"Of course I did, when I was a kid. But then I kinda realized, what's so bad about the way I am? So I started telling myself, 'Today I'm gonna beat the odds. Today I'm not gonna be a stereotype. Today I'm gonna be whatever.' I have to psych myself up on the daily. So yeah, I know how hard it is, but what you're doing . . ." Troy holds his hands in the air as if he's done talking and leaves me to fill in his blanks, but he doesn't take his gaze off my face, adding, "Do you even know what's pretty to you? I mean, not what people tell you is pretty. . . ."

I was all proud of my changes, hoping the world would notice, but he now makes me . . . want to run for cover. He's asking all these questions that, I don't know . . . I thought I had figured out. Now I want him to look at anything else besides my face. So I hold up my book and ask, "Are we working today?"

But Troy's not done. "You know that that stuff can give you cancer, right? It can burn your skin."

"It's not like I plan on using it for that long," I argue, but my brain is sending off an alarm bell. I didn't actually know that! " 'Sides, people do stuff all the time that'll cause cancer and they're fine." Like Dad's smoking.

"Genesis." Troy lowers his voice, looking right at me. "Here's the deal. You were dope *before* the auditions. Before the fancy hair. Before all of it. Because you weren't chasing the hype."

Chasing the hype. Hmph.

"Anyway, you still mad at me? I miss my friend, you know?" I say, leaning against the table.

"I'm not mad. Well, I was . . . you went off on me, and I was like 'whaaa?' " He rubs his hand back and forth, back and forth, over his own curls. "But it's all good."

"Good." I grin big, and it feels good. Troy *sees* me. And because of this, I want to help him, too. "Troy," I say, "it's time we talk about your violin act, 'cause you're pretty dope too; let me help you harness all your dopeness."

THIRTY

Mama's in the laundry room when I get home. My plan is to sneak to my room without her noticing me — noticing my hair and face — so I call out, "I'm home," before shutting my bedroom door. But then she responds with, "I'll be right there. I brought some boxes."

Shoot. I scramble to tie on my night scarf and try to shade my face. She opens my door, and I immediately turn my back and start digging in my book bag. "Ma, I have a ridiculous amount of homework," I tell her.

"Okay, but let me first tell you about the jobs I've been applying for . . . right out here." Mama sits on my bed. "So I don't want you to get too excited, because I haven't had any interviews yet, but —"

"Ma, can we please do this later? I just said I've got a ton of homework. Plus, I need to practice for the show."

"I know, I know, the show. But you'll want to hear this, come sit down." She pats the space next to her. I work my way over while pretending to look out the window. Mama takes my hand and rubs it. "Time is running out here, but I'm working on at least moving us back to the area. . . ."

I slide my hand out of hers, but she grabs it back. "Listen now, we should discuss one — wait, what . . . what is this?" Mama examines my fingers, holding them tight so I can't pull away. "You been playing in my makeup again?"

"No."

"Then why your fingers look like this?" she asks. Then she takes hold of my chin and inspects my face. "If it's not makeup, then explain what's on your face." Mama's eyebrows are scrunched in examination mode, and she cries out, "Oh no . . . I know what it is. I've seen these before. . . ." She stands up. "We need to see a doctor to be sure, but I believe it's . . . what's it called?"

"Vitiligo."

"Yes, that's exactly what it's called, vitiligo." She reaches for my hand again, as if she's about to haul me to a doctor that second. "I think that's what you have."

I turn away. "I don't, Ma." Sophia had just asked me how I was gonna explain these spots to my folks. To think that I was so close to claiming this condition, but our talk convinced me otherwise. And guess what? I still don't have an answer to this question.

"How would you know?" Then the look on Mama's face turns from fear to concern.

I hide my hands in my lap, wishing that this whole moment would just — *poof!* But no, Mama's still waiting for my response, and I drop my head.

Now she's pacing. "It's that brown bag nonsense, isn't it? Why my mother have to —" Mama keeps going, not giving me a second to answer, even interrupting herself. "I thought that after our talk and how I told you I was teased . . . I thought you'd realize that you are who you are."

Mama doesn't understand. She just

doesn't understand. So I tell her. I finally tell her, "I want to look like *you.*" Mama's eyes brim instantly with tears. And then I admit that it's a cream, and right away apologize for using her credit card. And boy, oh boy, I was not expecting her to blow up the way she does.

"You used my credit card?! You stole my credit card?!" And all of a sudden, I'm a bunch of irresponsibles, untrustworthies, and lacking of moral character. These are only a few of the words that I pick up. They sting the most because, well, that's how Dad's employers saw him. When Mama's tired herself out from fussing, and I'm ripe with the most awful, spoiled-milk feeling ever, she holds her hand out and with a voice full of bass, says, "Give it to me."

I take the box from my drawer, holding on to its sleek smoothness for a moment before finally handing it over. Mama scrutinizes it as if it's a repulsive artifact. And so I don't have to keep apologizing every day for some other stupid thing I've done, I better come 100 percent clean. She's taken my cream, so it can't get no worse. "And, something else . . .

Yvetteputarelaxerinmyhair."

It takes a moment for Mama to untangle the jumble of words, and when she does, her volume is on ten. "She what?!" All her brown bag guilt vanishes, and I swear, her whole body's gone rigid. "Genesis Anderson, have you lost your mind? You *know* how I feel about relaxers!"

"Mom, I'm sorry!"

"You've been a whole lot of sorry lately!" She wheels around and stalks out of my room, taking my jar of miracles with her, but she's right back, shouting, "And another thing, don't think for a second that you're gonna watch TV, listen to your lil' music — all that is cut off — gone! And hear me clearly, you can forget about sashaying in that show, too!"

The talent show?! Not the talent show! Mama can take away anything — *ANYTHING* — but not this, not this! "Please, Mama, just —"

"No, *please* nothing. With all the tricks you've pulled, you're lucky you'll even see the light of day." With that, she slams my door, leaving me to hear her yelling, "I'm done! I'm so done with it all!"

Mama's words bounce off the walls. *I'm done! I'm done!* One moment ago she was all excited about trying to keep us in Farmington Hills. And now she's fed up with me. And I can't even blame her, really, because . . . I messed up. And, aw man, when Mama looks at me, she probably only sees secrets, lying, and stealing — just like she does with Dad. What can I do now? Apologize again? Make a promise that I'll do better? She already heard that a million times from Dad. But it wasn't like I didn't have a good reason for it all, right? Naw, I can't even front. The stuff I did was just plain stupid. And wrong.

Now I feel worse, worse than ever. The . . . opposite of clean. I've got nothing — *nothing* — else up my sleeve. I go slam the drawer shut, but it sticks three-quarters of the way closed. I shove it again, but it's stuck. I reach in and find the jam — my list is sticking up. My list. There are now so many things that I can add to it. And I don't waste time doing it. I get a pen and write: #89: Because she ordered bleaching cream with her mama's credit card that she stole!

I stare at the sentence. I feel bad about a whole lot of things, but not about this — well, minus the stealing. The truth is, I would shave layers of skin off my body if I knew I'd be lighter. In two more days, I could've been truly light-skinned. And without my cream, what if — what if the spots change back?

I remember how on my first day I noticed Yvette playing basketball with her friends, later wishing I could be friends with someone like her. I was excited to be part of her group, even more thrilled when she did my hair. Now she hopes I'll go bald. That's what she said this morning when I explained that I had to drop out of the group. When I couldn't tell her why, just that I'm on punishment, she accused me of lying. *Lying!* Said I was being vague. Well, she was right about that, and I told her so. Yep, and even admitted that I was planning to quit anyway. I won't repeat it, but you can just about guess the name she called me then.

Sophia lifts her chin in Yvette's direction. "Good thing her eyes aren't lasers;

you'd be dead." I turn away, blocking Yvette's stank eye. "What else did she say?" Sophia asks, doing a full push-up, not the girl ones, on the knees, like I'm doing.

"She cracked on my face. Lame jokes." I won't admit to Sophia that those lame jokes stung because the splotches have gotten bigger. Shoot, I don't look *lighter.* I look — spotted! And the pride I thought I was gon' have — well, I'm feeling something, and it ain't that. "These things are hard!" I gasp between push-ups. "How many do we have to do?"

"Three sets of fifteen." Then she stops, resting on her knees. "How you really feeling?"

I collapse, laying my cheek flat on the mat. Her asking forces me to check in with myself, which I've been avoiding. Who wants to focus on drama? "I don't know. It's like . . . like a lot of pressure is on me. I wanted to win that show so badly. Of course, right now my mom won't even let me *do* it. . . . And I feel so . . . so *ugh* —" I don't want to say it, 'cause if I say it, I may get all emotional, and I'm not about to break down in this funky gym, especially with Yvette glaring.

"Coach is coming." Sophia quickly drops her chest to the floor. We grunt through our next set of push-ups, real convincing because Coach says, "Good job."

"You know, after that comic book thing, I still had to come back to school and face everybody. And I still had to do my work, acting like I wasn't breaking apart inside." Sophia goes back to her knees and claps away dust from her hands. "I wanted to confront Yvette, and my so-called friends, so many times. Ugh! I just dealt with it. Was I scared? Yeah, probably. And, well, you probably are too." Sophia rests a hand on my shoulder and says, "It's gonna be okay, okay?"

I shut my eyes, squeezing tight 'cause they're getting kinda wet. "How . . ." I pinch the corners of my eyes. "I can't even be in the talent show . . . can't even go."

"Yeah," she sighs. "There's that. . . . What're you gonna do?"

"What can I do?" I say. "Shoot, my mom went off so bad, you almost had to write my obituary last night." Then I add,

"Dang, I need to tell Mrs. Hill she's gotta scratch me off the program." Sophia's quiet, so I go on. "There's something else."

Coach blows the whistle and makes the end of class announcement. Everybody's jumping up and putting away their mats. I take Sophia's hand to make sure she's listening. "We may have to move at the end of the school year."

"Move? Why?" she asks, alarmed. "You just moved here!"

How do I answer without revealing Dad's habits or that he doesn't pay the rent? Best friend or no, Dad's addictions are not something I want to admit to anybody. So I tell her it's complicated. "But," I say with a fake cheeriness, "my mom's looking for another job, out here. And . . . well, you just never know."

And that's the part that gets to me . . . the never knowing.

THIRTY-ONE

Last night I kept wondering "What if?" Then I got to humming a Billie Holiday song and thinking about her story, her pain. It's . . . in some ways, I realize, not totally different from Dad's. Dad has a lot of hurt in him from his childhood, like Billie does. And in her photographs, she looks so alone. But she wasn't, she had her husband. Maybe . . . maybe Dad needs to listen to Billie and hear that he's not alone, either. And a CD might not be enough to get his attention. I now realize that what I'm secretly thinking is gonna get me into big, big trouble — I'm already in such big trouble . . . and . . . this is the very last, bottom-of-the-barrel thing that I can do. I don't have anything left but this. So before I set off for school, I quickly curl my hair, pack a dress and shoes, write a letter of what I'm doing and why, and leave it on the table with my list. Then I pray real hard for Dad to come.

And all day long, I kid you not, everybody's been buzzing about how the PTA's inside the auditorium decorating, setting up the lights and sound equipment. *They're taping it this year. They even rented a photo booth! They're putting the red carpet down now!* Kids try to sneak a peek, but the old man is at the door shooing them away. Even the teachers find it hard to keep us focused — well, all except Ms. Luctenburg.

A big red-and-silver banner is draped above the auditorium's doors that reads: A NIGHT WITH THE STARS: FARMINGTON OAKS MIDDLE SCHOOL'S ANNUAL TALENT SHOW. Red, black, and white balloons are posted on the sides of the doors.

"Told you they go all out," Troy says, sneaking up on me.

"Yeah, I see, you'd think it was *America's Got Talent* or something." Troy laughs, and just then, the same two jerks that I've seen him with in the halls purposely bump him.

"Yo! Einstein, I got a D on my test, no thanks to you," says the tall one.

"All you had to do was hook us up," snaps no-neck-guy.

"Hey, I already told you I wasn't gonna keep giving you my notes." Okay, I don't know if it's Troy's talent show nervousness or what, but he explodes! I'm talking in-yo-face-and-tired-of-your-picking explosion — Troy style. "Stop asking for them. I'm tired of bailing your sorry selves out."

"Yo, why you acting brand-new?" says no-neck.

Then, because Troy has my back, I have his. And because I'm amped, part scared for the show and part scared that Mama'll come yank me out of this school, I shoot off, "Hey, y'all live in freakin' Farmington Hills, go to a school without metal detectors, and don't gotta share desks — you not hard. So stop frontin' like you dumb."

"Who she?" the taller one asks Troy.

"Don't worry about her. I'm done trying to help you." Troy turns to me, smiling his great smile and says, "You ready, Gen?"

"I'm ready," I say, and we go into the library. When the door closes, I let out a very anxious breath. That's what it feels like to be down for your friend. Wow. I ask him if he's okay, and he tells me he's good. And this time I'm sure that he is.

Sophia joins us just as we settle in our beanbags. I can tell something's up because she's shifting from side to side. "Here, this is for you," she says, handing me a gift bag.

A gift? For me? I grin and sift through the fancy paper until I feel something hard at the bottom. It's a frame with a picture of us, the one taken in her room the night we had dinner. I've never . . . I've never had a picture with a friend before. "Sophia, I love this. Thanks."

"Yeah, you're welcome," she says, still shifting. Then she takes out a cloth from her pocket and proceeds to rub the lenses of her glasses so hard I worry that she's going to pop them out of the frames.

"Sit down, Sophe. I've got an announcement." I tell them both that I'm going through with the show. And right away, Sophia pipes up, "You sure? You might not live to see tomorrow."

"What do you mean you're 'going through with it'?" Troy asks.

"She hasn't told you?" Sophia says, now adjusting her beanbag. "You haven't told him?"

Then I do. I fill Troy in on the whole story. And I'm kinda thankful that neither one of them remind me of how stupid the cream idea was in the first place. I still don't know how I would've explained the color change!

The closer it gets to the end of our library time, the more my fingers want to twist my hair. I sit on my hands, and Sophia tells me to calm down for the fifth time. But my nerves won't settle. I do hope Mrs. Hill is right, that I have a gift, because it'll take more than that for me to win with only one night of practice. Troy, he looks cool on the outside, but he's fiddling his fingers too.

"Y'all are driving me bonkers. Would you both relax so I can relax? Geesh!" Sophia says at last.

"My bad," Troy says. "I don't know what's wrong with me. Usually I'm cool."

"I used to get like that too," Sophia

acknowledges. "Every piano recital where I had to play a classical piece, I felt like I had to be extra perfect."

"Yeah, but that's not why I'm nervous. I'm ah, doing things a little different this year since I've heard that classical violin doesn't cut it for talent shows."

"Where'd you hear that?" Sophia says, shocked.

Troy nods toward me, and I raise a finger in the air fast. "But that's not what I meant — well, okay, that's what I meant, but it just came out wrong when I first said it. I know, I know, I'm the worst," I say, covering my head.

"No, not the worst" — he laughs — "but seriously, our talk inspired me to try something different." Troy assures me that it's a good thing.

Us three being together got me feeling all tingly, and I try to hold on to this feeling throughout the day, especially in my next class. In chorus, Mrs. Hill keeps us focused with the graduation songs; otherwise I'd melt from the burning glares of Yvette, Belinda, and Jason, and Terrence's mean-mugging. At least Nia smiles at me.

As soon as we're dismissed from final period, you'd think it was the last day of school. Kids burst out of the rooms as if they're hyped on sugar. Some were actually running to the auditorium to claim seats. I ease into the hallway, on the watch for Mama — 'cause you never know — and go grab my outfit from my locker. But when I get to the foyer I hold back. There are even more balloons bobbing throughout the hallway. Kids are already crowding around the photo booth, taking pictures with friends. And the prize basket sits on a table surrounded by students "oohing" and "aahing." Suddenly I can't move. I turn away; maybe I should go home, after all. I push through the crowd, and then I hear my name. *My name.* It's Sophia, racing toward me with Troy behind her. He carries a bag in one hand and his violin case held protectively to his chest with the other.

"I can't believe you're going through with this," Sophia says excitedly. "If I ever break a punishment, I'll think of you — now go show Yvette you're no backseater."

"Come on," Troy says, offering me his arm. He leads us toward the talent holding area, which is in the cafeteria. We pass the red carpet for the runway, a few parent volunteers acting as paparazzi, the velvet rope leading to the auditorium doors, and eager parents already filing in the auditorium. I look for Mama and Dad, but I don't see either of them.

I tug on Troy's arm. "Wait. I'm not . . . I'm not sure I can do this. I mean, I've got this bad feeling."

"It's just jitters — everyone gets them," Troy assures me. "You'll be great."

Sophia adds, "It's good to be a little nervous — keep you on your game. Well, that's what my piano teacher always says."

"I guess," I say, chalking it up to nerves.

Troy opens the cafeteria door, and a slew of kids are already here preparing for the show. More trail in behind us. A modern dance group is prancing around in hot pink and sparkly spandex. An a cappella group is doing vocal warm-ups. Everywhere, kids are practicing dance steps, tuning instruments, or finding pitches. Jason and Terrance are in the corner spitting rhymes back and forth. Nia has her guitar over her knee and waves. Yvette and Belinda spot me from across the room and make a beeline my way, a third girl in tow.

Sophia raises one eyebrow. "Maybe they're the bad feeling you're getting," she says in my ear.

Yvette and her crew stop right in front of me. All posing with attitudes, crossed arms and lips pursed out. Kids near us are pretending to get ready, but they're really staring. I flash back to Regina standing with her crew in the yard, amid all our furniture, and I had promised myself that one day I wasn't gonna stand around letting people dis me. And today is that day.

"Wait," I get in first, holding out my hand like us Detroit girls do. "You're gonna tell me that I'm gonna be blinded by the lights, everybody'll laugh, and I'll stinkingly, ridiculously embarrass myself because I've never been in a talent show, right? Because you ain't here to wish me good luck."

"No, I come to tell you that I knew you were lying, talkin' about grounded. Yeah, right." Yvette refolds her arms, fuming. "Doesn't matter, you're gonna look mighty stupid when we walk away with the trophy."

"Yeah, well, you're gonna look mighty stupid if you don't." I turn my back on her and say, "Sophe, I'm going to go change."

It's my turn to leave them standing there, looking lame.

Sophia grins. "You go, big, bad Detroit," she calls after me.

Troy fist bumps me, then he says he has to go get fly.

"You okay?" Sophia asks as we head for the girls bathroom. My hands seem to be trembling. "Don't tell me they rattled you?"

"Not this time," I say. "I'm good." *Tell that to my hands,* I think. "But maybe I shouldn't do this. . . . My mom's gonna kill me." I shake my hands, releasing the tension. It then occurs to me that she's going to kill me anyway for ditching my punishment in the first place. Plus, what other choice do I have? "No, forget it, I'm doing it, I'm fine."

"Sure?" And when she knows for sure that I am, she leaves to grab her seat.

At the last house when I did the final sweep, I remember thinking how I'd hoped a change would happen with this new move. And you know what? Things have definitely changed. I touch my fine hair and the splotches on my face. I also remember vowing that I'd never sing in public. No matter what. Another big ol' change.

My shirtdress falls right under my knees, and when I wrap my black leather belt around my waist it cinches up a little bit. I turn around to see if my butt pokes out, but the mirror is too high. I take off my sneakers and socks, and slip on my good black ballerina-like flats. I raise my arms and twist about, considering how I might pose onstage. In my imagination, this is how I'd get ready for my concert. I gently finger my curls that now look like I stood in front of a fan for a few minutes, which is cool because it's a straight up Yoncé style, except much shorter. And when I go to put on my lip gloss, I really look at my face, my face with all the random patches of light on it. I did this to myself — on purpose. *I did this to myself.*

Girls come in and out, some change too, others slyly peek at me as they wash their hands. It's my cue to hurry up. By the time I get back to the cafeteria, the show has already started and everybody's in a frenzy. Even the parent volunteers aren't much help for all the backstage insanity. Yvette's fussing at the new girl, and Jason and Terrance are huddled together, arguing over something. Troy's on edge too, pacing back and forth with his hands going through the motions of playing his violin. And yes, he is definitely fly in his jeans, blue shirt and vest, and brown-and-blue fedora cocked to the side.

"Group two," a volunteer calls. "Showtime!"

"That's us," says a boy from the a cappella group. They rush backstage.

The order of acts is posted on the walls around the room. My name is listed after Troy's, with the song title of "A Surprise Arrangement," which Mrs. Hill suggested. It's time for me to warm up my voice, so I find an empty corner to do the exercises that Mrs. Hill taught me. Jitters go through my body, as if I have the flu. I practice the breathing techniques, but the jitters are still here.

Two dance groups go on and off, and the fake Eminem. When he comes back to the cafeteria, the confident swag he left with is gone, and a girl pats his back. His eyes are glassy like he's about to cry. Terrance calls over to him and says, "Yo! Should've karaoked Post Malone."

And that's why I'm really glad that I didn't sing a hook for those jerks. Thank you, Sophia!

"All right, Bring the Rhythm dancers, you're on!" calls the volunteer. The girls in the modern dance group screech and scream, and run out the door.

I check the list again and count the acts before me. Yvette's group is called One Star Trinity. I stifle my laugh. One star of three? Troy comes over too. "Almost showtime," he says, resting his arm over my shoulders. "By the way, what's the 'Surprise Arrangement'?"

"By the way, what are *you* playing?"

He laughs. "Good one. You'll see."

Before the modern dancers are back in the room, the volunteer announces that Jason and Terrance are up next. I don't even have the urge to see their performance. When they're done, they come back all amped, talking about how they "killed it!"

When Nia's called, I tell her to break a leg. She thanks me, and then Troy and I sneak backstage to watch. We're not the only ones — Jason, Yvette, and Belinda are there too.

Nia sits on the stool, props her guitar on her knee, and adjusts the microphone. Into the mic she says, "I'd like to perform for you an original piece called 'Stand.' " Her fingers strum the strings, and then she sings. Next thing I know, I'm bobbing my head. I peek out at the audience, and everybody's rocking along too. When she goes into her last refrain, she starts drumming a beat on the face of her guitar and sing/raps about the world and making a change. Finally the beat stops, and she sings the chorus once more, ending with a high note that seems to ring in my ears even when she's done. People jump up clapping. I'm so happy for her that I bum-rush her with a hug. "You are so dope!"

When Yvette and her group go on, Troy goes to grab his violin, and then we creep backstage once more. They wear the same short sequined dresses, sing the same song, and perform the same dance steps Yvette had taught me, and she's still front and center. I hate to admit it, but they're fantastic. Their harmonies sound like one incredible voice. And their moves are on point. I'm impressed with how quickly the new girl picked it all up too. The crowd goes wild, as if they were at a concert. Dang, Yvette just might win.

"Wish me luck," Troy whispers, half groaning. "I have to follow *them.*"

"Break a leg," I say instead. "They say wishing luck is bad. You got this."

After the emcee announces Troy, he goes onstage and hooks his violin up to an amplifier. I'm hoping he doesn't up his classical song to classic rock. Troy taps the beat out with his foot and begins playing. And I swear the entire audience takes one huge gasp because instantly, we all recognize the song — "Stay with Me." And it almost . . . almost, even without vocals, almost sounds like Sam Smith is right here. Troy's making his violin sing! He moves his body as if the music is bottled up inside him, fighting to get out. I've never seen anything like this. Never heard anything like this. By the looks on the faces in the crowd, neither have they. And when Troy teases his bow across the strings for the final note, the crowd cheers so loud that the building shakes. Okay, maybe not that loud, but they cheer the loudest I've heard so far.

"Awesome!" I say, grabbing him tightly, as he dips behind the curtain. "You were so, so, so awesome!" Other kids backstage excitedly give him dap too.

Then I hear my name. My stomach goes spastic. "Genesis, you're on!" And now Troy's telling *me* to break a leg.

I'm doing this! I tell myself as I head for the curtain. *I'm doing this!* I tell myself as I walk toward the microphone. *I'm doing this!* I get fierce with myself. Then, I go there. I draw those voices, those voices that hold me back. *Look at you with that nappy hair; it can break a comb. Look at you with that wide nose and thick lips. And*

don't get me started on how black you are.
Life is going to be harder for you.

I recall every bad memory, every negative word, because when I sing, I'm gonna conjure the loneliness of Billie Holiday, the joy of Ella Fitzgerald, the soul and longing of Etta James. I'll sing for every girl who feels like . . . feels like *me.*

When I take the microphone, I peer out into the audience to see if Mama or Dad is there, but all I can do is blink in the blinding stage lights. Then I hear it. A snicker here and then there.

"Hello." My voice cracks. "I'd like to sing a little medley I put together. Thank you." I have no music. It's all *me.* I tap a rhythm with my right foot, and pat my thighs with my hands. I take a deep breath. I got Billie's gold. I got Etta's soul. I got Ella's scat. And that's what I start with: light, peppery, Ella Fitzgerald with a Genesis Anderson scat.

Someone shouts, "You better sing, girl!" And then I hear it. The audience, they're clapping and snapping along with the beat. I trail off with a "da-dat-dat-doo-wah," then I summon Etta. I let each word soar. I swoop down to hug the little girl sitting on the curb with all her furniture. I visit the girl in the basement with the wrinkled brown bag passing from hand to hand. I kiss the lonely girl who hears ugly taunts from the mirror. I experience every single moment. And I'm not afraid. I am not afraid.

At last, I fill my lungs with as much air as I can take, and I belt. I do. I let it all go in one long breath, hitting a note that even surprises me. When I'm done, I collapse my shoulders, but quickly straighten them. And when I bow, the applause — it startles me. I shield my eyes and peer into the crowd. Everyone's . . . standing? For me? I hurry offstage and Troy comes toward me with Nia close behind, both bombarding me with hugs. Then there're others, too, who I don't know.

Wow.

Powerful.

Girl, you worked it.

I hug and thank everybody, and quickly break away to the cafeteria. The volunteer announces another act as I find a peaceful place to . . . breathe. Troy sits with me; he doesn't say anything, just covers my hand with his. We sit there for a long time, the quiet after the storm.

Sophia dashes in. "They're about to announce the winner," she says breathlessly, and dashes out again. All the acts squeeze onstage, and the emcee is congratulating everyone. Nia stands on the other side of me with her guitar across her back. The rhythm dancers hold hands, the white rapper keeps his head down, Jason and Terrance high-five each other as if they've already won, and Yvette and her girls are right in front, of course.

"And now, what you all have been wanting to know — are you excited?" The emcee teases the audience with rhetorical questions and long pauses. "Okay! Here we go! Our second runner-up is —"

Did Dad make it? I wonder.

"Nia Kincaid! Give it up!" The audience cheers and whistles.

Nia got third place! She hugs me and gets her trophy. She deserves it, for real.

"Last year I didn't even get third," Troy says.

"It's not over yet," I tell him, squeezing

his arm.

"This was a tough show to judge," says the emcee. "So much talent in this school! Our first runner-up is — One Star Trinity! Let's hear it for these superstars!"

Dang! I wanted to beat them! Ugh! Now I'm dealing with Yvette's egotistical smile, and the attitude she's giving me with that stupid trophy she's now parading across the stage with. *It's not over,* I tell myself.

"Drum roll, please." *Let it be me, let it be me, please let it be me.* "Farmington Oaks' first-place winner of our annual talent showcase is . . . Isn't this exciting?" The audience groans. "The first-place winner is . . . Troy Benson!"

Troy Benson? Troy?! "You won!" I yelp. He's too stunned to move. "Troy, you won!" I say again, pushing him to the front. The audience is going berserk! And so am I. Troy's winning makes me forget about Dad, care less about Yvette, and erase my wanting a trophy. Troy finally won! Everyone's jumping all over him, even as the curtains close. Mrs. Hill's thanks to the volunteers can barely be heard 'cause we're still screaming "You won!" We head back to the cafeteria to get our stuff, I'm carrying Troy's trophy, and he's got both arms wrapped around his gift basket.

"Thank you, Genesis," he says, putting his winnings down. When I ask for what, he explains, "If you weren't so mean, talking about me living in a bubble, then I might not have changed my style."

"Well, now at least I don't feel as bad as I did before," I tease, setting his trophy over with his stuff.

We finally get to the foyer together, where, as expected, people start to surround him, sweeping him away. And almost first thing, I spot Mama. She stands against the wall, looking right, looking left. Looking for me. In her hand is my list. She finds me and we lock gazes. Mama weaves her way over to me. The pages, trembling in her hand, are pressed to her chest. There's so much sorrow, guilt, and joy in her glassy eyes.

People stop to congratulate me, and I thank them quickly. And, as if she can't stand it any longer, she grabs and holds me for a long time. "I'm so proud of you," she whispers. When she releases me, her fingertips gently stroke my face. "So very, very proud."

Just then, Sophia's at our side. "Oh my gosh." She bear hugs me. Sophia *hugs* me. "That took a lot of guts. You should've won, Genesis, you were great! And Troy, can you believe it?!" Sophia squeals excitedly. "He was awesome!"

"He was all that, for sure."

Sophia agrees. Then she greets Mama with an "Oh, I'm so rude! Hello, Mrs. Anderson. Can you believe Genesis?!" Then turns back to me. "You did it! Now let me go find Troy — Troy *won*!"

After Sophia rushes off, I blurt, "I know you're gonna kill me. But I had to do it, Mama, I *had* to, and I can explain why."

"I know why," Mama says, holding up my papers. "I read your letter."

The foyer is packed with parents, kids, little brothers and sisters. I attempt to put on my best "Mama" smile for the PTA paparazzi. Cameras flash, as do more compliments. But there's still no sight of Dad. So I ask, "Did Dad come? He read my letter?"

She must see the desperation in my eyes because she tells me, "He . . . he was here. And yeah, he read it." Then she adds, "Gen, he wasn't in the best condition. . . . He left after you performed."

Should I be happy that he came — even drunk?

We stay around for a little while longer, enjoying this moment. I find Mrs. Hill in the crowd and in Mrs. Hill's fashion, she opens her arms, and I fall right into them. "Girl, you did it! You did!"

"Yes, I did, Mrs. Hill," I say, showing all thirty-twos. Then she chides me for even wavering about not doing it.

"I know, I get it now," I say. Then I introduce her to Mama.

"Your daughter is something special," Mrs. Hill tells Mama, beaming.

"That she is." Mama's eyes are getting watery now.

"Oh, I forgot . . ." I open my bag and get the Etta James CD.

Mrs. Hill closes my hand around the CD. "Keep it. A gift. For you."

THIRTY-TWO

A sound, something like a whimpering puppy, wrestles me awake. *It's only a dream,* I tell myself and roll back over. Except it's not. I strain to hear where the noise comes from. I peek out my window. Nothing. I creep to my door and crack it open. It's coming from inside the house. I tiptoe toward the sound.

In the dining room, I find him slumped on the floor, against a box, directly under the chandelier.

"Chubby Cheeks?"

"I hate that name," I say.

"Why? You'll always be my Chubby Cheeks."

"Stop calling me that." Every time he says that name, it takes me right back to that basement. I turn to go.

"Wait," Dad says. And of course, of

course, of course I do. He tries to pull himself up using the box, but only succeeds in knocking it on its side. "Oh God . . . look at me."

He looks like one of Mama's patients in the nursing home. I don't want to feel sorry for him. Still, I stay. "What do you want?"

"I've gone to a meeting . . ." He reaches out to me. "Tell yo' Mama for me. She won't listen. I'm going, for real . . ."

Now he wants to go to AA, after all this time?

I want to leave, but can't . . . 'cause maybe, finally, he really is trying. And because . . . he's . . . my daddy. I step out of the shadow so he can see me. "Mama told me you came . . . to the talent show. . . ." Dad grapples with the box again. I push it up to his back, so he can lean on it. I'm wanting to ask what he thought, was he proud, did he cheer — but, I can't bring myself to form the sentences. And since he doesn't offer anything, there's nothing for me to do but walk away.

Just then, Dad speaks. "When I saw you on that stage . . . I was so . . . amazed."

He wipes wetness from his cheeks. "I never seen you like that . . . didn't even know it was in you. And I thought self-ishly . . . 'Listen to her, sings jus' like *me*. *Look* jus' like me, too.' "

I've always wanted to hear him say things like this to me — undrunk. And he's finally saying it, after everything — everything that's happened, everything I've done . . . I just gape at him. He's *hated* that I look like him! That's not just being selfish, it's . . . it's hypocritical!!

"Dad," I burst out, "how you gon' say that — now?" I can't stop what's coming out of my mouth and not sure I want to. "You told me I didn't take after you. You told me that plenty times. . . . 'You ain't nothin' like me,' you said. Made me hate looking like you! Made me hate looking like . . . like me."

Now it's me who's sniffling.

"Gen?"

I don't get it. Why couldn't he have said any of these things before . . . just once?

"Genesis?" he says, stronger. I meet his eyes. "Me saying those words to you . . . were because . . . I didn't *want* you to be

437

nothin' like me — not act like me, look like me. But everything about you was me. I thought if I pushed it away . . . then . . ." Dad takes a deep breath and blows it out. "You wanted to know why I don't talk about my family?" I nod. "My mama . . . she blamed me for what happened to Charlie. She did . . . told me over and over she wished it was me dead, steada Charlie."

My chest tightens. Dad's mama said that?

Dad continues, "She called him her pretty little boy. Me? I was never-gon'-amount-to-nothin'-like-yo'-black-nappy-headed-triflin'-daddy." Drool slips from his mouth and he wipes it away with the back of his hand. "Turns out, she was right. She was *right.* Now tell me, you'd think I'd want my baby girl to be anything like that?

"I'm a mess. I messed up my life, yo' mama's life, and yours. But when I drink," he goes on, adjusting the box again, "I feel like a winner. When I drink, I drown out her voice. . . . The other night, when you asked me what you did —"

What I asked him? I think back . . . oh yeah. *You drink 'cause you hate me?*

"I saw myself," Dad mutters. "I saw myself . . . askin' my own mama that same question . . . and I couldn't think of nothing to say 'cept what she said to me. But . . . Genesis, you gotta believe me when I say this . . . I don't wanna lose you."

A lump the size of a walnut is stuck in my throat. Now I know why Mama wants so much to protect him. I wanna cry for the little boy that was dogged by his mama. The one who tried to save his brother from the bats. He seems so — empty. And yeah, I do this. I sit next to him.

"On that stage, Chubby Ch— Genesis . . . you were . . . incredible."

"But you left."

"But I *saw* you. You didn't deserve me being there like that. . . . And, I, uh . . . All I could think was, why couldn't I be a better father?"

Even though he doesn't apologize, his regret is a small drop of comfort. And I know for certain you gotta start somewhere. Maybe he will change, eventually.

"I didn't win. . . ."

Dad pats my knee. "Oh, you won. In my eyes, just being up there, you won. You ain't need no trophy for that."

The walnut is now the size of a grapefruit. Still, I gotta tell him the truth. "I wanted to, for you." Now he squeezes my knee. "Dad, I *am* like you. I made a mess of everything." Dad shushes me, letting me know it's okay, but it's not okay. "In the letter, I told you that I did something horrible to my face. . . . Well, I put some cream —" The words get stuck, but I fight to get them out. "I thought that if . . . if I could —" I can't finish, I'm choking up for real now.

"I know, I know what you're about to say," Dad says quietly. "Don't you think I felt that, wanted that every time my mama went on about Charlie . . . and then looked at me like, like I was —"

"I get it, I do," I say, putting everything, every single piece together. "You drink to drown out your mama's voice. . . . I hear voices too. And I drown 'em out. . . . I . . . I do things to myself to make me . . . beautiful."

Now Dad's breaking up.

I wipe my face on my pajamas. My mind's blown away with — this. This moment. There's nothing else to do but sit quietly. And of all songs, my mind plays Billie Holiday's "Good Morning, Heartache," as if it's our theme. Then I get to thinking about her hard childhood and struggles with her sickness. What would she have wanted to hear? Or even Ella, dealing with memories of being put away in that orphan asylum. And surely Etta, too. They all had big, big hurts. It's right there, hidden in their music. And I believe what they needed to hear — what Dad needs to hear — what I wanna hear —

"Dad," I say, "you're not alone. I'm right here." And Dad, he takes my hand, and his levees break.

THIRTY-THREE

What's not okay is that I've got to stay locked up in my room — with nothing but my bed, dresser, and a bunch of boxes. Mama was moved by my performance, but not enough to release me from my sentence. For breaking my punishment, she grounded me for even longer — shoot, I'm liable to sit here till my hair turns gray. I even pleaded my case and told her all about Dad opening up about his family and our long talk last night — which was the point of me breaking my punishment in the first place. You know what she said? "Good, I hope it brings him closure." Then she sent me back to my room. *Back to my room!*

"Can you at least have pity on me . . . I didn't win a thing!" I shout through my cracked door.

"Use this time wisely," she calls back. "Think about how you can make better choices."

"I have already," I mutter. And I'm not lying; I really have. Like, I've worked on my novel study questions for English class, and I really thought about my answers, like for myself. I figure, it's not like the books that Troy read, but it's a start. And Troy, he won! If I had phone privileges, I'd call him right now.

I finish my homework, which doesn't take long — even with me dragging it out. It's only about two o'clock, and honestly, I've already learned my lesson. *This is torture,* I think, kicking a box. Dad's not even around to — I don't know, talk about what we talked about last night. He woke up about noon and told us that he won't make any more promises, that his actions will speak for him. Not shortly after, he left. I kinda want to hear him tell me one more time that he doesn't want to lose me.

I sit for another hour, reflecting on my choices until Mama knocks on my door. She comes in before I even answer. It's not a good time to discuss how Sophia has privacy with a door lock, but whenever we move to a place of our own, I'm definitely bringing it up. "I'm not sure if you want this," Mama says, holding out my list.

The List. "Not really," I say, extending my hand to take it. My blotchy hand. I can't believe I was so close to finally changing. No, no, no. I can't believe I did this to myself.

"Wanna talk about it?"

"It's just a list that some girls started . . . you can see what happened next." Stupid girls. Couldn't even count.

"You believe everything on there?" Mama asks.

I scan the paper, flipping it over, and, oh my gosh, this is another thing that I can't believe that I did to myself. "I guess so," I say, adding: "Some of this stuff was really lame, though. Like Number One: She smiles too much; Number Eighteen: She always trying to be somebody's friend. Like I said, lame."

Mama bites down on her lip, holding her words back. Finally she asks, "What about . . . Number Seventy?"

"Number Seventy?" Ouch.

She can't stand being this black.

The words stab me. After last night's talk with Dad, I realize one thing: Everybody's in pain. Billie. Etta. Ella. Grandma. Mama. Dad. Me. Even Chyna and Porsche. And for me, it was trapped between the lines of this paper. I don't even know why I kept it. It's nothing but a reminder that I was one of the bad ones. And I added to it. *Me.*

I look at Mama and the darkness under her eyes; she's been through a lot. Growing up with all the traditions and rules might not've been as rough as Dad's mean mama, but it sure wasn't easy. Dealing with Dad might've hurt her too, not to mention what I've done. I wonder if she now regrets marrying Dad, because if Dad was truly trying to marry up, and if, say, she married down to spite Grandma, then it hasn't turned out too well for her. And since I didn't turn out looking like her, then everything would fall back to #70 and that brown bag. So, I ask, "Why'd you marry Dad?"

"What?" Then Mama shakes off her

shock. "That's out of the blue." When I don't respond, Mama goes on. "I married your father for love. Yeah, I noticed his dark skin, but I wasn't bothered by it. . . . I just wasn't. To be honest, he was my type — tall, dark, and handsome." Mama laughs, probably at her cliché. "My parents were mad, of course, but like I told you before, there was so much about him to love . . . funny, affectionate, caring, charismatic . . ." Mama trails off as if remembering the good old times. "I love who *I* love. And now . . . it's time for me to forgive those I love, you know?" Mama then dips her head to me, reminding me of the list.

"Oh yeah," I say, glancing back down at the paper. "Number seventy. I don't know what to say." I've been trying to lighten my skin for Dad, at least that's what I told myself. Just had to look like Mama. But now I know, it was for me. I think about that night on the back porch, me asking Dad why he hates me, and I never thought to ask myself. Why? Why I hate *me*? Gosh, I feel stupid. Stupid for the cream, bleach bath, exfoliation, lemons — all of it. Troy's right, I've been caught up in the hype and what everybody thought of me, and I'm tired of it. I just want to look in the mirror and be okay with myself, that's all. "Ma, I can't do this anymore."

Mama gives me the *what-are-you-talking-about* face.

I don't tell her that I'm talking about all the trying I've been doing since last October. So I tell her, "I'm done with this list."

"Good," she says, nodding. "Want to start another one? A positive one, like, what you love about yourself? I can help."

"Naw," I say, tearing up the paper over and over again until it looks like confetti. I laugh inside because we should really have a party after saying bye to this fancy house and hopefully starting fresh in a new one. I even have friends — real friends — to invite. But seriously, I say no because this list thing was never my idea. I want to figure out what I like about myself, but I want to do it on my own — no lists or help from anybody. So I tell Mama, "It's a good idea, but I'm kinda done with lists for right now. I just kinda wanna start all over . . . begin again."

"That sounds like a good decision," Mama says in her thinking voice. "I love it. Just begin again."

Then I think of something, and real sad-like I say, "But . . . I guess I can't."

"Why?" Mama asks alarmed.

"Because . . . ," I pause. "Because this punishment stops me from starting anything new." Mama laughs, and I can't help but to burst out laughing too. And we carry on like this so long that we forget what we're even laughing about in the first place. I like when we laugh. And I like that I'm funny. And I'm sure I like a whole lot of things . . . and truth is, I can't wait to discover 'em all.

ACKNOWLEDGMENTS

In 2011, in my graduate school's lecture hall, a speaker shared the good old adage: "Write what you know." So, I sat in front of my computer and did exactly that. It was my first adviser, Claire Rudolf-Murphy, who informed me that I had to at least add paragraph breaks throughout my story. Thank you, Claire. I added them, as you'll see.

And it was Jane Resh-Thomas who responded with focused questions that forced me to think more deeply about my story. What was it I wanted to convey? Oh, I had no idea. I was just writing what I knew. And thank you, Jane, for urging Laura Ruby to convince me to press through with the story. When *Genesis* was packed away and never to be explored again, Laura coaxed it out of the recycle pile and helped me to fall back in love with it. Thanks, Laura. And thank you, dear Marsha Qualey, for your wisdom in further developing the draft.

My writer's group kept me accountable for getting my revisions done. Thank you, Andrew Cochran, Elizabeth Verdict, Jane O'Reilly, and Melissa Taleb.

The themes in this story went well beyond what I knew and experienced. And my girl Tracee Loran was always a phone call away for the in-depth analysis, long discussions, and shared venting of these issues. Thank you, Tracee.

In 2014, Anne Ursu asked to read *Genesis*. Now, when someone like Anne Ursu says, "I want to read your manuscript," well, you had better say yes. But my manuscript was in shambles. However, I knew that I couldn't keep someone as busy as Anne waiting. That should've been motivation enough, right? But I needed a deadline — I work better with deadlines.

That's when my friend Maria Blackburn set one and announced, "And we'll celebrate with cake." Cake! That did it for me. I wrote and wrote and met my deadline — and thank you, Maria, for bringing not just a regular grocery store cake, but a Suárez Bakery cake!

Finally I sent it off to Anne, who also gave me feedback and has been a mentor and major champion of mine. I can't thank you enough for all you've done.

I'd like to thank my agent, Brenda Bowen, and her then assistant, Wendi Gu, for pulling *Genesis* from the slush pile and recognizing its potential.

And a huge thanks to my editor, Caitlyn Dlouhy, for pushing me to delve deeper, staying true to the characters, and keeping the "voice" authentic. And thanks for using a green pen; it's not as traumatic as a red one. I'm amazed at how *Genesis* has evolved. And now it's as if we're proud parents crying, "Our baby has grown up." I've learned a lot from you — and am still learning — and on a brighter note, at least you didn't have to send me a note about paragraph breaks.

Nailah, my daughter. My inspiration for Nia. You'll never know how much it means to me when you say, "I'm proud of you, Mom." Those words have gotten me through some rough patches — not only in my writing life, but life in general. Your encouragement has motivated me more than you'll ever know. I love you. I love you. I love you.

My mother, Phyllis Williams, thank you for always being on my team no matter what. Thank you for spoiling me, cracking jokes, and being you. You make me laugh even when the world is tense. I love you.

I also owe a tremendous thanks to my #teamAlicia and #teamGenesis folks: Christine Stone for offering your beautiful mountain home so that I could write and revise in tranquility; and when I got stuck in a rut and was beating myself up, Debbie Kovacs said one sentence that has opened my eyes as to how we can support one another. She said, "Stop it. I will not let you talk about my friend that way." Thank you; I now use that phrase to help others. Also, here's an enormous THANK YOU for every individual who has emboldened me during this journey.

And lastly, I'd like to thank Detroit. Growing up in the city, I've learned one thing is true: Nothing stops Detroiters.

ABOUT THE AUTHOR

Alicia Williams is a graduate of the MFA program at Hamline University. An oral storyteller in the African American tradition, she is also a teacher who lives in Charlotte, North Carolina. *Genesis Begins Again* is her debut novel.

The employees of Thorndike Press hope you have enjoyed this Large Print book. All our Thorndike, Wheeler, and Kennebec Large Print titles are designed for easy reading, and all our books are made to last. Other Thorndike Press Large Print books are available at your library, through selected bookstores, or directly from us.

For information about titles, please call:
  (800) 223-1244

or visit our website at:
  gale.com/thorndike

To share your comments, please write:
  Publisher
  Thorndike Press
  10 Water St., Suite 310
  Waterville, ME 04901